READY TO SOAR

A CLEAN SMALL TOWN ROMANCE

MCKENNA FAMILY ROMANCE SERIES

LUCINDA RACE

MC TWO PRESS

DEDICATION

This book is dedicated to the following people:
My mom,
Thank you for giving me wings to fly.

This book wouldn't have been possible
without the LR posse—
Shirley – for telling me to keep writing
Cheryl – for your text messages
Rick– for his patience while my nose was
buried in the laptop
Megan and Emily– for inspiring me every day
to live my dream.

Manufactured in the United States of America First Edition
E-book- ISBN 978-0-9862343-8-5
Print – 978-0-9862343-9-2

PROLOGUE

QUICK NOTE: If you enjoy Ready to Soar, be sure to check out my offer for a FREE Price Family Romance novella at the end. With that, happy reading!

It was a glorious day, perfect for a wedding. In a few short hours, Kate's twin brother, Shane McKenna, would marry Abigail Stevens, Kate's best friend, and the love of his life. Kate thought it was amusing that Shane was marrying a girl he'd spent his youth chasing and teasing.

Kate knew the couple was meant to be together. Several months before, Abby and Kate were enjoying lunch when Abby told her that before her mother died, she'd told Abby that she would find a place to call home, a place where people cared about their friends and neighbors. And then tragedy struck. Abby lost both her parents and then her sister and brother-in-law, Kelly and Tim, who died in a car accident, leaving Abby alone in the world with the exception of her nephew, Devin. Abby's wedding day would be bittersweet; she missed her family but she was officially becoming a McKenna.

Abby stood in the kitchen doorway wearing a bewildered look. Devin was happily squishing a banana chunk in his chubby hands while the floor was littered with cereal.

Abby wore a sleepy smile. "Please tell me some of that mess made it in his mouth, too."

"Good morning, Abigail. Shane wanted you to sleep in, so he gave us a key and asked us to take care of Devin. And we made coffee." Ellie beamed at the little boy. "And we've been having lots of fun, haven't we, Dev?"

Kate poured Abby a mug of steaming hot coffee. "Take a seat. We're starving, so what would you like for breakfast?"

"I'm too nervous to eat. Coffee is fine." Abby giggled. "I didn't expect to see anyone this early. I'll admit it's nice to wake up to calm, smiling faces. Let's enjoy coffee, and then if you don't mind, I'd like to run through the shower. What time do we have to leave?"

Ellie chimed in, "Abby, today is your day and there is no need to rush. I dropped the dresses off at Shane's yesterday."

"Mom, Grace, and Gram have everything under control at the lake. Our job is to get you and Devin to the wedding on time. Don will be over in a bit in case you've forgotten something that has to go out to the lake house today."

The sisters shooed Abby out of the kitchen. "Devin is fine. Go soak in a bubble bath. You have three hours to primp," Kate called as Abby floated on a cloud up the stairs.

"You've thought of everything!" Abby called over the banister. Once again, Shane's family was making the day run smoothly. Her life had changed since moving back to her hometown. It had been a difficult decision to pack up, sell her parents' and sister's houses, and move from the eastern shore to the hills of Western Massachusetts. In the beginning, her grief had been overwhelming, losing her parents and sister within a span of twelve months. Abby didn't know how to take care of herself, let alone a small child. That's when fate stepped in. Abby and Devin had wandered into What's Perkin', Cari McKenna Davis's coffee shop. Even though it had been years since she had seen her, in typical McKenna fashion, Cari welcomed Abby and Devin with open arms.

Abby sank into a hot, fragrant bubble bath, her mind wandering back to those dark days after Devin's grandparents kidnapped him. Edward and Louise Martin had decided Abby wasn't a fit parent. A custody battle ensued, playing out for many long, tense months. In the end, Abby retained custody and was now in the process of legally adopting the boy. The relationship between Abby and the Martins remained strained but tolerable. Today, putting the past firmly behind her, Abby Stevens was starting a future with the man whose heart beat in sync with hers. Shane's family was an added bonus. Instantly, Devin had grandparents, aunts, uncles, and three cousins. Abby's life was turning out just as her mother had predicted. Abby pulled the plug on what was left of the bubbles and stepped out of the tepid water to begin the final primping process.

She scrutinized her reflection. Short strawberry-blond curls were enhanced with a crescent headband that added a dash of pizzazz.

Carefully applying her makeup to enhance her blue-gray eyes, Abby used shades of purple and gray eye shadow, dusted her cheeks with fairy-pink blush, and then swished on some dark-brown mascara. Abigail Stevens was ready to get married.

Gingerly, Abby took the white garment bag from the closet, picked up the tote bag, and floated down the wide staircase. The moment she stepped into the kitchen, a hush fell over the room.

"Abby, you look like a princess," Ellie gushed.

Abby was radiant. "I'm ready."

Don carefully took the garment and tote bag. "I'll put these in the car and come back for Devin's things."

For now, Abby and Devin were moving into Shane's home until they could decide where they would take up permanent residence. Abby loved being lakeside but enjoyed the convenience of town, so everything was up in the air.

"Okay, girls, let's change my last name."

The guitarist was ready and waiting…

Abby gave a slight nod. The familiar chords of the wedding march filled the air. Heads turned to catch their first glimpse of the bride. She took a deep breath and nodded to Kate and Ellie. Ellie went first, carrying Devin, followed by Kate, and then Abby glided down the flower-strewn path.

Shane thought his heart would burst from his chest. Abby was exquisite. Her long white dress was simple—a sleeveless scooped neckline—and the sun shimmering off the beading created a vague rainbow effect. Sterling roses completed the picture-perfect bride. If he hadn't already fallen in love with this woman, he would have at that first glance.

Abby's hand was in the crook of Ray's arm. As they entered the gazebo, Abby's eyes locked on Shane, handsome in a dark tux with a lavender rose boutonniere. The sun was dimmed by his brilliant smile. Ray placed Abby's hand in Shane's and took one step back.

The minister smiled at Shane and Abby. "Who gives this woman?"

Ray answered, "I do." He took his seat next to Cari.

The minister moved smoothly through the ceremony while Shane and Abby gazed into each other's eyes. When the minister announced it was time for the first kiss, friends and family cheered and clapped. Devin looked around at the happy faces and gleefully joined in, clapping his little hands.

Shane and Abby turned to greet their family and guests. Devin strained in Abby's direction so Ellie passed him to her open arms. Shane placed a protective arm around his bride and a steady hand on Devin.

The minister announced, "I'm pleased to

introduce, for the first time, Shane, Abby, and Devin, the newest branch on the family tree."

Kate watched her twin, his bride, and their soon-to-be adoptive son. She said a small prayer that they would be blessed to share the same bond in marriage she had with Don, the love of her life.

1

—————

Kate's dream of a warm sandy beach was interrupted by the shrill sound of the phone ringing. For a split second, Kate wasn't sure if it was real or imagined. Wondering who would call so early, she rolled over, picked up the phone, and mumbled, "Hello?"

Don pulled the blankets over his head, muttering in protest at the intrusion. He hesitated, realizing she was trying to pass him the phone. "Who is it?" he grumbled.

"It's your mom. I'm having a hard time understanding her."

Don sat up, sleep forgotten. "Mom, what's the matter?" Concern clouded his dark-brown eyes. "Is he okay now?"

Kate listened to the one-sided conversation, unsure what was going on but getting the gist that someone had been hospitalized.

"Of course. Kate will need to get coverage at the shop, but we'll be there. Either late tonight or first thing tomorrow." He listened to his mother for a few more minutes. "I'll call you when we get on the road, and don't worry, Mom. Dad will be fine; he's strong."

Don disconnected. Kate slid close, wrapping her arms around his waist. The minutes dragged as the couple sat in silence. Kate felt compelled to say something.

"Don, what did your mother say about your dad?"

"Mom called the ambulance last night. Apparently, Dad was having chest pains yesterday while he was working in the vineyard."

Exasperated, he continued. "I don't know why he doesn't leave the heavy work to the field hands. But of course, Dad being Dad, he didn't say anything. After dinner, Mom noticed Dad kept rubbing his arm. He claimed he pulled a muscle or something. Mom thought his color was off. That's when she called the ambulance. It was the only way Dad was going to the emergency room. They admitted him for observation and tests, but the doctor is fairly certain it was a mild heart attack."

Don looked at his wife. "We have to go see them, and Mom needs me to talk to the doctors. You know my sisters and brothers always expect me to do the tough stuff when it comes to our parents."

"Of course. I'll talk to Mom. I'm sure Ellie and Abby will help." Kate caressed his cheek. "Don't worry, we'll leave right after lunch and be at the winery before dinner." Kissing him tenderly, she flipped back the covers. "I'm going to take a shower. Why don't you make some coffee?"

Distracted, Don nodded. Needing reassurance, he asked, "Kate, do you really think he's going to be okay?"

Kate sat down on the bed and squeezed his hand. "Donovan Price, other than you, your father is the most stubborn man I have ever met. He'll be fine because the alternative isn't an option for him."

"I know you're right. I can't picture Dad in a hospital bed. I can't even remember a single time when he was really sick." A deep, ragged breath escaped him. "You're right. Dad will be fine." Don leaned in and kissed his wife. "I love you, Katie."

"I love you too. Try not to worry; we'll get through this together."

Don gave her a little push off the bed. "We'd better get moving. There's a lot to get done in a few short hours. I'll take care of the bed before I make coffee."

Kate dashed into the bathroom, making a mental list of clothes she would need. She wasn't going to have a lot of time to pack before leaving for work, so while hot water ran down the drain, she packed her makeup bag.

Kate flipped on the kitchen lights at What's Perkin'. She loved this time of day. Kate tied on a fresh apron and turned on the ovens to preheat. Walking through her morning routine helped quiet the worrisome thoughts. What condition would Sam Price be in when they arrived in Crescent Lake? Kate thought about the last time they were at the vineyard. Don and his father had exchanged harsh words regarding his choice to work for Shane's landscaping business. Sam was old school and demanded Don, as the oldest son, return home and take over the daily operations at the winery. Don loved the growing process— planting and pruning—it was his true passion. Sam said it was time that Don work with his sisters. Tessa would teach him about marketing, and Anna, the chemist, would teach him about new wines. His brother, Jackson, was happy to manage the fields; he had no desire to be in charge. Leo, the youngest, had a successful car repair business and preferred beer to wine, so that left Liza, who was happy to stay at home with two small children. Although Don and Sam left things on good terms, the issue of Don returning to Crescent Lake Winery was unresolved; it was the elephant in the room at every family gathering.

Cari was surprised to find the shop glowing when she arrived. Mouthwatering aromas drifted from the open windows. She discovered Kate up to her elbows in batter. It was clear she had been baking for some time. "Good morning, Sunshine," she called, breezing into the kitchen. Cari got a thrill each morning she entered What's Perkin'. Her hard work resulted in a business to be proud of, and as a bonus, she got to share its success with her oldest daughter.

Kate glanced up. "Hi, Mom."

Immediately, Cari could sense something was troubling Kate. "You're here early."

"Sherry called this morning. Sam was admitted to the hospital, and I need to leave after lunch. We're driving to Crescent Lake and we want to get there before dinner. I'm going to call Abby and Ellie. Hopefully they can help with the counter so you can run the kitchen. I don't have any idea how long we'll be gone. It all depends on Sam's prognosis." Tears filled Kate's eyes. "I'm concerned about Sam, but I'm worried the same old argument about Don taking over is going to come up. I don't want to live in Crescent Lake. Our home is here."

"I thought Don made it clear he wasn't interested."

"Mom, you know my in-laws. The family and winery are everything to them and they've never been happy Don chose to live in Loudon and work for Shane. They put a lot of pressure on him. On us."

Cari nodded. "Honey, I understand about deep family ties, and I have always believed that everything happens as it is supposed to. You and Don need to be there for his family. His parents need your support."

Kate wrapped her arms around her mother. "I know you're right; I'm just scared. What if Sam is really sick and has to retire, or worse?"

"You and Don will cross that bridge when you get to it." Cari squeezed her daughter and smiled. "Why don't you give me the rundown on what you planned for specials over the next few days? It's been a while since I've had the kitchen to myself."

With a slight grin, Kate said, "Just do me one favor, Mom? While I'm gone, don't re-arrange the kitchen. It took me six months to get it organized and the flow is perfect."

Amused, Cari said, "You're a little protective of my kitchen, aren't you?"

Kate smirked. "Darn right, I am. A chef's kitchen should never be trifled with."

"Not to worry. I promise you'll find every-thing exactly where you left it. I'm going to call Ellie, Abby, and Grace. I'll have plenty of help."

Cari started the coffee as she thought about her family. There was one thing she was sure about. They always stood together in good times and bad. From the day her first husband, Ben, died, her children cemented their bond. They weren't Stepford children—they fought like cats and dogs—but heaven help anyone who tried to hurt one of the McKenna clan. Over the last couple of years, her family had grown. She found love with the man next door, Ray Davis. After they were married, Ray's son, Jake, and his wife, Sara, had triplets, two boys and a girl. Most recently her oldest, Shane, married Abby Stevens and they legally adopted her nephew. The blessings continued to come once Cari had chosen to live in the present and stop grieving for what was lost.

Cari dialed the phone and listened to endless ringing. She was ready to hang up when she heard a breathless, "Hello?"

"Ellie? Is everything okay? You sound out of breath."

"Everything's great. I just got back from a run. Now that I'm finished with school, I've decided to exercise."

"Do you want to call me back or, better still, can you swing by the shop before you go to work? There's hot coffee and Kate just pulled cranberry scones out of the oven."

Cari worried about her youngest daughter, a petite blond pixie who looked like a gust of wind could knock her over. But if anyone mistook her for a pushover, they would be in for a rude awakening. Ellie was a powerhouse in heels.

"Breakfast? Sounds good. I'll be there in less than an hour. I don't have to be at work until late morning and I have an idea I'd like to run past you."

Cari smiled to herself. Ellie was always coming up with new ideas. Since the day she graduated from college, she had been working on, as she called it, her life plan. "I'll be here. Love you, Pixie."

"Love you, too. Bye, Mom."

Next on Cari's phone list was her best friend, Grace. From time to time Grace enjoyed working in the shop, especially when she wanted to get away from her home office and job as a research analyst. Her schedule had enough flexibility to let her come and go as needed. Once Cari explained Kate's emergency, Grace said she would stop by so they could set up a work schedule.

Last was Abby. Again, Cari gave a brief summary of what was going on. "Do you think you could help out a bit?"

"I'm so sorry to hear Sam is in the hospital." Abby empathized with Don. Facing a parent's life-threatening illness was heart-wrenching. Her father had a massive heart attack and passed away before her mother, who died from cancer. "What do you need me to do, Mom?"

Cari's heart warmed each time Abby called

her mom. Before the wedding, Abby had approached her future mother-in-law and asked if Cari would mind. Cari said it would be an honor and hoped Devin would consider her and Ray his grandparents. "I was hoping you'd help me bake for the next few mornings, before Shane goes to work. Preparing muffins, breads, and soups would be helpful. Ellie and Grace will cover the front. Ray and the boys will pitch in too if needed."

"I'm sure Sara would like to help if we can get someone to watch the triplets," Abby suggested. "She might enjoy the adult conversation."

Cari hesitated. "You're right, but I'd hate for her to feel obligated. I'll call her later, after I have a schedule. This way I'll know where I have holes. The new office manager Sara hired has her real estate business running smoothly. Good idea, Abby."

Cari pulled out a calendar and penciled Abby in for several early morning shifts. Next, she would figure out when help would be critical for the remainder of the day. The shop should be the last thing on Kate's mind; Don's family needed her full attention.

Kate walked up behind her mother and peeked over her shoulder. The calendar had been divided into sections and initials filled in. Planning was her mother's forte.

"Geez, it didn't take long for you to replace me," Kate mused.

Cari glanced up. "You're irreplaceable, but I've been thinking the shop has grown since the early days. It's apparent we need more than the two of us plus family filling in when we need an extra hand. When you get back, we should hire someone for the front and maybe a part-time baker."

"I agree, and we should have talked about this before today. If we had someone trained, you wouldn't be scrambling while I'm out of town."

"Don't worry, Kate. Emergencies happen. The shop will be fine."

"Hey, Mom. Hey, sissy." Ellie waltzed in,

dressed in her casual yet elegant country chic outfit. Short blond hair framed her big blue eyes.

Cari knew Ellie took great pains with her appearance and everything she touched.

"Morning, Pixie." Kate smiled at her little sister, who wasn't just five years younger, but also the complete opposite of Kate—brunette vs. blond, tall vs. short, and green eyes vs. blue. Despite the differences, the resemblance between the sisters was unmistakable.

"So, what's going on? Why are you and Don rushing off to the winery?"

"Sam was admitted to the hospital with chest pains and they kept him overnight. When Sherry called early this morning, she asked us to come for a family meeting. We don't know if it's about Sam's health or Don and me moving there. Who knows… maybe it will be both. But that leaves Mom shorthanded. I'm hoping you'll have some free time to help."

"I'll talk to Karlene. I'm sure I can re-arrange my hours at the gallery. Not to worry. I'll make it work."

"Isn't the gallery busy right now?" Cari interjected.

"We opened a new exhibit so the weekends are busy. I have to write another press release for this show to generate some buzz, but otherwise there isn't much to do during the week. Besides, we're talking a couple of days, not months."

Kate was relieved. The customers loved Ellie and she could handle the hectic pace, leaving Cari to the kitchen. "Great."

"So, if that's all, can I still have breakfast? Running makes me ravenous and I could eat more than the scone and coffee Mom promised."

"Is that your way of asking for something more substantial?" Kate grinned.

"Well, if you're offering, I'd kill for some eggs, sausage, or whatever is easy." Ellie laughed.

"Come on. I'll feed you before you fade away."

Ellie poured two cups of coffee and grabbed a cookie on her way into the kitchen.

"I saw that, young lady," Cari teased. Ellie laughed as she left the room.

Cari was swept up in the morning rush as her attention was diverted to the customers coming and going. Grace stopped by and, as usual, jumped behind the counter to fill orders and ring up sales. When there was a break in the action, Cari filled Grace in on the details of Kate's trip. Without hesitation, she agreed to help when the shop was at its busiest.

"Can you start tomorrow?" Cari brushed her bangs back. "This will be just like when we worked in that restaurant that summer during college, remember?"

"What I remember is you made it look easy. You were always chatting up the customers and made great tips. I was a terrible waitress, running around trying to deliver orders, which were usually wrong. Thank heavens I chose the business world. These days I don't have to be nice or smile to make money."

"GF, please tell me you'll smile at the customers. If you're lucky, you might even rake in some tips." Cari chuckled.

"What time do you need me tomorrow?" Grace hoped Cari would say a time when the sun would already have peaked over the horizon.

"A little before seven? I'll get in by six and get things going. You'll run the counter. Customers start coming shortly after seven."

Grace cringed. "I'll be here. Do I get free coffee?"

"Don't you usually?" Cari smirked as she reached under the counter to hand Grace two dark-purple T-shirts.

"I'll see you in the morning, and thanks for the shirts." Grace peeked her head into the kitchen and said goodbye to the girls.

Cari glanced at her schedule. She wasn't worried about the shop, but she couldn't shake the feeling Kate might be right. Sherry and

Sam had been pushing the kids to move to Crescent Lake and take over the winery since they got married. Don had been working the distribution side of the business when he met Kate. He made the decision to move to Loudon to marry Kate while his brothers and sisters remained happy in their roles with the family business. Cari had no idea what they would decide if the meeting was about Don assuming the position of CEO. It was a difficult situation for everyone.

"Time will tell," Cari mused to herself. She popped her head in the kitchen. "Ellie, when you're done with breakfast, come out here so we can add you to the schedule."

"On my way." Ellie reviewed her mother's notes. "Looks good to me. I'm going to make a couple of copies so I can give one to Karlene, but then I need to leave. I hate the one-hour drive to the gallery, but until I figure out what's next, I'm going to soak up all that I can from Karlene—she is a very savvy business-woman. Not unlike you, Mom. Just a different product." Ellie flashed her dimples as she took the papers into the small office in the back.

"Stop buttering me up, kiddo. Your pay scale is the same," Cari teased.

"Oh, all the food and coffee I can consume? Sweet!" Ellie gave her mom a quick hug and like a whirlwind, she was off again.

Kate watched her sister leave. "Ellie will never go quietly, will she?"

"No, I don't think so. That's more your speed, Kate."

Mother and daughter grinned and went back to work.

2

Kate surveyed the back seat. Two tote bags and a small cooler. She thought of the larger suitcase in the trunk. Why did she always need to overpack? They were only going for a couple of days. Thankfully, Don didn't care how many bags she took. At the beginning of married life, he learned Kate didn't travel anywhere light.

"Don, if you're ready, I think we have everything."

"Just a minute." He jiggled the door handle to make sure it was locked and jogged down the walk. "Do you mind driving? I don't think I can concentrate on the road." He ran a hand over his blond crew cut. "Kate, I'm scared. What if something is seriously wrong with my dad? He isn't getting any younger and he still works the fields like he's my age."

She slid behind the driver's seat, adjusting her belt. "Don't borrow trouble. Your dad is strong and stubborn. His body might be giving him a warning to slow down a bit, but I don't think it will be anything he can't manage." Kate gave Don's hand a reassuring tug.

"I know you're right. I can't help but worry. We've never been summoned home before." He turned to face the window. He didn't want his wife to see the tears in his eyes.

She turned the key and the car purred to life. After backing out of the driveway, she headed toward the highway, doing her best not to worry. The sounds of gentle snoring drew Kate's attention. It was good he was sleeping. The next few days promised to be stressful. The miles steadily clicked away while the jazz station kept her company.

*D*on shook the fog from his brain as the familiar site of his childhood home came into focus. How long had he been asleep? He drank in the beauty of his wife, eyes closed, behind the wheel.

"Honey?" he said softly.

Kate smiled. "You don't need to whisper. I'm not sleeping, just waiting for you to wake up."

"How long have we been here?" Don looked around, wondering where everyone was hiding.

"Just a few minutes. I wanted to enjoy our last moments of calm before the family…" She didn't finish her sentence before the front door opened and Don's mom ran down the porch steps.

She approached the car with a wave and a smile. "I just heard the car. I am so relieved you're here, and your father will be thrilled."

Don greeted his mother with a warm bear hug. "Hi, Mom. How's Dad feeling?"

"He's doing much better, and if the test results look good, he can come home tomorrow." Sherry turned to Kate. "You look lovely, dear." She embraced Kate with genuine affection. "Come inside. I'm sure you could use something to drink after the trip."

She led the way as Kate grabbed a tote bag and her purse. Don took the other tote and cooler and retrieved the suitcase from the trunk. Following close behind the women, he scanned the fields. Everything seemed to be in fine shape. He turned his attention to what his mother was saying, hoping for a clue as to why they had been summoned.

"We can drive over to the hospital after you get settled." Sherry studied Don. "I hope you can just wait on your questions. Please? How about a snack? I'm sure you must be hungry."

"Mom, we're fine. Where is everyone? I

thought we would have dinner together and go to the hospital as a family." Don fought to keep the irritation from his voice.

"Jackson is somewhere on the property. You know how he keeps himself busy, fixing equipment and hovering over the vines. He'll be around at some point, but he said not to wait on dinner; he might be running late. I'm sure Tessa is in her office, working on the website, building our customer base or some brilliant marketing plan." Sherry took a breath and continued to fill in the couple on all the recent happenings around the winery. "We've seen a nice increase in foot traffic due to her efforts. People always mention something about her postings on the website. I'm sure she'll be along in about a half hour. Leo probably has his head in an engine at the garage. It's a shame he doesn't take more interest in growing things as opposed to fixing up those wrecks. But your dad said Leo is building a good business, so I guess that's something. Anna, the last I heard she was in the lab, working on a new blend for a novelty red wine. You know once your sisters set their minds to a new project, they'll find a way to make it work. And Liza is inside with the boys. Steve is on a business trip so I asked them to come over early."

Don could hear the sounds of small children playing emanating from deep inside the house. He pulled open the door and bellowed, "Who's in my house?" The sound of little running feet answered him.

He knelt on the floor, anticipating two bundles of energy hurling themselves at their uncle. He swung them up into the air to squeals of delight. His sister, Liza, was close on their heels.

"Donovan, be careful with my children. They sound loud but they're two and three and have little bones."

"Oh, you worry too much, we're just having fun!" Don carefully tossed them onto the sofa cushions. "Boys, we have to listen to Mommy."

Without missing a beat, the two towheaded boys slid from the sofa and ran into the kitchen calling, "Grammy!"

Don followed at a more sedate pace. His mom was chopping vegetables and slipping them into the oven to roast. "I hope a frittata and bread will be enough for dinner," she mused.

The boys went out to the back deck after getting a celery stalk with cream cheese from their grandmother. Liza took a few moments to make a phone call before going out to supervise the kids.

Kate observed Sherry. Although she was average height and slender, Don's coloring came from his mother—the blond hair, deep-brown eyes, and those amazing Nordic cheekbones were all maternal—but his height and body structure was powerful like his father's. She knew from experience that Sherry didn't like another woman cooking in her kitchen unless invited. "That sounds delicious. Please let me know if you'd like help."

"Thank you, dear, but you spend all day cooking for others. While you're here, I like to cook for you." Sherry gave her an absent-minded smile.

Don took Kate's hand. "I appreciate you offering to help Mom."

It was like this each time they came to visit. Kate would sit by and watch Sherry run around cooking for the brood without letting Kate lift a finger. With a shrug of her shoulders, Kate took a seat at the breakfast bar. Pleasant conversation flowed about What's Perkin' and the ever-expanding McKenna family.

The sound of footsteps on the porch drifted inside. "Mom, I think the rest of the family has arrived. We're going to have some wine out front. Come out with us." Don passed a tray of glasses to Kate before grabbing a corkscrew and taking a couple bottles of chilled wine out of the refrigerator.

"That's a fine idea, son. I'll join you in a few moments. I just need to tend to the oven." Sherry turned her back on the retreating couple.

⚜

*D*on pushed the screen door open, happy to see Tessa, Anna, and Jack sitting on the porch. Anna squealed and hopped up. "Kate, Don! It's about time you got here. Mom thought you'd get in earlier." Anna kissed Kate on the cheek and punched her brother's arm.

"Careful," Don said in a playful growl. "You wouldn't want me to drop the wine, now would you?"

Anna giggled and inspected the label. "The Blanc is a great choice."

Tessa greeted Kate warmly, but threw her

arms around Don's neck, planting a big kiss on his cheek. "How is my dear big brother?"

Don pretended to wipe off his cheek. He studied his sisters. They were both tall and had curvy figures, dark-auburn hair, and deep-brown eyes; most people mistook them for twins and were surprised to discover they were three years apart. Anna was the oldest but at times acted like a teenager, whereas Tessa had always been very serious. Liza joined them. Don had never realized before how different she was from the rest of the family. She was short, had blond curls and hazel eyes, and was the only sibling to have children.

"It's good to be home," Don said. "Jack." He put one of the bottles on the wicker table and stretched out his hand.

Jack grabbed it and pulled him in with a clap on the back and a hearty shake. "'Bout time you found your way west. What took you guys so long?"

Don knew he wasn't asking about the

drive. This was the primary reason visits to Crescent Lake were reserved for holidays. Less time to answer questions about when he and Kate would make the winery their permanent home.

"Wine?" Don diverted Jack's attention by opening the bottle and pouring its contents. "Mom has dinner in the oven, and then we'll go see Dad."

Kate declined a glass. "You all enjoy, and I'll be your DD tonight."

"Kate, you just got done driving," Jack protested. "Have some wine and relax. I'll drive. You can return the favor some other time. Besides, I'm not a huge fan of white wine." Jackson held up a glass of iced tea and handed Kate a wineglass.

"Well, if you're sure. This is one of my favorites." Kate took a tiny sip.

"Thank you, Jack. It is delicious." She gave him a warm smile.

Jack watched his sister-in-law sit back and enjoy her wine. His brother got all the luck when he literally ran into Kate. If Jack had known being a salesman was going to find his brother the love of his life, maybe Jack should have gotten out of the vineyard years ago. He envied what Don and Kate had… but he'd certainly never tell anyone how he felt.

Kate glanced at Jack and asked, "Any hot dates lately?"

"Nah, I would need to go out to meet someone and I'm too busy around here to be out carousing at night. Besides, I'm waiting for you to find me the perfect girl."

Don chuckled. "Jackson, I married the only perfect girl. You're going to have to settle for slightly less than perfect."

"Well, sooner or later she'll show up. Hopefully she'll walk through the door of the maintenance shop and even then, I'd have to trip over her." That statement was so close to the truth everyone laughed.

"What is going on out here?" their mom asked as she joined her children while two little boys held her hands.

Still chuckling, Don filled her in. "Jackson said the perfect woman will have to come into the shop and then let him trip over her before he'd notice."

"Don, be nice to your brother. He just hasn't found the right girl. But when he sees her, trust me, he'll know what to do." His mom waved her hand, indicating for Tessa to move her feet off the stool. "We have a few minutes before dinner. Is there any wine left?"

Kate passed a glass to Sherry. "Here you go. It's nice and light."

She took a sip. "I've always enjoyed a small glass at the end of a long day. Today is no exception. I just wish your father was here." Tears hovered in her brown eyes.

Tessa put her arm around her mother's shoulders. "Daddy is going to be fine. This was just a warning. You know the doctor has been after him for the last couple of years to slow down. And he'll be home tomorrow. In twenty-four hours, we'll have a glass of wine together."

"This was quite a scare. I'm not ready to lose him." Sherry set her glass on the table and got up. "Let's eat. I want to get to the hospital before it gets late. Your father is anxious to see Don and Kate."

*D*on walked into his father's hospital room. He feared the worst. To his surprise, Sam Price was sitting up and watching the evening news. What was left of his dinner was pushed to one side.

His dad turned the volume down on the television and grinned. "Well, there's a sight for sore eyes; my oldest son and his beautiful wife have come home."

In one short sentence, Don knew exactly what his father meant; it hadn't been a slip of the tongue. Sam Price was ready to hand the reins of his winery to Donovan and Kate, the next generation of Prices to own and operate Crescent Lake Winery.

"Hello, Dad." Don stretched out his hand, shaking his father's in a double-handed grip. "You gave us quite a scare. We heard your test results look good and you'll be home tomorrow."

His dad dismissed the comment and reached for Kate. "Kate, give an old man a hug."

"It's good to see you, Sam." Kate gave him a warm embrace. "You look fit."

"Kate, I wish you would call me 'Dad.'" His dad made this same comment each time he saw her.

Don jumped into the conversation before Kate could respond. He knew Kate didn't feel comfortable calling anyone "Dad." That was reserved for her father's memory. "So, I took a quick look around, and everything looks good."

His dad took the cue and easily moved the conversation back to the moment. "How long are you kids staying? A week?"

"We can stay for a few days. Cari got the

family to pitch in at the café and Shane's crews are busy." Don looked at Kate. "Maybe three or four?"

She nodded. "Mom and I are hiring a new cook and I need to get back for interviews. Besides, the shop is really busy this time of year with the tourists and part-time residents. They're great for business but inventory goes fast."

Sam nodded in appreciation of the effort that went into running a successful business. "How is your family? Don told us your brother recently got married."

"Everyone is doing great. Mom and Ray send their best for a speedy recovery."

"So, I guess you're wondering what happened to your old man." His dad paused for a moment, as if collecting his thoughts, but the family knew he loved to have everyone's attention when he spoke. It was part of his charm. "The doc said I had a mild heart attack. I've been dealing with high blood pressure and high cholesterol, both of which I take medication to control. I've also developed the middle-age spread despite the physical work I do every day. I'm in a high-risk category for heart problems. The good news is, this was a warning, a wake-up call if you'd like." His dad gave Don a hard look. "I need to make some changes. But what that means exactly, I don't know yet. I do know I can't wait to get out of the hospital and get home to my own bed. I don't know how anyone sleeps in here with all the noise."

He attempted to make light of the conversation. Don knew he was trying to bring them around to the idea of taking over for him, hoping they would step up and realize this was the right thing to do for the family. His dad did a double take. "Where's Leo?"

Liza hastily spoke up in defense of her twin brother. "Daddy, he's at the garage. You know he has that car to deliver in a couple of weeks."

"Well, I would have thought he'd show up to see me." Indignant, he turned to his wife. "This is what happens when your boy starts his own business. It takes him away from his family!"

"Sam, hush. You know not everyone is born with wine in their blood," Sherry admonished. "We agreed to support him in this venture. He works hard and has proven to have a good head for business. Besides, I know for a fact he was here this morning before he went to work."

"I know, but can you blame a man for wanting all his children together, hovering around his hospital bed? It makes a man feel good."

"We're having a family dinner tomorrow night and Leo will be there. He promised." Sherry waved Anna away from the end of the bed where she fussed with the bedsheets. "Speaking of dinner, what would you like?" A gleam came into Sam's eye. "Remember, we have dietary restrictions we're going to follow."

His dad visibly shrank; he wasn't a man who'd change what he didn't want changed.

"Whatever you want to make is fine with me. But I want dessert *and* wine."

Everyone started talking at once about the endless possibilities for dinner. Their voices were loud and carried down the hallway.

"Excuse me!" A deep male voice got their attention and the quiet was instantaneous. "Thank you for your attention." Anna stared at the man dressed in light-blue scrubs standing in the doorway. "Sam, what is going on in here? You're disturbing the other patients." He looked around the large group, filling the room to capacity.

"Sorry, Colin. This is my family. Let me introduce you to my kids." He pointed to Don. "My oldest, Donovan, and his wife, Kate. That's Tessa standing next to her mother, and Jackson and Anna at the end of the bed, and of course Liza and my two grandsons. Everybody, this is Colin. My nurse."

Anna murmured hello and studied the floor.

Colin nodded to each in greeting. "Okay.

Well, Sam, I would appreciate it if your family would keep their voices down." Colin's gaze strayed to Anna and her cheeks flushed bright pink. "Anna, are you feeling okay?"

Mortified, she muttered, "I'm fine."

Colin took one last look around. "Alright then. Sam, you need to get some rest so the family should leave soon." Colin gave each family member a stern look. He did his best to catch Anna's eye, but, unsuccessful, he left the room.

Jack spoke up. "Okay, everyone, let's go. Mom, are you going to stay for a while?"

She nodded. "Actually, I'm going to stay here tonight. I really don't want to leave your dad. Colin had a sleeping chair brought in for me last night."

Don heard the catch in his mom's voice. "Then we will see you both tomorrow." After hugs and a round of goodbyes, everyone vacated the room. Don stuck his head back in the door. "What time should we come back to pick you two up?"

"I'll call after we talk to the doctor." Sherry looked at Sam, who nodded. "That way you're not waiting around." Don gave her a wave and left.

Sherry took Sam's hand. "So, what are you thinking?"

"I don't know if Don and Kate are ready to pull up stakes. Did you see how Kate lit up when she talked about the shop? But this would be theirs—all of it. They'd have to promise to keep Jack and the girls in the business, Leo and Liza on the board of directors, but I would give them free rein to make any changes. Let's call Bill tomorrow and see if we can pull a rabbit out of the hat. I do have a few tricks left up my sleeve." Sam rubbed his whiskers. "Sherry, you know I push them to be the best they can be."

"Sam, you're a softie, but I'm the only person who sees that side of you. Maybe it's time to show the kids, too." Sherry worried about her husband's relationship with their children. She firmly believed everyone knew they were loved, but there were times she didn't know if her children reached for the stars for themselves or for their father. "Maybe this heart episode will help you lighten up on the kids." The comment hung heavy in the air.

The master of avoidance, Sam turned the volume up on the television. Before he got totally immersed in the news, he stated, "Sherry, I don't know what will happen if Don doesn't take control of the business. We need a solid plan before dinner tomorrow night so he and Kate can't say no."

Sherry leaned back in the chair. "If this idea doesn't pan out, you'll think of something. You always do."

3

Kate listened to Don's rhythmic breathing. Careful not to disturb her husband, she slipped out of bed and tiptoed from the room. The house was silent in the early morning hour. On a typical day, she would be in the kitchen at What's Perkin', up to her elbows in batter. Stepping into the spacious kitchen, she made a beeline for fresh coffee, silently thanking Sherry for setting it up after dinner. Kate poured a mug and stepped onto the back deck. Fields of lush grapevines sprawled as far as the eye could see. In the cool morning air, Kate thought of Sam. She was happy he was coming home but wondered what the topic was for the family meeting.

A noise caused her to turn and peer into the kitchen. It was Sherry.

"Good morning, Kate. You're up early." Sherry joined her on the deck and tipped her head back, soaking up the first rays of the sun.

"Good morning. I thought you were staying at the hospital. Is Sam okay?"

"He's fine. I wasn't sleeping well and keeping Sam awake so I called Jack to pick me up."

"A good night's sleep is important. But you could have called Don; he would have picked you up."

"It's fine. I'm home and ready for today. Are you always up this early?"

"Unfortunately, this isn't early for me. The shop opens at seven and we pride ourselves on freshness so I get the baking done before the sun is up."

"I'm sure your customers appreciate your

devotion. How long has your mother been in business now?" She sat down in a chair.

"Jeez, eighteen years. She opened the shop about a year after my father died. In the early days, it was therapy, helping her work through the grief. Her passion was cooking and there wasn't a shop like it in Loudon or any of the surrounding towns. The business flourished and my brother and I helped out. Ellie too when she was old enough. I decided on culinary school because of my mom. I love cooking as much as she does. When I graduated, I thought about moving to a major city to conquer the world, but that didn't work out. Instead, I went to work at the shop." A small, satisfied smile played over her face. "And I'm proud to say business is booming. But you know most of that story."

Casually, Sherry asked, "Do you ever regret moving home?"

"Not at all. Don and I have a good life there. We love our house; I have a lot of freedom at the shop, and my family surrounds us. I'm not sure if you heard, but we have one niece and three nephews. Shane and Abby have an adopted son."

"Don is very lucky to have married into a family very much like our own. It's a shame you get back so infrequently." Sherry and Kate fell silent. The words hung heavy in the air.

At a loss, Kate asked, "Would you like me to make breakfast for everyone?"

"It's just the three of us. The girls will grab something after the gym and Jack thinks coffee is all he needs to start his day. But if you'd like to cook, feel free."

Surprised that Sherry was giving her free rein in the kitchen, she hopped up, anxious to start. "Any requests?"

"Whatever you'd like to make, but I haven't shopped recently." Sherry leaned back in the chair. "If you don't mind, I'm going to sit right here and enjoy the peace and quiet."

Kate stood for a moment. "Let me take care

of everything." For the first time, Sherry allowed Kate to see she was exhausted from the stress of Sam's illness. Kate was determined to be more supportive and understanding while she and Don were in town and resolved to make time to visit more frequently.

Half-asleep, Don stretched out his arm. Groping the empty space, he propped himself up and glanced around the room. He rubbed a hand over whisker stubble and begrudgingly got up. He had hoped to stay in bed this morning but hadn't planned on being alone. He pulled on a T-shirt and shorts. He got a whiff of breakfast and his mouth began to water—no one made breakfast like his mom. Eager to get to the kitchen, he dashed down the stairs two at a time and stopped short.

"Where's Mom?"

Kate pointed to the deck. "Why don't you

bring her a refill? Don, just look, she is exhausted."

He wrapped his arms around her waist and gave her cheek a quick peck. "You're very sweet."

Kate leaned back into his arms with a soft laugh. "Don't worry, I made some of your favorites. Now go, pour your mother some coffee, and set the table, please."

"Your wish is my command, love." With a mock bow, he grabbed the pot and an empty mug and joined his mother.

Kate watched the two of them; the love between mother and son was obvious. It was good to see Don happy. She turned her attention back to the stove before the bacon burned.

Moments later, she called out, "Breakfast is ready!"

Don pulled Sherry to her feet and held the door as they entered the kitchen.

"My gosh, something certainly smells good." Sherry grinned. "This is a treat—

having my breakfast prepared by a professional chef!"

"I hope you're hungry and you like it. I made a German puff pancake, berries, and bacon." Kate carried three plates to the table.

"Is this all?" Don teased.

"There is plenty more. Sherry, I don't know how you kept your sons fed. If Jack and Leo are anything like Don, he's a bottomless pit."

"Did I hear my name?" Jack came sauntering into the room with a huge grin on his face. "Whatever you made, is there enough for me?" Jack stood at the counter surveying the pans.

"Help yourself." Kate anticipated Jack would stop by. The boys had been close growing up, and despite the physical distance between the brothers, they talked often.

Don grumbled good-naturedly, "Don't eat too much, little brother. I'm counting on seconds."

"By the looks of your plate, you don't need

seconds." Jack heaped his plate high, leaving one very small slice.

Kate gave Don a playful warning glance. "Don't worry about Don; he's grumpy in the morning."

Sherry watched her boys' banter. "Will you two ever stop poking at each other?"

Don grinned, his mouth full, and gave his head a fast shake. He swallowed. "Nope."

Kate was pleased everyone enjoyed the pancakes. Unlike a traditional pancake, this one had a custardy texture. The men and Sherry devoured all traces and sat back in a food coma.

"Don, will you help me clean up?"

He nodded. "Do we have to start right at this moment? I'm too full to move."

"Kate, is this on the breakfast menu at What's Perkin'? I've never been in during normal business hours."

"No. We serve breakfast sandwiches, traditional pancakes, waffles, or omelets, and a daily special. Of course, most people get items to go during the week. On weekends, we have more table-based business. Lunch is a different story; that's big every day. Our menu consists of soups, salads, sandwiches, and a seasonal daily special. I try to make the specials enhanced versions from traditional ingredients. It keeps my creative toe in the pot and introduces our customers to new flavors."

Sherry grew thoughtful. "I didn't realize you use your culinary skills. For some reason I thought it was more of a bakery and less of a café."

"When Mom opened it was a bakery and coffee shop. But over the last five years or so, it has evolved into a restaurant. However, we don't serve dinner; family time is important, too. That is one of the reasons we're looking to hire another cook and maybe a waitress or two. Mom and I don't take much time off." Kate looked at her husband, hoping he wouldn't say anything about starting a family.

As if reading Kate's mind, Sherry continued. "Well, of course, when you have children, you'll need some time off, dear. It's hard being a full-time working mother. Back when Don was born, I was managing the office. Then Jack came along, and I had to put my foot down and tell Sam to hire an office manager. Thank heavens he did or I would never have had the next four babies."

Kate's heart constricted in her chest. She forced a smile and got up from the table. "I'd better get these dishes done."

"Mom, we've got cleanup under control. Go ahead and do what you need to do. I'm sure Dad is chomping at the bit." Don got up and placed a comforting hand on Kate's shoulder.

"Are you sure? After all, Kate made a lovely breakfast; she doesn't need to clean up, too." Sherry looked around the room.

Did she sense the undercurrent of tension?

"Sherry, we insist. By the time you're ready,

the kitchen will be tidy. Do you want us to go with you to the hospital?" Kate had regained her composure and tried to dismiss the dark cloud that threatened to settle over the morning.

"No, you two stay here and relax." Sherry smiled. "Jack, will you be here when I get back with Dad?"

"I have to head out to the south field and check on the guys. I should be back around noon."

Sherry patted his cheek. "See you then."

After their mother left, Jack looked from Kate to Don. "What is going on with you two? What did Mom say that has you both on edge?"

Kate was close to tears, surprised by the gentleness from Jack. She gave a slight nod to Don.

Don kept one eye on Kate and the other on Jack. "If you tell anyone, I'll kick your butt into next week."

"Who would I tell?" Jack's concern was obvious on his face.

"We've been trying to have a baby and it seems it's not as easy as we thought. So, talk about babies is a little hard for us at the moment." Don spoke quietly. He didn't want his mother to overhear the conversation.

"Hey, you guys. I'm really sorry. I'm not sure what to say."

"If Mom brings up the topic again, can you change the subject? We'll tell the family when we're ready. You're the only Price who knows what is going on and I want to keep it that way."

Kate loaded the dishwasher while the guys talked.

"You've got it. Kate?" Jack said. "If you need something, I'm here for you. I'm sure you're more comfortable talking with another girl, and I'm just a guy, but, well, you know, we're family." He pulled his sister-in-law into a bear hug and quickly released her before she cried. In an attempt to lighten the mood, he said, "So about that breakfast. Any chance you can show Mom how to make that pancake?"

Grateful, Kate smiled. "Sure, I'll supersize the recipe so you can get enough."

*D*on watched Kate and Jack. He was lucky to have a kindhearted brother who was supportive of his wife.

"Tell me what's been going on in the fields." Don walked his brother to the porch. Over his shoulder, he called to Kate, "Be right back. I'm going to walk Jack to his car."

"I've got your number, Donovan Price. I'll be done by the time you get back." Kate's laughter followed the men to the porch.

"Don, I'm really sorry about the whole baby thing. I wouldn't have brought it up if I had known."

He looked over the grassy yard. "It's harder for Kate than for me. She feels like she has let me down. I don't care if we adopt; one way or the other we'll have kids."

"I wish there was something I could do to help. But man, I'm at a loss."

Don eased the subject back to the family business. "So, tell me, are we expecting a good harvest?"

"So far it's been a warm and fairly dry season. I'm anticipating high yields this year. The last spring frost was long before the buds started to pop. Growing grapes, like all crops, doesn't make for sound sleeping. I'm always worrying that it's going to rain too much or not enough. At this point, we're going to have grapes to sell, especially the Riesling. Did Anna tell you about the new blend she's working on?"

Don nodded. "Yes. What's she got up her sleeve, or should I say in her beaker?"

"She wants to create a light summer blend that is a bit sweet while being easy to drink, something fun to be serve chilled. She's combining a red with the Riesling. Time will tell if it will be drinkable." Jack was confident Anna would find a way to accomplish her goal; she usually did. "I need to get going. Are you driving Mom to the hospital?"

"I'd like to. Just in case anything happens, then she'll have help. But you know Mom is very stubborn." Don grinned. "Guess we all know where we get it from."

Jack chuckled. "You're going to have your hands full with both of them. I wish you luck." He jogged down the steps. "Catch you later."

Don watched Jack head down the driveway and take a left toward the garage. More than likely, he would take a four-wheeler to the field. It was easier to navigate the vines for a quick overview. He would never admit he missed walking around the warehouse, checking on all aspects of winemaking. He was happy with his life, and Kate meant more to him than the grapes. Don had wanted Kate to move to Crescent Lake after college graduation. There was one problem. He hadn't asked Kate; he just assumed she would get a job nearby and they would live happily ever after. She had been furious, called him an inconsiderate clod, and how dare he assume she would fall in line like a good little girl. She broke off their relationship and moved home with her family. He came home to lick his wounds and spent a lot of time going out with old friends and burying himself in work. Within a few months, he concluded life without Kate wasn't a life he wanted to live. After telling his parents he was going to ask Kate to be his wife, he moved to Loudon and proceeded to win her back. He never regretted his decision, but there were moments when he missed the view from this front porch and everything that went with it. Drinking in the warm earthy air, he turned to go in search of his mother.

"**D**onovan, I am perfectly capable of driving to the hospital." Sherry was becoming more exasperated as the minutes ticked by. "You're being obstinate, insisting you drive me into the city to pick up Dad."

"Mom, look at it this way; you get to spend some quality time with your favorite son." Don wore his most charming smile in an attempt to sway her.

"Well, I must admit that is a very persuasive argument." Sherry pretended to weigh her options. "Alright, you drive. However, on one condition." Eyeing her son, she waited until she had his full attention. "Your father has been through enough so you will not say anything to upset him. And no questions about tonight! Understood?"

With a mock salute, Don said, "Yes, ma'am."

"Give me a few minutes. I want to ask Kate if she would mind making a dessert. You know how much your father loves his sweets."

• • •

Sherry breezed into the kitchen. "Katelyn, I'm not sure if you have been kept in the loop, but Don has insisted on driving me to the hospital." By Kate's lopsided smile, she knew. "I was wondering, could I ask a favor?"

"Certainly, how can I help?" Kate's curiosity piqued.

"I really hate to ask but I won't have enough time to get everything done. Could you make dessert? It doesn't have to be anything fancy."

"Absolutely. Is there a farmers' market nearby?"

Sherry jotted down the directions. "While you're there, would you pick up salad fixings, too? I'm going to grill chicken."

"Consider it done." Impulsively, Kate hugged Sherry.

"My goodness, dear, what was that for?" Sherry beamed at the unexpected gesture.

"Thank you. I hate sitting around twiddling my thumbs."

"Oh? Don tells me how hard you work at the café. I want you to take a break from cooking when you're here."

Kate's face flushed crimson. "I had no idea. I thought you didn't want my help."

"Dear, I want you to feel comfortable and I assumed you knew I admired your skill in the kitchen. In fact, I agonize over everything I cook when you're here. Seems to me we've had a classic communication breakdown." Sherry checked her watch. "My gosh. Don! We need to go. Sam is going to think we forgot about him."

Kate watched Sherry hurry out of the room, amazed at what had just happened. She went from feeling like an outsider to more of a family member, all with one short candid conversation.

Kate followed Sherry outside. "Don?"

He stopped and jogged up the steps. "We'll be back in an hour or so."

"Okay, I'm going to the farm stand to pick up a few things for dinner. Any requests?"

Don kissed her lips. "Whatever you make will be delicious, but Dad's favorite is strawberry rhubarb pie." With a gleam in his eye, he gave her one last kiss and, in a few long strides, slid behind the wheel.

Talking to the wind, she said, "I guess that's your way of asking for pie." With a spring in her step, she retrieved her handbag and keys. If she was going to make a dessert, she had better get going.

Don pulled away from the house while looking in the rearview mirror at his smiling wife. "I'm not sure what you two talked about but Kate seems happy." Don glanced sideways at his mother.

"It seems we've had a misunderstanding. I

thought I was being nice encouraging Kate to relax when you are here, and Kate thought I didn't want her help. I'm afraid I've made your bride feel a tad unwelcome. Also, I confessed she intimidated me with her culinary skills."

"You told Kate she intimidated you?" Don hoped his mother didn't make things worse. "I can't see how that will make things better."

"I am sure Kate will be a little more comfortable now that I've learned I shouldn't try to do it all. Your sisters have never been interested in cooking. So, that has always been my domain. I guess it's time I learn to share the joy of feeding our family." His mom patted his arm. "Son, please don't worry. I'll do my best to have Kate feeling like she's an important member of our family in no time."

"If you say so, Mom. I have to ask, is this part of yours and Dad's new scheme?"

Don's mom flashed him a look and refused to answer.

"I know, no questions or comments before

dinner. I have a pretty good idea what the main topic of conversation will be tonight and that's the last thing I'm going to say on the subject."

Sherry looked straight ahead, hiding a smile. Don and the family had no idea what was coming. Well, maybe they had some inkling, but nevertheless, the magnitude of the news would cause quite a stir.

4

Sam and Sherry sat on the airy front porch, soaking up the sights and sounds that stretched in front of them. For the last forty years, this had been their favorite spot to unwind with a glass of wine and each other. There had been good times and bad, worrying about their children, the crops, or their business. But through it all, they had the strength from each other to weather the storms.

Taking a deep breath, Sherry broached the

subject that was the elephant on the porch. "Have you thought about what you're going to say to the kids?"

Sam's wineglass hovered near his lips. He took a small sip and grimaced. "This isn't wine."

"No, it's iced tea. Humor me, just for today, dear."

Sam set the glass down. "I've done some thinking when I was lying in that darn hospital bed. I'm going to be completely honest, about everything."

"And that means what exactly?" Sherry prodded.

"If I don't stop working and dealing with the stress of running the company, I won't be around long term. Sherry, you know it is that simple. Potentially, I have a serious heart condition. This latest episode was a warning I heard loud and clear. You know what the doctor said. If I had been by myself in one of the back fields, I might not have been so lucky.

As much as I don't want to turn the reins over to anyone, I have to do it. My hope is that I can oversee things and be an extra hand when needed." Taking a sip of his iced tea, he contemplated his next words.

"Do you think the kids will overreact?"

"You know our children. Each one will handle the news differently. Ultimately, I'm worried about Don. He'll be torn between stepping into the role he'd dreamed of since he was a child following you around, and his life with Kate. If you remember correctly, once he figured out she was the only girl for him, he packed up and moved. I had hoped they would return long before now, but as the months turned into years, I've known this day would come." Sherry turned and reached for Sam's hand. "This morning I discovered my attempt to give Kate time to relax has actually made her feel like an outsider, a guest in our home."

Sam blinked hard. "So, all this time Kate had no idea we considered her a daughter, and not just the girl who married Donovan? Shame on us. How could we have been so insensitive to overlook her discomfort? I can understand why Don and Kate kept their distance, especially when Cari accepted our family with open arms. We sure messed that up." Sam grew thoughtful. After a time, he said, "What do we do now? How can we fix it?"

"Rest assured I've already started down that path. I gave her directions to the farm stand and asked her to help with dinner preparations. I never understood cooking is her passion that she shares willingly with family, friends, and strangers alike."

She glanced over her shoulder to make sure they were truly alone. With eyes gleaming, she continued. "I have an idea."

"I know that look. We've been together far too many years for you to get anything past me, woman. What are you cooking up? And pardon the pun." Sam smiled. Over the years he'd learned that some of the best business ideas came from his wife after she uttered those four simple words.

"We build, or I should say Kate builds a bistro off the tasting room. You remember when we talked to our accountant and the contractors a few years ago. The numbers looked very positive then. I think she could serve light luncheons each weekend, and if she wanted to, we could add private parties. Jack could create an outdoor wedding spot and we could set up tents for larger events. She'd run the kitchen and be as hands-on as she wants. Then, when they have children, she could still run everything and have a staff that would work exclusively for her. It's a win-win for Crescent Lake Winery and Don and Kate." Satisfied, Sherry leaned back in the chair.

"For our business that's a brilliant idea—new ways to grow—but you have conveniently forgotten Kate is in business with her mother. How do you convince her to leave Cari? Because I think Kate would view the move as abandoning her mother."

Sherry's smile dimmed. "Don said it was never Kate's intention to permanently stay in Loudon. She has become comfortable in her role. She told me Cari is going to start looking for additional help. Maybe Kate would see it as good timing all the way around. They could hire a pastry chef and the kids could jump in with both feet at CLW. It would take time to finish the construction, but it's a perfect way to make the transition, and I think we should discuss it tonight with the rest of the plan."

Sam nodded slowly. "It might work, but let me do the talking. You can be a little pushy with your ideas when you get on a roll," he teased.

"Then it's settled. Tonight, after dinner, we tell the kids everything and let them ask all the questions they want. It will take time for them to adjust to the changes, but I'm confident they will." Thoughtfully, she continued. "I am worried about Leo. He's not going to want to work for the winery. He loves what he does with car restoration and Liza wants to be a full-time mother."

"For heavens' sake, Sherry, all we're asking is they sit on the board and attend quarterly meetings. I'm sure they can spare a few hours a year. They have a good head for the business and they have a financial stake in its success." Exasperated, Sam leaned back and closed his eyes. "I'm tired and I want to rest until everyone gets here," he said, effectively ending the conversation.

"That will be in five minutes, Sam. Tessa just parked her Jeep, which means Anna isn't far behind."

"Okay, so five minutes." Sam kept his eyes shut. "Just drink your wine and breathe. It's going to be an eventful evening."

Sherry watched her youngest daughter glide up the stone walkway. Her hair was pulled off her face with a clip and long waves tumbled over her shoulders. Large dark glasses were perched on a pert nose, hiding her deep brown eyes from view. Sherry wondered how it was possible all her children, except Liza, inherited her eyes when Sam had the most interesting shade of hazel, full of flecks of gold, green, and brown.

"Hello, sweetheart. Is Anna going to be here soon?" Tessa stepped onto the porch. Sherry offered her cheek for a peck.

"Yes, she is right behind me. I offered to drive but you know Anna; she likes to drive with her top down and the wind in her hair." She glanced at the door. "Where are Kate and Don?"

"They'll be out soon. Kate was checking on the timer and Don went in to get a few more glasses."

"I'm going to see if I can help. Can I get you something?" Tessa peeked at her father and tapped the top of his head. "Dad, I know you're not sleeping so you can open your eyes."

Sam grunted. "How could anyone get any sleep with all this jabbering?"

Laughter answered him as Tessa stepped inside.

"One down, four to go." Sam sat up straight in the chair. "Here comes Anna, driving like a hellion as usual."

In a cloud of dust, a late model VW bug screeched to a halt. The door flung open and Anna came bounding up the steps. "Hey, Dad, Mom, what's up? Good to see you got home okay. Don did good." Anna kissed her parents' cheeks and flopped down on the glider. "So, where is everyone? Tessa's Jeep is here but I don't see the boys or Liza and the kids."

Before she could get an answer, the screen door burst open and Tessa came out carrying a tray of delectable-looking appetizers. "Perfect timing, sis. Kate's handiwork." Tessa offered her parents first choice. Don emerged with another tray of small plates and wineglasses with Kate close behind him with bottles of wine.

Anna stood up. "I'll take those for you, Kate."

Don set the tray on a small side table. "Hey, little sis, do anything amazing today?"

Grinning, she said, "Oh, you know, played in my lab with grape juice—all fun stuff."

"Sounds like a good day in your world. Maybe in the next day or so I'll wander in to see what you've got fermenting."

Sam watched closely to see how Anna would react to someone hanging around her space. Typically, she worked in solitude, and he wondered if it would bother her to have Don checking on her projects.

"Sure," Anna replied, attempting to cover her surprise. "It's been a while since you've come around. I love showing off my latest and greatest blend. I've been playing with some interesting combinations, but I'm sure Jack told you."

"Well, I've never been good at sitting idle and Dad needs to take it easy for a few more days, so, well, you know, I thought it might be interesting to catch you in action." From the corner of his eye, Don noticed Kate watching him and quickly changed the subject. "I wonder when Liza and Leo are going to show up. I'm starving."

Sherry could feel the tension ramp up a notch between Kate and Don when talk had turned to the winery. "Kate, would you like to go into town with me tomorrow? There is a new shop I'd like to check out. I think they might carry some of our wines."

"That would be nice, Sherry. I didn't realize you were involved in the distribution end." Kate wasn't sure what was going on but she was going to have a serious talk with Don later.

"It's good for me to keep my fingers in the business. With local shops, we've found it's better if I check them out. If it seems like a good opportunity, I approach them about a wine consignment arrangement. Once the wines start to sell, they typically place a nice stocking order." Sherry smiled. "These days this is the only direct contribution I have to the business."

"I had no idea." Kate understood the core conversation of the evening was about CLW and to be fair she was going to listen more than talk. However, she fully intended to keep a close eye on Don's reaction to whatever came up.

During Sherry's explanation, Jack and Leo arrived and helped themselves to what was left on the tray. Liza had the little guys in tow, struggling to carry a basket of toys between them.

"Sorry we're late. We had a few tears over what toys could come to Grammy's house." Liza pointed toward the boys; Johnny and George were struggling to get up the stairs without spilling the contents.

Jack hopped up and helped his nephews get the basket into the house without putting a hole in the screen door.

Leo piped up, "When's dinner? I missed lunch."

"That seems to be a common question with this family. I guess we should go in." Kate stood by her father-in-law's chair, ready to help Sam if he needed it.

"If everyone would grab a bowl or platter, we can eat." Sherry shepherded her kids like ducklings to water with Sam and Kate, arm in arm, bringing up the rear.

"I hear you were busy today." Sam eyed Kate with a wicked gleam. "I must say I'm looking forward to dessert; I hope you've whipped up something decadent."

Kate squeezed Sam's arm. "I don't think you'll be disappointed. We have strawberry rhubarb fruit sorbet, and for anyone who wants a little something more, shortbread cookies. I thought about pie but wanted something kid-friendly."

"I love cookies and you know my wife isn't much of a baker; she makes incredible meals, but dessert, not so much." With a conspirator's wink, the pair took a seat at the table. "But don't tell her I told you. She'd have my head on a platter," Sam chuckled.

When the Price family got together for a meal, it was much like the McKenna clan, full of laughter, but louder. Shadows crept across the backyard and the table was cleared of dirty dishes, making room for dessert.

"It's nights like this I'm glad we screened in this porch or these darn mosquitos would have driven us inside by now." Sherry spoke a little louder than she had intended. Getting a signal from Sam, she ushered the little boys inside and turned on their favorite DVD before returning to the back deck.

Sam put his spoon down and cleared his throat, and instantly his children's eyes were glued to him. "Well, I'm very happy everyone was able to come for dinner tonight, especially Don and Kate, dropping everything to come home." He paused for dramatic effect. "I know you are all wondering why your mother and I want to talk to everyone. I would like to ask that you let us finish, then you can ask questions, and everything is up for discussion. However, I don't think we will get full resolution tonight."

Sam again paused and took a sip of water. "For the first time in many years, I'm not sure where to begin." Drumming his fingers lightly on the tabletop, he continued. "Your mother and I have decided it is time to step down from running CLW and turn it over to the next generation."

The silence was deafening.

Just as Sam feared, the family had panic on their faces.

Don glanced around the table. "Dad, is it your health? Is there something you're not telling us?"

"I have a mild heart condition and high blood pressure. This recent episode was a rather unpleasant warning for me to slow down or it might get worse." Sam didn't want to alarm anyone so he tap-danced around the words "heart attack." "Honestly, I think it's time your mom and I travel if we want, sleep late, and not have to live each day by the clock and seasons. For our entire married life, we have put in long hours and sacrificed to keep the business growing for the family. We're ready to reap the rewards of our hard work."

"But Dad," Tessa cried, "you are Crescent Lake Winery. You're a part of everything we do—new wines, marketing, distribution, growing, even the tasting room. None of us know how to do what you do and make look so easy."

"Tessa. Kids. I'm not packing up my office tomorrow and heading for parts unknown. I'm going to take a back seat and let you"—Sam's gaze slowly circled the table—"all of you, step into the roles you have been working toward since you were babies." Sam studied Don, the implication hung heavy in the air. Everyone knew Don had been groomed to follow in Sam's footsteps, to become the president and CEO of Crescent Lake Enterprises. Well, everyone except Kate.

"Dad." Leo broke the heavy silence. "I don't have any interest in growing, bottling, selling, or anything to do with wine, other than drink it occasionally. I'm happy working on cars and that isn't going to change."

Sherry was quick to speak. "Leo, we know you and Liza aren't interested in the business. But if you agree to be on the board of directors with your sisters and brothers, we feel that is a good compromise for us all. You can be impartial as you're not involved in the day-to-day operations but you have sound business logic."

Leo grinned. "Cool. Well then, I think I can speak for both of us; we're happy to be on the board and be the tiebreaker as needed."

Liza spoke up. "I think it's a good compromise. Someday I might want to work at the winery, when the boys are in school, so for me, staying involved on a limited basis is the perfect solution. Thanks, Dad, for including me."

Sam nodded while his baby girl spoke up.

Over the years, Liza had developed a habit of letting Leo take the lead for both of them.

Sam addressed Jack next. "You'll manage the operations side of the business. You've been doing most of the work for a long time, but over the next few months I'll turn contract negotiation for all maintenance supplies and equipment over to you. For the next year or so, I'll help you with the contracts, but I don't foresee any issues and you'll get comfortable fairly quickly."

Jack nodded, but seemed a little disappointed. It was obvious he wasn't going to get a crack at the big chair. He had never wanted the job, but maybe he would have thought it was nice to have been considered.

"Tessa and Anna, nothing will change for either of you in the short term, although, Tessa, if you are interested in sales, that might be a good challenge for you. Go on a few distribution calls and check it out."

Tessa's eyebrow arched in surprise. Sam knew she had expected Sam to turn over the reins to her, considering Don lived in Loudon and was completely out of the business. She would adjust given time.

"Sure, Dad, I'll give it some thought."

Anna had sat quietly and watched the events unfold. "That's great news, Dad. I'm happiest in the lab."

🍷

Since Sam started to speak, Kate's heart had been hammering in her chest and heat had flooded her cheeks. Don had better set his parents straight, she thought, right away before the conversation got out of hand.

"Kate. Before I talk with Don, I would like to request that you listen with an open mind." Sam paused, waiting for her to look more receptive.

Slowly, Kate nodded. "Of course, Sam, Sherry. I'm happy to listen to what you have to say."

"Before Don met you, he was handling the distribution of our wines nationally, working with large firms to generate sales, and he was a natural. He believed in the product and was passionate about our business. When Don came to us and said he was moving to Loudon, we accepted the news under the premise he would be back and bring you with him. At the time, we thought you would become a chef in an area restaurant. But Sherry and I understand that after working with your mother, working for someone else wouldn't be enough to satisfy you long term. We are proposing you open a bistro adjacent to the tasting room. If you'd like to open it up to larger events, we can develop a long-term plan."

Speechless, Kate stuttered, "You want me to open a restaurant here, at the winery? I don't know what to say. That is very generous of you. Do you have any idea how expensive it is to do what you're suggesting?"

Sam smiled. "But of course, we do. We've run numbers with the accountant and talked with a contractor." He continued. "Kate, we didn't put any plans in concrete, no pun intended. It would be built to your exact specifications. You would have complete control." Sherry and Sam nodded, grinning like Cheshire cats.

Kate turned and looked at her husband. "Did you know about this before we got here?"

Shocked at the undertone in her voice, he said, "Absolutely not. This is the first I've heard of the plans for a restaurant." Don could understand how Kate would feel betrayed if he had lured her here under false pretenses. "Honestly."

Kate addressed her in-laws. "As I'm sure you understand, this has come out of the blue for me and you've given me a great deal to think about." Her chair scraped across the wooden deck. "If you'll excuse me, I need some air." Kate hurried out the back door, desperate to escape.

Leo looked from his mother to father. "Well, I don't think that went according to your plan."

The family sat in silence in the cool night air, listening to sounds of children's giggles in the next room.

Don glanced at his family and without another word rushed after his wife.

5

Don stood on the front steps frantically searching the shadows until he made out the faint outline of Kate sitting under the old apple tree. He jogged over and dropped onto the bench, taking her hands in his. He asked, "Kate, why did you run from me?"

She glared at him. "How dare you let them ambush me? It would have been nice if you had told me their plan. At least I would have been prepared. Instead, I was blindsided. Did you think I'd be more apt to agree if I didn't have time to think about the implications of their offer?" She dragged her hands away and stalked to the fence line.

"What are you talking about? Do you think I knew and didn't tell you? Right from the beginning of our relationship, we both agreed to be totally honest and that hasn't changed. You have to believe me; I had no idea they were going to tempt you with your own restaurant." Don was angry with his parents but now was not the time to get into that topic. "Honey, I completely understand where you are coming from, but you do have to admit the offer is very generous."

Kate's voice ratcheted up. "Are you saying we should forget about the life we've built in Loudon, pull up stakes, and move here so that you can run the winery? I can't believe we're having this conversation."

"Don't put words in my mouth. What I said was, it was nice of my parents to think of you when they developed a plan for the family business." Pacing, Don continued. "Kate, I've never made it a secret that I love the wine business, but I would live anywhere with you. Our marriage is more important to me than anything else. But in all honesty, I never considered my father would want to retire." Don looked to the heavens' stars dotting the sky. "Dad's hospitalization has made me think. Maybe I *could* take over for him. I'm not saying we move here but I'm wondering what I can do from home, and maybe come up a few days every couple of weeks. It would mean furnishing the cottage my parents gave us for a wedding present. I can't live with them." Don let the idea dangle in the air, hoping Kate would move beyond her anger to see this as an opportunity for their future.

"Don, I can see you have given this some thought," Kate challenged. "But since when have you wanted to run CLW? You told me your passion was working outdoors with plants and trees, not in a stuffy boardroom."

"That's not exactly what I said. I do love working outside but the challenge of business has always been a part of who I am. I was born to run CLW. I put that dream aside for you, but Kate, it's time for us to make a change. I don't regret my decision to move to Loudon and work for Shane. Actually, it's helped get me ready for this day, to accept the responsibility of my family's business." Don crossed the dew-covered grass to where his wife stood.

"We don't have to make any decisions tonight but we need to talk about this tomorrow. Kate," he implored, "I love working for your brother but it's his business, not mine. I'd like to have something where I leave my mark, where my decisions are my mistakes or my success." Gently, he drew Kate into his arms. "Let's not argue tonight. Tomorrow we'll find a way to make this work for both of us." He pointed to the starlit sky. "It's a shame to let the moonlight go to waste."

She sighed and allowed him to gather her into his arms. "You're right. Tomorrow is a better time to talk, once emotions, namely mine, have settled down."

"You know," Don whispered in her ear, his warm breath causing her to sigh, "we could go upstairs and get even warmer."

She looked into his eyes. "We aren't doing anything of the sort in your parents' house."

"Why not? We're a married couple." He nibbled behind her ear.

"Stop that before you get something started you can't finish," Kate playfully admonished.

Pulling her hair back, he continued to nuzzle her neck. "Who says we have to stop?"

"I do." She pulled her hair down. "We'll have plenty of time for that when we are in our own home."

"We need to furnish the cottage, then we can canoodle all we want."

"That is another subject for another day, Mr. Price. For the moment we should go back to the house so I can apologize to your parents."

Tenderly, Don cupped Kate's face in his oversized hands as he dropped a chaste kiss on her mouth. "As you wish, my love."

Caught off guard by the tenderness mixed with underlying passion, Kate pulled Don closer, returning his kiss with enough fire to fan the flame of passion, leaving them breathless and wanting more. With ragged breaths, Kate murmured, "A reminder of where we left off. In a few days I do believe we'll remember."

In the bright moonlight, Kate's deep-green eyes shimmered with promise. "I won't forget," Don said in a deep, husky voice.

"I'm counting on that." Grasping his hand, they walked back to the house.

Sherry and Sam had sent the rest of the family home, giving Don and Kate space to talk without expectations from the rest of the clan. Sherry finished stacking dishes in the dishwasher when she said, "Sam, they have been gone a long time."

He glanced at the clock. "It hasn't been that

long, and we should have talked to Kate and Don without the other kids around. We sprang the bistro idea on her, and let's face it, we've bounced the idea around for years. What were we expecting, Kate to jump up and down with excitement? Basically, we're asking her to uproot and start over."

"Isn't that what Don did when he moved to Loudon?" Sherry sniffed.

"Dear, it's different for a man to leave his family. It is more commonplace. You have to remember the circumstances surrounding the McKenna family. Kate's father dying when she was ten years old, leaving her mother, twin brother, and little sister to build a new life. She is a sensitive young woman and that family is closer than most. I'm not surprised Don fell in love with her. Without hesitation, they welcomed Don as a son and brother. He couldn't have picked better in-laws."

"You're right. Of course, the McKennas are wonderful people, but I wonder how long he would be content working for someone else when he was cut from your mold—ambitious, driven, and an innate businessman."

Don and Kate found his parents in the kitchen. Kate spoke in a firm but quiet voice. "Sam, Sherry, I'm sorry I walked out. It was rude and I apologize."

Sherry walked around the counter. "We're sorry, Kate. Sam and I should have talked with the two of you first. We didn't exactly think ahead. It was thoughtless and we apologize, too."

Relieved, Don interjected, "Sounds like everyone is sorry. Before you guys start asking questions, Kate and I have to figure out what we are comfortable doing in the short and long term. So, until we're ready, can we table the discussion?"

Sam knew his son well and understood negotiations were afoot. "Of course, son, we're here whenever you are ready." He gave them a broad smile. "Now, how about a couple more cookies?"

Kate shook her head. "No, thank you. I'm

dead on my feet." She gave a sideways look at Don. "Are you coming?"

"Right behind you. Good night, Dad, glad you're home where you belong." He stooped to kiss his mother's cheek. "Good night, Mom, see you in the morning."

Once the kids were out of earshot, Sam looked at his wife. "Don has a plan to become involved in the business. I can feel it."

"You may be right, but until they are both ready to talk, we shouldn't ask any questions. Let them come to us."

"Agreed."

"Now, we should go to bed too. You've had a few very long days, dear."

Sam pulled himself from the chair. "I can't wait to sleep in my own bed."

Everything was as it should be, Sherry thought. Her children were healthy and her husband was home. Tonight, she would sleep soundly.

At the opposite end of the house, Kate studied the shadows dancing on the ceiling. Irritated, she could hear Don's slow, deep breathing. How could he sleep when they had things to discuss and decisions to make? Her thoughts were illogical and getting a good night's sleep always helped make things easier in the light of day, but as much as she wanted to succumb, her mind whirled with scenarios.

On one side, Kate and Don could return to Loudon, pick up where they left off two days before, and forget about the winery and bistro. However, realistically, that wasn't an option. She loved Don and wanted him to be happy and fulfilled with his work, just as she was as a chef. Maybe Don's idea of traveling between the winery and Loudon could work. To his point, she could finally set up the cottage as a second home. If she and Cari hired some decent help for What's Perkin', she could spend time here, with Don. It was a good compromise. Tomorrow they could stop by the cottage and see what needed to be done. Satisfied, Kate snuggled close to her husband and fell into a dreamless slumber.

A light breeze stirred the dotted Swiss cotton curtains. Kate rolled over to wake Don as it was going to be a busy day, but she was surprised to discover the sun streaming through the window and the bed empty. Kate sat up, dark hair tumbling over her shoulders. "Don?" Silence answered her. Sliding out of bed, she pulled on shorts and a colorful tank top, secured her hair into a quick twist, and left the room. Kate was confident she'd find Don in the kitchen.

Kate entered and the conversation came to an abrupt halt. Sam and Sherry looked focused on their coffee mugs. Don turned to his wife.

"Good morning, Sunshine. Sleep well?"

Don placed a kiss on her lips. "Coffee?" He set a mug on the counter.

"I hope I didn't interrupt anything important. I can go upstairs if you'd like to finish your conversation." Kate didn't attempt to hide her irritation.

"Of course, you didn't interrupt anything," Sherry quickly reassured Kate. "We were apologizing to Don again. Last night didn't go as smoothly as we envisioned. The last thing Sam or I want is for you to feel pressured. We just thought you should have options."

"Sherry, I appreciate the time and trouble you and Sam took to investigate an establishment tailored to my needs. It is a very generous offer. But for now, I think we should focus on how we can get Don back into the business by commuting between here and Loudon." Kate thought a pin would drop. "Don and I haven't hammered out the details, and some of this he's hearing for the first time. After lying awake for quite a while, I did some serious thinking."

Don sat down, waiting to hear where Kate was headed.

"Don reminded me that we have a cottage here but we've never taken the time to furnish it and make it a home. So today, we're going over to poke around. I want to see what it needs for furniture so Don can be comfortable when he's in town. From there we should go to the office and have Don walk around, talk to the people, and set the stage for his return, part-time at this point, of course. We'll set up an office for him in Loudon so he can keep in touch. This means he'll give notice to Shane, but that won't be a problem." Kate paused and smiled. "Don, have I missed anything?"

He grinned. "Honey, I know this will take some getting used to but I'm sure it will all work out for everyone." Don turned to his parents. "What do you both think?"

Sam was speechless for a moment. "Well, I think we can make it work. If you want to be here and in Loudon, it will take organization of meetings and such. It's definitely worth a try."

Sherry beamed. Her son was going to take over the family business and Sam could move into semiretirement, jumping in when needed but at a much slower pace than today. "If you two want to drive by your place and go to the winery, you'd better get going. If you don't have your key with you, there is a spare hanging on the hook in the mudroom."

"Just let me have breakfast and we'll go." Kate was pleased that they didn't try to change her plan. After all, she thought, this was a great compromise.

Don took the car keys from Kate. He couldn't wait to get to the cottage. Driving down the two-lane road lined with vines heavy with grapes, he couldn't help but grin. Secretly he had hoped one day she'd want to decorate but each visit had been filled with activities and family. With the exception of the day his parents gave it to them, he couldn't remember the last time they had gone to their cottage.

Kate glanced at her husband. "It's nice to see you happy. Maybe we should make more time to hang out with nothing to do. This is heaven to be driving in the warm sunshine, windows down and fresh air."

Don grinned. "We're here." As they turned in the drive, the cottage captured Kate's attention. Colorful flowers spilled out of the window boxes and the grass was neatly clipped. She had never thought about keeping the yard tidy. "Don, who has been taking care of the place?"

He pulled to a stop in the half-circle drive, dashed around the car, and opened Kate's door. "I'm not sure. We'll have to ask Mom." He held out his hand. "Ready?"

She stepped onto the gravel drive and stopped to admire the view. "I had forgotten how beautiful it is here."

"Sort of reminds me of our place in Loudon. Nice, quiet neighborhood." Don tugged her hand. "Let's go inside and see what else we forgot."

"Hold on." Holding up her trusty notepad, she said, "I need to make notes." She studied the façade. "I'd like to change the color, inside and out, make it pop, make it reminiscent of a traditional cottage. I'm sure your parents can help with recommendations for painters."

Kate marched up the front steps to the small covered porch with Don close at her heels. "We'll need to plant some flowering shrubs. They'll give it curb appeal." She jotted a note. Don unlocked the door and pushed it open.

"After you." Don let Kate enter the house, praying her enthusiasm would continue.

She paused on the threshold. "Do we need to replace the wood? It's beautiful, but do you think it will be durable, like tile? And a small bench for taking off shoes." Taking a deep breath, she sighed. "Oh, look at the backyard." Kate crossed the kitchen area into the great room. "Don, did you remember it was this cozy?" She turned a full circle, taking in the staircase that separated the house and created privacy for the master bedroom tucked at the opposite side of the kitchen. "I love the wainscoting; we should leave it alone, freshen up the walls with ivory paint, and on the floors, some colorful scatter rugs." Kate ambled into the kitchen. She passed the French doors that opened onto a full-length deck. "Maybe we could add a pergola to filter the sun."

Don nodded and held his breath. He was pleased with her ideas, but knew the expensive room was looming.

Kate studied the galley-style kitchen with a keen eye. With arms wide, she sighed. "I love the openness of the kitchen in relation to the rest of the house, but it needs work. I think a center island with a six-burner professional-grade stove, surrounded by marble counters and a large farm sink under the window. The cabinets are ample but I'd like to see glass fronts on the top and over here"—Kate walked to where a standard refrigerator sat—"this will need to come out, remove this cabinet, and put in a sub-zero commercial grade unit. And, of course, we need a dishwasher." Kate knew the rough estimate, as they had just finished the kitchen in Loudon. To Don's credit he didn't cringe.

"All this is doable. Anything else a must?"

Kate walked down the hall toward the master bedroom. "I think a stackable washer and dryer could go here and relocate the linen closet to the main bath." She stepped into the master. "All that is this needed is a fresh coat of paint and furniture. Pretty easy." Kate wrapped her arms around Don's waist. "I can make this a home away from home for us if this is what you want."

"Do you want to look upstairs? There may be some painting or renovations you'd like to have done at the same time." He attempted to steer her toward the stairs.

"No, we don't need to worry about the up-stairs at the moment. But we should make sure the fireplace is checked and order wood before it turns cool." Kate easily dismissed the conversation of the extra bedroom and sitting room.

"Let's go outside, then we should go to the office. While you're busy, I'll make a list of things to discuss with your parents. If possible, I'd like to talk with a contractor tomorrow."

Efficient as usual, Kate was already planning five steps ahead. Don said, "We don't have to rush, honey. Don't you want to enjoy the process of turning the cottage into our home?"

"I have to get back to work. You know Mom is short-staffed. I'm hoping she was able to get the advertisement in the paper. Once we get some help, I can be here a few days every couple of months."

"Months, not weeks?" Don didn't hide his disappointment. "Okay then, tomorrow you handle the contractor. Before we leave I'll have a meeting with the staff. I want to make this transition as painless as possible for everyone."

Kate looked at him with one eyebrow cocked. "I didn't realize you'd take over immediately," she said coolly.

"Katie, I've been gone from the business for six years. I'm sure a lot has changed. I need to get up to speed, especially working remotely. I'll need to come back in a couple of weeks and, more than likely, be here for a week. Will you come with me?" Don realized he was holding his breath and slowly exhaled.

Her temper flared. "I can't keep running out on What's Perkin'. I have responsibilities too, remember?"

Sensing an argument, he chose to sidestep it. "No big deal if you can't make the next trip. I'll have some long days, and if you stay in Loudon, maybe you can hire someone and that will free you up for another visit. After all, at some point, you'll need to check on the contractors."

Kate slowly nodded. She was beginning to realize two homes were just the start of the complications they were about to encounter. "We should get to the office," she said flatly.

With little conversation, the couple pulled out of the driveway, leaving the lighthearted feeling behind.

Kate attempted to break the tension. "I'm sorry. This is a lot for me to get used to in a really short period of time. Don, be patient with me, please?"

With a side look, he could see hurt in the depths of her emerald eyes. "Of course. I love you and in time we'll figure this out."

She visibly relaxed. "How many full-time employees does the winery have?"

"I'm not sure. It's the growing season so we'll have temporary field help. Do you remember Peyton Brien?"

"Vaguely. I know the name. We met once during my last visit before graduation. She was that cute brunette who seemed to have a crush on Jack."

"That's the one. She manages the tasting room and store. Peyton is a good friend to all the Price kids, but I don't think she had a crush on Jack. Dad said she works full-time now. I'm sure we'll see her today." Don pulled up to the tasting room entrance. "Let's poke around and see who we can find. I'm sure Anna and Tessa are sequestered in their offices."

Kate glanced around and saw Sherry's handiwork in the flower beds and fountain. "I don't remember the gazebo, is that new?"

"Nothing escapes you." He smiled. "Mom said there was a couple who had their first date here, wanted to get married on the property, so she had it built. Since then, they've held a few more events in the gazebo. Turns out it was a good idea."

He held the door and she entered the cool, dimly lit room. "Hello," Don called. "Is anyone around?"

A petite brown-eyed brunette popped up from behind a long wooden counter. "Don, is that you?" With a squeal, she ran around the end to give him a big bear hug. Pulling away, she grinned. "Kate, it is great to see you again.

It's been too long. How long are you in town this trip?"

Casually, Don draped his arm over Kate's shoulders. "We came when Mom called about Dad being admitted to the hospital. I'm sure you've heard, Dad wants me to take over the big chair. For now, I'll go between here and Loudon while doing my best so Dad can ease into retirement."

Peyton said, "Cool. I guess that means you're my boss." She stepped behind the counter. "I was doing inventory. We're expecting a big weekend, but can I pour either of you a glass of wine?" She pointed at the wall clock. "It's afternoon."

Kate glanced at Don. "No, thank you. But I will take a bottle of water if there is any cold?"

"I always have the fridge stocked. Help yourself." Peyton pointed to the wooden screen. "It's back there."

Kate crossed the room. "Honey, would you grab me a bottle, too?"

"Sure, Peyton?"

"I'm all set. Thanks anyway."

"Who is this cute little boy in the picture on the fridge?" Kate called to Peyton. "I don't think I've seen him before."

"Owen, my son." Peyton busied herself.

"I didn't know you had a son. How old is he?" Kate asked.

Peyton scrubbed an invisible speck on the counter and said softly, "He's five."

"He's a cutie. He's got your eyes but he must have gotten the blond hair from his dad." Kate handed the picture to Don.

He studied the image and glanced at Peyton, then back to the picture. "He's a good-looking kid. Does he look like his dad?"

Peyton bristled. "He's not a part of our lives."

"Too bad. A boy needs a father."

"Owen has *me*."

Don passed the picture to Peyton, unsure how to respond. "Kate, we'd better get to the office before Dad sends out a search party."

"Peyton, thank you for the water and I'm

sure we will be bumping into each other from time to time."

Peyton murmured, "I'm sure we will."

Once they were out of earshot, quietly Kate said, "Owen's father must be quite a jerk for Peyton to have that kind of reaction. But I give her a lot of credit. After spending time with Abby and Devin, I know how hard it is for a single mother."

Don sensed there was more to this story than what Peyton was willing to say. In the meantime, he was going to see what he could find out from Jack.

6

———

For the next few days, Don spent long hours with Sam. Kate was busy ordering furniture and hiring contractors. Sherry happily agreed to oversee the work and promised to send Kate pictures regularly. Despite talking to Cari several times a day, Kate felt awful that she was shouldering the bulk of the work; she was anxious to get back into the kitchen.

Kate was on the porch swing waiting for Don to get home. The moment he stepped on the steps, she announced, "The car is packed and I'm ready to go."

"Well, hello to you too, dear wife." Don appreciated Kate wanting to get the long drive behind them so they could sleep in their own bed. It seemed like they had been away forever, when actually it had been just shy of a week.

"Hello, my husband." Kate greeted him with a chaste kiss.

"Surely you can do better than that," he teased. After a quick glance around to see if they were alone, Don wrapped his arms around Kate, pulling her close. "I've worked hard today."

Before Kate could answer him, a discreet clearing of a throat stopped Don mid kiss. He turned to see who interrupted them.

"Mom, I was going to give my wife a proper kiss hello. Can you give me five minutes?"

"It only takes you five minutes to give her a proper kiss?" Sherry winked at Kate. "I was going to surprise you. I've packed a cooler for the drive, so you won't need to stop unless you want to stretch your legs."

Embarrassed, Kate disengaged from Don's arms. "Sherry, that's very sweet. Thank you." She glanced at him. "We were just talking about what time we'd be heading out."

Reluctantly, Don released his wife. A real kiss would have to wait until they were home. "From what Kate's said, the car is packed and ready so we'll say goodbye to you and Dad and be off."

"He's in the kitchen." Sherry held the door open. "Are you coming?"

"Yes, ma'am." Don and Kate entered the dim interior.

Sam was sitting at the kitchen table, rifling through papers, and looked up when they came in. "Don, you should take these and re-view the new distribution contracts. I'm thinking we may want to change the rebate." Sam slid the papers across the table.

Don took a cursory look and handed them back. "I've got these on the laptop; you can keep them for when I call tomorrow."

Don stuck out his hand and Sam stood up, giving it a firm shake. "Drive careful, kids." Sam looked at Kate. "We'll see you soon?"

"I'm not sure when exactly. Mom has a few interviews lined up so that will take up a lot of my time. But I promise I'll be back just as soon as I can." Kate hugged her in-laws, promising to call when they got home.

Slipping behind the wheel, she buckled up and waited for Don to do the same. "Ready?" With a grin, she turned the key and the car purred to life. "Sit back and watch the world zip by. If you want, take a snooze; I'll wake you when we're home."

Don leaned back with the intention of mulling over a few ideas. He had just accepted a huge responsibility and he didn't intend to let his family down. In less than fifteen minutes, the sound of snoring filled the car. Taking a peek at him, Kate's mind drifted. How was she going to convince Don the long distance of the winery wouldn't become an issue? They could make it work with him traveling every couple of weeks. Of course, he would need a comfortable car for the drive; his truck was a gas hog. Kate made a mental to-do list for the shop while the miles ticked away. At dusk Kate pulled in front of their garage door. It was opening slowly when Don stirred.

He blinked several times and rubbed his hand across his eyes. "We're home already? Guess I was more tired than I thought. I'm sorry I wasn't better company."

"No worries. You know me, I love driving, and it gives me time to plan. But for punishment you can bring in all the bags."

"Happy to help, and then I want a real 'welcome home' kiss." Don gave her a wicked grin that caused Kate to blush bright pink.

"I'm sure that can be arranged," she called over her shoulder and unlocked the door.

Don grabbed the bags from the trunk and hurried after Kate. He made his way to the bedroom and dropped them in the corner, pulled back the blankets on the bed, and went to see what was keeping his wife.

She was peering in the refrigerator. "I set up the coffeepot, but you'll need to come by the shop for breakfast. We don't have anything that isn't fuzzy or an unnatural shade of green. Maybe you can run by the grocery store after work."

"Sure. Don't worry about a list. I'll pick up the usual items and we can always get takeout if we're too tired to cook tomorrow night."

Don pulled Kate into his arms. "I'm going to talk to Shane first thing tomorrow and see how long it will take to hire my replacement. But I'm going to recommend he consider promoting Tom Hamlin. He does a great job with the projects he's run and deserves a chance at more responsibility."

She chewed her bottom lip. "Are you sure you want to tell Shane now? You're not sure if the remote office and traveling between Loudon and Crescent Lake is something you will want to do long term."

Unprepared for her hesitancy, he said, "Kate, I'm taking over the winery. Did you think that was lip service to my parents?"

She pulled away. "I didn't think you'd leave my brother shorthanded, that's all."

"I'm not going to leave him in a lurch, and if he needs help, all he has to do is ask. If I didn't know better, I'd think you just went along with everything because you felt it was a passing idea and once we were home I would change my mind." Don's temper was beginning to get the best of him and he didn't want to say something he'd regret. "Kate. Do you support me taking over the winery or not?"

This was the moment she had been dreading. He had her pegged. Kate had spent the last few days humoring him. One look at his face told her it was best to tread lightly. "If this is what you want, then of course I support you. I'm surprised you want to get started right away, that's all. I thought you'd be doing it part-time."

"I can't run a large company part-time. I'm either all in or nothing. You understand, right?"

She crossed her arms over her chest. "Of course, I do. This is a big change for me. For us. I thought we would ease into it, but I guess you're ready to walk away from McKenna Landscaping and be totally focused on Crescent Lake Winery. You have to realize that up until a week ago, I had no idea you wanted to be involved at CLW. I thought you left that behind when we got married."

"I didn't think I could have both you and the business. Now I see it was shortsighted. I should have talked to my parents to see if we could have set up this arrangement years ago. I need for this to work, Katie."

"Well, now you have the best of both worlds, me and your dream job." Kate was done with this conversation. "I'm going to get ready for bed; it's been a long day." With her spine ramrod straight, she marched down the hall.

Don ran a hand over his buzz cut, wondering what the heck had just happened. They went from the potential of a romantic evening to Kate literally walking away. He struggled to understand why she was so upset. He had never kept it a secret that he loved the thrill of the business world, or had he? The distance would cause some issues but he was sure they would find a way to work around them. Ultimately, he had hoped Kate would grow attached to the idea of the bistro and they could live and raise their family in Crescent Lake, but at this moment he had doubts that would become a reality. Moving from room to room, Don clicked off the lights and double-checked the exterior doors. He hesitated at the threshold of their bedroom. He could hear Kate sniffling. In a few long strides, he was at her side.

"Honey, what's wrong?" Gently, he wiped tears from her cheeks.

"I'm worried our life is going to change so much you'll be too busy to keep trying to have a baby," she wailed. "And we'll grow apart. I love you so much and I don't want your new job to come between us. It almost did once before."

Don smoothed back her long dark hair, noticing her face was extremely pale in the soft lamplight. "Oh, Kate. I love you too and nothing, not this job or traveling for work will drive us apart. No matter where we are, the journey home will always end with you, so put that worry out of your head. For us, together is our home."

She snuggled into his arms as they lay on the bed. Don continued to comfort her. Within moments, he felt Kate relax. He was ready to pick up what they had started in the kitchen as Kate's deep rhythmic breathing reached his ears. He resigned himself to one more night of waiting to show his wife how much he adored her before drifting off into a deep slumber.

In the morning Kate woke refreshed and

slipped out of bed to let Don sleep. Last night had been emotionally draining and she was anxious to get to the shop. She was curious to see how Mom did while she had been gone. Whistling tunelessly, she pulled into her spot behind the store. Kate was surprised to see the lights on and her mom's car in the parking lot.

"Hello? Mom?" Kate shouted as she entered the kitchen.

Cari's head popped up from behind the counter. "Kate!" She grinned. "The prodigal daughter returns," she teased. "I wasn't sure what time you were coming in, so I came down to get things started. Ray is making coffee."

"Jeez, looks like you're doing just fine without me." Kate tried to hide her disappointment.

"Of course, we missed you. This place isn't the same without you. But remember, I used to run this business solo for many years and it's good to know I still can. I'll admit it helps to have Ray pitch in and do what needs to be done." Cari never thought Kate would be sensitive about the shop, but quickly reminded herself that over the last several months Kate was easily upset as her longing for a baby grew more intense.

"Tell me, how are Don's parents?" She watched a flash of something unreadable flit over Kate's face.

"Suffice it to say it's a long story and one we don't have time to talk about right now. But I do want to talk it out with you. I'm a little disappointed in Don."

"Oh?"

"Well, his parents handed him the winery on a silver platter and he didn't say no. Today he's going to tell Shane he's leaving the landscaping company and running the winery between here and Crescent Lake." Kate stated facts without emotion. If she said anything more, Cari suspected she might start crying.

"I see." Cari nodded quickly, putting together the obvious scenario. "We should talk about this later." Handing Kate an apron, she stated, "Time to bake."

Grateful for the change in subject, Kate tied it on and turned to see what was sitting on the cooling racks. She announced, "I'm going to make tea breads."

Cari left her daughter, hoping that baking would soothe her and give Kate an opportunity to think. She joined Ray out front.

"I'll be home a little late today. I need to spend some time with Kate after we close. It sounds like Don is back in the wine business and this time he's in charge. I have a strong suspicion Kate is hoping it's a temporary change."

Ray said, "Then I'm going to make myself scarce. Cari, you may want to get that help wanted ad in the paper a few more times. I have a feeling Kate and Don may be spending some time in Crescent Lake." Ray kissed his wife goodbye and headed off to work.

She paused to think about the possibility of hiring someone full-time. Over the past week she thought it would give her some free time but now wondered if that had been a pipe dream. Her thoughts were interrupted by the first customer of the day. Wearing a warm smile, Cari focused on the flurry of morning activity and the day evaporated along with the baked goods in the case.

Kate flipped the CLOSED sign on the door and stood with her back to the sidewalk. "Were you this busy last week?"

Cari wiped the counter off before answering, "Typically, sales were strong. I don't think any more or less. Are you still worrying about the time you were gone?"

"I feel like I abandoned you," Kate said quietly.

"Kate, sit down." She pointed to a chair. "We'll have tea."

*K*ate sat and stared as the traffic meandered down the street. She loved this view and wondered how many times over the last eighteen years she'd sat in this very spot. When she was a teenager, she'd dreamed of becoming a world-class chef. Culinary school was the first step toward fulfilling her dream until one spring day when she literally ran into Don. Her chef coat was covered with iced tea and she had to detour back to the apartment to change, which, of course, made her late for class. Over the next several weeks, she kept seeing him around the city and did her best to avoid him. She didn't have time to date. Kate wasn't going to get derailed from her life plan. However, one beautiful day she stopped to enjoy the courtyard on Fed Hill and Don appeared with a peace offering—cold drinks and cookies from the best bakery in town. From that point until graduation, whenever he was in the city, they spent all their free time together. As a wine salesman, he was up and down the northeast coast, but Don always made it a point to call her every day. After graduation, she thought Don would pop the question. Instead, he suggested she get a job in Crescent Lake. She wasn't ready to give up on her dream and was furious he would suggest she blindly follow him. Brokenhearted, she moved to Loudon to lick her wounds and figure out the next step, and while doing that, she went to work for her mother.

Cari could see Kate's mind had drifted. Giving her some space, Cari prepped the counter for the morning, waiting until it was a good opportunity to break Kate's mood.

Kate exhaled and Cari walked over. Steam rose from the pretty floral teacup Cari placed on the table. "Milk?"

She nodded. "Please."

Cari set the tiny pitcher down and took a seat.

"I guess you're wondering what happened in Crescent Lake," she stated.

"Other than updates regarding Sam's health, you didn't say much."

"Bottom line, Sam wants to retire and Don needs to take over. The other kids will remain in the jobs they have today with Leo and Liza as board members. But day-to-day operations will be Don's responsibility. So today, he's giving Shane his notice. He'll set up a home office and go to the winery once or twice a month for meetings. The first couple of trips will be to reassure the employees he has no plans to make any drastic changes." Kate's voice was filled with bitterness.

Surprised by the turn of events, Cari said, "It sounds like Don has given this a lot of thought, and I'm sure he's going to be a terrific CEO. From a strictly business perspective, his father made a good choice."

"You haven't heard the best part," Kate snorted. "They have this plan to build a bistro on the property. They even hired a consultant and did a feasibility study from a logistical side as well as projections for return on investment capital. It's like dangling a carrot in front of a horse, well, or so they thought."

Slowly, Cari said, "What do you mean?"

"I didn't bite, offering me a bistro when I'm in business with you, like I'd pick up and leave you high and dry. Can you believe their audacity?"

"It sounds like a very generous offer. I seem to recall your dream was to open a restaurant."

"Well, yeah, while I was in school. But that was a pipe dream. You need me here; we have plans to expand." Kate glared at her mother. "Don't we?"

Mildly annoyed, Cari said, "You moved home after college to nurse a broken heart. Then Don moved here and said he would rather live in Loudon than lose you. Do you remember that? He gave up his career and took a job with your brother. Don walked away from his family business to marry you. If you asked Don, I'm sure he would say he'd do it again tomorrow, but isn't it time you support his choice of a career?"

Kate chewed her lower lip and toyed with the teacup. "Do you think I've been selfish?"

"I wouldn't say selfish, specifically, but you've been wearing blinders. You're a lucky woman to have married a man with morals and family values." Cari didn't want to hammer the point.

The two women sat in silence. "I guess I have been a little harsh. I didn't want to decorate the house his parents gave us and it has been standing empty all this time."

Cari let Kate mull over her thoughts.

Looking brighter, she said, "Did I tell you Sherry is keeping an eye on the kitchen renovations and the painters? And I've ordered furniture. In a couple of months, Don will stay at the cottage, instead of with his parents."

"And what about when you go to the winery?" Cari pushed her point.

She looked surprised. "What do you mean, 'when I go'? I can't leave you."

"You need to stop using me as an excuse," Cari gently admonished her daughter. "It's time we hire a cook and front of the house staff. I'm not going to work six days a week forever. Ray and I are talking about enjoying life before we get too old."

"You guys are old." She chuckled.

"No, we're not decrepit, but I've been thinking I want to cut back. I've worked hard for years, Kate, and the majority of those years I was alone so it didn't matter. But now I have a wonderful husband and I want us to spend quality time together. For that to happen, there have to be changes here."

"Why does everything have to change?" Kate wailed as tears threatened to spill from her troubled eyes.

"Katie, without change there is no growth and we need to continue to grow in all aspects of our lives. Believe me, I know better than anyone the truth in that statement. For years, I was stuck grieving. Losing your dad caused me to become emotionally crippled. Sure, I started the shop, raised three children, and from the outside, I had moved on, but the reality was, I hadn't. Not until my sanctuary was damaged did I start to change how I lived life. It took an act of nature, but the tree did more than damage my house, it cracked the protective shell I built over the years, layer by layer."

Kate was stunned. "There isn't a time limit on grieving, Mom. Maybe it wasn't the time for you to let go of Daddy until the storm."

Cari shrugged. "Maybe not. But I didn't do anything to help myself move on either." She grasped Kate's hand. "Keep your options open, Kate, and remember your life is with Don, whether you live in Loudon, Crescent Lake, or on the moon."

"I know, Mom, and when I get home tonight, I'm going to tell him I support him. I'm going to make sure that when Don is at the cottage it feels like our home." With a smile, she stood up. "Thanks, Mom, for the tea and the talk. I feel much better." In one quick motion, Kate cleaned up the table. "Tomorrow we place an ad and I'll call JWU—maybe they can recommend a pastry chef looking to get their feet wet in an establishment like What's Perkin'."

With a bounce in her step, Kate went into the kitchen, calling goodbye as the door slammed behind her.

Cari remained at the table wondering how Kate could be overlooking the most important point she had tried to make. Don had sacrificed his career to be with Kate. Maybe it was time for Kate to realize her marriage was more important than where she lived.

She went through the usual routine of closing up. Talking to herself, she said, "One thing is for sure; we're on the cusp of change and the road is going to get rocky before we reach our destination."

7

*D*on's truck was parked in the driveway when Kate sailed into the kitchen. All she needed to do was find her husband, wrap her arms around him, and apologize.

"Don?" she called out as she walked through the house.

"In the spare room," came a muffled response.

Kate was surprised to discover the room had been rearranged to make space for an oversize worktable. On it sat Don's new laptop, printer, and various other office supplies. "Well, looks like you've been busy today," she said brightly.

Don looked up from the mess of wires. "You're in a good mood."

She planted a kiss on his mouth. "I need to tell you I'm very sorry for the way I've been acting. I should have paid more attention to your feelings and stopped being so insecure. If running Crescent Lake Winery is your dream, then you have my complete support and everything else will work out. I'm going to make sure the cottage is comfortable and homey. You'll be able to concentrate on business while you're there and get back to Loudon and me quickly." She gave him another lingering kiss. "I think we should pick up where we left off last night. If you're still interested, that is," she said coyly.

"I like the way you think. Did you lock the door when you came in?"

She turned her head and batted her deep-green eyes graced by dark lashes. "I'm one step ahead of you." Gently, she tugged his calloused hand. "Come with me and let me finish apologizing."

He followed Kate to their bedroom. She pulled the shades and flipped back the covers. She felt him watch her every move, waiting for her to welcome him into her arms. Kate's body flushed with warmth, anticipation of what was to come. Her husband knew how to make every fiber of her being quiver. There were times where Kate yearned for his touch, impatient to be consumed by the intensity of their love, but tonight she wanted to move slowly. He seemed to sense her pace and respected it. Timing was everything.

Kate was an arm's length from her husband. He watched as she released her hair and it tumbled over her shoulders and down her back. Moving slowly, she stepped out of her sandals. Grabbing the hem of her shirt, she pulled it off and tossed it to the floor. In jeans and a skimpy white lace bra, she nodded.

Instantaneously, his clothes joined her shirt.

Just as the first time they came together, she marveled at the perfection of his long, hard body. Muscular from physical work, deeply tanned arms and neck, his legs like granite, hard yet silky to her touch. Her gaze skimmed over him, noting he was ready for her. Slowly, she stepped from her jeans and took one step toward him, closing the distance by half, her body awash with anticipation. She took the final step, standing heat-flushed skin to skin.

"I need some assistance," she said in a soft, husky voice.

He reached around and with one finger dropped the first of two final barriers between them. His hand trailing down her spine, his finger caught the edge of lace, and with a tug, only air separated the couple.

Kate caressed his chiseled features, losing herself in the molten depths of his velvet-brown eyes. With a slight shiver, her mouth stopped just before the kiss. Don hesitated, impatient to wait another moment. Her mouth claimed his hard, pulling him into the swirling vortex of emotion.

Maintaining their connection, he swept Kate off her feet and tenderly placed her in the center of their bed. Her arms locked around his neck. She pulled him closer, unwilling to let anything come between them. She surrendered to the sensations he was eliciting from her body. Before succumbing to the final peak, she regained her focus and began to mirror Don touch for touch. He groaned in pleasure. She continued to fan the flames, bringing Don to the edge of pleasure. Moving ever so slightly, they came together, only as one who knows the other well can do, each of them urging their love forward to the very cusp of heaven. Emotions flooded their senses, leaving them drenched in each other's arms.

Shadows had crept through the room before either of them could form a coherent sentence. Don turned to gaze lovingly into his wife's eyes. "I think we should stay at my parents' more often. If this is what you're like when we get home, abstinence is worth it."

She giggled. "Maybe we could pretend we stayed at your parents'."

He grew serious. "Kate, I know change can be unsettling. But I'm awfully glad you understand why taking over for Dad is important to me. If I didn't have your support, I wouldn't be able to be as successful as I hope to be."

"I understand now. I'll admit at first I didn't, but after talking with Mom today, I get it, and I'm ready to do what I can to help." She snuggled in his arms. Lazily, she drew small circles in his chest hair. "Are you hungry?"

He snorted. "I'm always hungry." He pulled her hand to his lips and grinned. "Oh, do you mean food?"

"Food first, and then if you're feeling up to it, we can revisit this exact spot." With a gleam in her eye, she knew what his answer would be.

"Now that's the way to support your husband." Sitting up, Don passed her a robe.

"Let's have eggs; they're quick and provide plenty of protein for late-night activities."

"I'll cook and you clean up. Over dinner, tell me about your conversation with Shane." She twirled her hair into a loose bun and the couple went to the kitchen.

"There's not much to tell. Shane said he's been ready for the announcement since I started working for him and agreed Tom Hamlin is a great choice to step into my role, and that was it."

She cracked eggs and listened as she whisked them up. A part of her wished Shane had made it a little harder for Don to leave McKenna Landscaping, but the other part of her expected nothing less from her twin.

*

Cari ran a help wanted advertisement in the paper and Kate contacted her alma mater. Within a few days, they had several interviews scheduled for a counter person and a bakery chef. Don had spent long hours reviewing reports Sam had sent to him and was planning his first trip to the winery. He asked Kate to go with him, but once she explained they were interviewing, he dropped the subject. He promised to go by the cottage and give her a full report. Sherry had been sending pictures but there was nothing like fresh eyes to give her the details.

Kate was stirring cookie dough when she heard Don talking with her mom. He was on his way out of town and she expected he would come to the kitchen via the coffeepot. This would be the first time they had been apart for any length of time since they were married.

"Hey, beautiful." He walked through the swinging door.

"Hi, honey. Are you all set to hit the road?"

He pecked her lips and relieved the cooling rack of a signature blueberry muffin. "Yeah, I had to run home and grab some files I forgot. I'm not sure if I'll need them but better to have them with me. I parked the truck out front and it's got a full tank of gas." After quickly devouring the muffin, he wiped the crumbs from the corner of his mouth and reached for another one. "We're going to have to look for another car so I don't have to take yours all the time."

"I don't mind the switch; I like tooling around in the truck." Kate grinned. "You know, there's something a girl likes about driving her man's truck."

Chuckling, he patted her backside. "I have to get going. I'll call you tonight?"

"Okay, I might have dinner at Mom's so call my cell." She wiped off her hands and slipped her arms around his waist. "Drive carefully and take lots of pictures at the cottage. I'm anxious to see how it's coming together."

"Yes, dear." He held her tight, inhaling her light floral perfume. "I'm going to miss you," he murmured.

"Ditto." She swallowed her tears.

He called goodbye to Cari as he left through the back door. She moved to the stove, checked the cookies, and set the timer for a few additional minutes. She leaned against the counter and gave a big sigh.

"I heard that," Cari called from the front.

She walked to the pass-through window. "It's official. We've started a new phase in our marriage. I'm not sure I'm going to like sleeping alone for the next few nights."

"Why didn't you go? You could have spent a few days poking around the town, checking out restaurants and maybe coming up with an idea for the spare room in the cottage."

Kate leaned on the windowsill. "I don't need to furnish the upstairs right now, and when we're there, we eat with the family so checking out restaurants isn't really necessary."

"I wasn't thinking about going out to eat. I meant to check out the competition."

"Mom, I know where you're headed and I

don't plan on opening a bistro. I am perfectly content here."

"Are you sure? I think you should give it some serious thought. It's a great opportunity, one that doesn't come around every day. How long do you think Don will want to travel between two homes? Your husband is going to immerse himself in the business. It's only natural he'll have to spend more time on-site. He has aggressive expansion plans for the winery and wants to make his mark. A bistro could help him to do just that." Cari didn't look at her directly; she was trying to take a subtler approach. She continued. "What's Perkin' was my dream, Katie. You are a very talented chef, not just for bakery and luncheon items. In my humble opinion, I don't think you have given this idea enough consideration."

"Mom," Kate said sharply, "we're not going to talk about this anymore." She snapped the towel off her shoulder and turned away from her mother.

Cari seemed baffled. "Why are you deliberately turning your back on the future? Do you think your marriage will be strong a year from now if you and Don spend the majority of your time apart?"

Frustrated with the silence, Cari turned her attention on cleaning an imaginary spot off the counter.

A flurry of customer activity diverted her mom's attention while Kate stewed. She had never doubted the strength of her marriage but suddenly she was thinking about the separation and the toll it might take. After all, she mused, Don had moved to Loudon to win her back after their big breakup. If that wasn't a testament to their love, what was?

When her mom was alone again, Kate stopped working. "Mom?"

"Hmm?"

"Do you think this could harm my relationship with Don?"

"Some separation between partners is healthy; you shouldn't be joined at the hip. It keeps the relationship strong and it gives you things to talk about and share. But if you stop sharing the day-to-day ups and downs, yes, a marriage can start to show the stress." Her mom was standing in the doorway to the kitchen. "The two of you need to talk about what your future holds and you really need to make sure the decisions are in the best interest of you as individuals and your marriage. If you want to have a family with Don, you need to live under the same roof. I'm not saying that needs to be in Loudon or Crescent Lake—only the two of you can make the decision—but maybe it's somewhere in between."

Kate's shoulders drooped as her mother spoke. "Are you saying you don't want me in Loudon?"

"That is not what I am saying and I'm not telling you what to do. The advice I can give is to help you make well-informed decisions with your eyes wide open. If you choose the wrong path, you might not get another chance. Maybe Don will work here every other week or maybe a few days every week. But you have to talk about it. Don't just assume it will work out."

Slowly, she nodded. "You're right, Mom. On his next trip, I'll go with him. Check out the area and work on the cottage. When we talk tonight, I'll ask him when he plans on going again. Once I know, then I can plan a few days off." Kate smiled for the first time in several hours. "That's if you can spare me."

"We'll work it out, and who knows, maybe we'll have some help by then, too."

Cari picked up the ringing phone. "What's Perkin'."

She grinned and pointed to the receiver. "Yes, the position for counter help is still available. Do you know where the shop is on Main Street?" Listening, she nodded. "Correct. Can you come in tomorrow at three?"

Cari jotted down a note. "Wonderful. We will see you tomorrow and please bring a copy of your résumé. Thank you."

"Our first interview. How did she sound?"

"Well, *he* sounded promising!" her mom

exclaimed. "His name is Lucas Ford. He was a waiter at the White Inn, until he injured his back. He wants to stay in the food industry but needs something less strenuous. If he has experience with people and food, it might be a good match."

"But it's a totally different pay scale, Mom. Fine diners are typically big tippers and the White Inn pays above scale for its entire staff. If he was any good, he was making bank." Kate thought for a moment. "I know the sous chef. I'll give her a call and see if there are any tidbits she can share."

"Can you call before tomorrow?"

"I'll do it right now. Pass me the phone."

She punched in a series of numbers and waited for someone to answer.

"Hello, Jenny? Kate Price." She paused. "Sorry, McKenna. I know you're in the middle of prepping for dinner service but I wanted to ask if you knew Lucas Ford?"

She took notes as her old schoolmate rattled off details. "That's right," Kate said, "We are looking for front of the house help and he's applied."

Her mom held up her hand as if to ask what she was saying.

"Okay, that's great. Thanks a lot, and if you're ever in Loudon, look me up at What's Perkin'."

After a quick goodbye, she hung up. "Good news. He was an excellent waiter and pretty much ran the dining room. He got hurt about six months ago and tried to go back to waiting tables, but the trays aggravated his back and he had to give it up. Jenny thinks he would be an asset to our shop and can upsell like crazy. She said they were sorry to lose him."

"That certainly is a good recommendation. All that's left is to see if we think he's a good fit with us."

She gave her mom a high five. "Hopefully one position will be filled and I'll get to work on finding someone for the kitchen."

"Let's not get our hopes up. I'm not going

to stop interviewing if we have other inquires."

"Understood, but Mom, if someone can handle the pace of the White Inn, this should be a slam dunk."

"Honestly, that's what I'm worried about. He may find our little shop dull by comparison." Her mom shrugged. "I love this place just as it is."

"I do too, Mom. We will find the right people, don't worry." She felt lighter as she closed down the kitchen. When she got home, she'd make some calls and it would fill the long, lonely evening that loomed ahead of her.

Cari poked her head into the kitchen. "Are you coming for dinner?"

Kate shook her head. "No, I think I'll pass tonight. I'm going to relax for a little while and then go to bed early, but thanks anyway. Tell Ray I said hi."

Her mom pecked Kate's cheek. "See you in the morning."

"See you tomorrow."

Quiet descended over the shop. Kate always liked this time of day, a busy day behind her and a new one on the horizon. Picking up her handbag and keys, she secured the door, ready to face the empty house.

"I can do this. I'll have a glass of wine, relax, and wait for Don to call."

She made the short drive home. She unlocked the kitchen door and discovered a large bouquet of wildflowers sitting on the counter with a note propped against the vase.

Flowers for my love. When you look at them, remember, I'm with you, always.

Kate leaned in and drank in the heady scent of summer. "Don, you are a sweet man."

She kicked off her shoes and poured a glass

of lemonade, then wandered into the living room.

"Well, this is nice. It's quiet and there is a nice gentle breeze coming in the window." Kate leaned her head against the pillows and the next thing she knew it was dusk. She sat straight up, distinctly aware she wasn't alone.

"Who's there?" she demanded to the room.

"Kate, it's okay. It's me, your dad."

Panic-stricken, she leaped from the chair and ran into the kitchen to grab something for protection. Flipping on the lights, she scanned the room. "Who's there!"

"Katie-bell, it really is me. Put down the rolling pin," the deep masculine voice implored.

"How do you know that nickname?" Her breath came in short, shallow gasps.

"Because I gave it to you."

"No, my father did. Get out of my house! *Now*!"

A dark-haired man seemed to materialize from thin air. "Katelyn. Please listen, it's me.

You know I used to visit your mother when she needed me. I was pulled here, to you. If you don't believe it's me, ask me something only you and I know."

Her pulse raced and heart pounded. "How do you know my mother used to talk to my father?"

"Kate, I told you, it's me, Daddy."

She stood totally still, her mind racing. "Why did I go to culinary school?"

The man wore a soft, faraway smile. "When you were five years old, I bought you an Easy-Bake Oven. When you opened it, you announced I had forgotten the most important part. I'll never forget what you said. 'The hat, Daddy. I need the poufy white hat. Otherwise, how will anyone know I'm a chep?'

"When I tried to tell you, it was a 'chef,' not 'chep,' you informed me it was okay that I couldn't say it right, but you were going to be the best chep in the world and the first thing you were going to make was a birthday cake for your Ellie. So, needless to say, I went out and I bought you a chep hat."

She slumped onto the bar stool and started to cry. "Daddy? Is it really you? It has to be since I've never told anyone that story."

"Yes, Katie. It's really me."

"Why are you here? Mom said you had gone and didn't think you'd be back."

"Mom doesn't need me, but if I'm here, that means you do."

"I don't think so. Don, my husband, is away on a business trip but he'll be back in a few days." Her hand flew to her mouth. Fear wrapped icy fingers around her throat. "Daddy, are you here to tell me Don's dead?"

"Oh no, Kate. Don is fine. If you're worried, call him right now."

She grabbed the phone and dialed. "Don?" She held back a sob of relief.

"Honey, what's wrong? You sound odd. Are you okay?"

"I fell asleep in the chair and had a bad

dream. I needed to hear your voice. But I'm okay now so you can go back to work."

"Are you sure? I was going to give you a call after I had some dinner and thought we could have a nice long talk." Don waited for her to speak. "Kate?"

"That sounds nice." She struggled to control her emotions. "Call me later."

He hesitated. "Alright, if you're sure?"

"Of course, I am. Talk to you in a bit. Love you."

She disconnected and looked at her father. "He's fine."

Her dad gave her a gentle smile. "I know, baby girl. Now let's talk about what's going on with you. I'd like to have you tell me every detail of your life since, well, you know, but we don't have enough time tonight."

"How long can you stay with me?"

"It varies. I never know for sure. Like now, I feel that I'm out of time. But when I come back again, don't be afraid. I'll never let anything hurt you, Katie."

She watched her father fade before her eyes. "Daddy!" she cried. "Wait!"

Once again, the house was silent. Perplexed, Kate sat wondering what she should do next. Straightening her shoulders, she went into the kitchen, heated up leftovers, and waited for the phone to ring. Talking to Don would be a much-needed balm for her frazzled nerves.

8

When Cari got to the shop, she found Kate had the cooling rack overflowing. "Good morning. You must have slept well," she said as she firmly closed the back door.

"Hi, Mom. You're here early." Kate glanced up as she dropped a spoonful of batter onto a cookie sheet.

"I wanted to check the machine and talk to you about a couple of questions I have for our meeting today with Lucas." Cari tied on her apron and went about her morning routine.

Taking a deep breath, she blurted out, "I saw Daddy last night. He was in my kitchen."

Cari sunk onto a stool and watched as Kate methodically measured the dough. "Are you sure you weren't dreaming?"

Color flushing her cheeks, Kate shook her head. "At first, I couldn't see him; I could only hear him. But after a few minutes, there he was standing next to the counter. He didn't look like Daddy, more like the essence of my memory, if you understand what I mean."

Slowly, Cari nodded. "I know exactly what you're saying. He appears a bit softened around the edges. But his voice is strong and comforting."

"It was exactly how I remembered. At first, I was scared and I demanded he tell me something only I would know. He reminded me about my first Easy-Bake Oven. Then I knew it had to be him. Before I could really talk to him, he was gone."

"Based on experience, he'll be back. I haven't seen Ben since Ray and I married."

Cari had a hunch why Ben had appeared to Kate. "Has he ever come to you before?"

"No, this was the first time. What do you think it means?" Kate wiped her hands and slid the trays into the oven.

"It's simple; you need him."

Puzzled, she said, "What do I need help with? My life is wonderful."

"I think when you figure out why he's here, your life will be different." Cari slid off the stool. "Time to open." She pointed to a few trays. "Are these ready for the case?"

Kate nodded. "Oh, and today's special is lemon scones infused with lavender."

She grinned and pushed the kitchen door open with her backside. "They sound delicious. I may have to sample one." The door swished closed behind her.

Kate turned up the radio to catch the local weather, effectively creating distance between the customer rush and the kitchen.

Ray walked in and deeply inhaled the wonderful smells lingering in the air and smiled.

Every day she reminded herself that her life without Ray would be empty. She thanked the stars they came to their senses and recognized love before it was too late. After a twenty-plus-year friendship, it hadn't taken long for them to tie the knot. Good things really did come to those who had the patience to wait for them.

"Good morning, Mrs. Davis!" He planted a kiss on his wife's cheek.

"Good morning, Mr. Davis. How can I help you?" she teased.

With dark-blue eyes gleaming, he said, "I don't think that's on the menu, so can I have two blueberry muffins and a large coffee?"

"You do realize there haven't been more than ten days since I've opened that you have eaten anything other than blueberry muffins and coffee. I'm amazed your skin hasn't turned blue."

Ray gave his wife a suggestive wink. "How do you think I got these baby blues?"

She let the remark slide and glanced into the kitchen. Seeing Kate was absorbed in her recipe, she whispered, "Guess what happened to Kate last night?"

"Hopefully nothing. Since it was the first night she and Don were apart." He leaned on the counter and took a sip of coffee.

"Ben came to see her." Cari glanced toward the kitchen to make sure they were alone. "Kate wasn't sure if it was really him, but he reminded her of a story only the two of them would have known."

He gave a low whistle. "Why now?"

"Well, you know I firmly believe Don and Kate are headed for some pretty serious hurdles in their marriage. I have a feeling Ben is here to guide her. Heaven knows she isn't listening to me. Every time we talk, she seems to understand little snippets, but she is still missing the big picture."

"Which is what exactly?" He knew Cari was worried about the kids but she hadn't shared what she believed was the real issue.

"Kate has no idea the toll these living arrangements will have on their marriage and their ability to have a baby. It isn't a secret they've been trying for a long time, but how can they get pregnant if they aren't even under the same roof? On top of that, Don's parents offered to build her a bistro connected to the winery. Her dream was to have her own place, not to work here. Her loyalty is binding her to Loudon."

"Cari, have you stopped to think maybe her dream changed? Maybe this is where she wants to be long term."

"Ray, you might not remember, but when Kate moved home, she was nursing a broken heart. She was going to live with me for six months or so and look for a position in a city or resort. It was easy for Kate to let things drift along while she licked her wounds. Before she made the leap, Don moved to Loudon, wanting to patch things up. They've been here ever since."

"Are you saying you want Kate to move?"

"Of course I don't. I love having our kids close, but I am a realist. I don't want her to sacrifice her future for the present." She scowled at Ray. "Would you want Jake to feel tethered to your carpentry business if he had an opportunity to live a different dream?"

"I see your point but I'm confused. Do you think Ben will convince her to follow her dream?"

"Yes. That is exactly what I think he intends to do. His visits with me were always about encouraging me to move forward, to spread my wings and soar."

He nodded thoughtfully. "Ben got you to move forward. You had better get hiring."

"The gentleman coming in today, Lucas Ford, has great references so we'll see if he clicks with us. That will be step one, then kitchen help. Kate and I need to talk about our options."

Ray glanced at his watch. "I gotta run, honey, but I'll see you later and I'll cook tonight."

She gave him a sweet smile. "Now that would be really nice, coming home to a dinner for two." Cari stood on her tiptoes to give him a quick peck and a playful shove toward the door. "Now, off with you. Go make your customers happy, and wish me luck with hiring."

He blew her a kiss and called back over his shoulder, "Luck!"

She watched her husband jog down the street to his truck. "I sure did hit the jackpot the day I realized I was in love with that man."

"Did you say something, Mom?" Kate called from the kitchen.

"No, just talking to myself." She chuckled. "If you're ready, let's talk about what questions we should ask Lucas."

Kate sat down at the counter. "Well, he's had a lot of experience waiting on people, but we need to gauge how he'll feel about standing behind a counter and bussing a few tables. I also want to know if he has any lifting restrictions. He'd have to carry trays between the kitchen and counter. How will he be at handling a cash register? In addition to credit cards, which are easy, we still have a lot of cash transactions and our register is the old-fash-ioned kind."

Cari nodded and made notes. "What about weekend availability? That should definitely be a question."

"I'm sure he's used to weekends, but we can ask. He might not realize we're open early or that weekends are crazy busy." Kate looked at her watch. "I'm going to tidy the kitchen, If we think he's a good candidate, I'll give him the nickel tour."

"Kate, before you do, how did your conver-sation with Don go last night? Did you get a chance to talk about tagging along on his next trip?"

"He said everything was good so far. He set up his office, and Sam was in for a while, filling him in on employees he hadn't met yet. And yes, I told him that next time I'll be with him and get the lay of the land, so to speak."

"And what did he say about your plan?"

"I'm sure he was surprised, and then he asked about leaving you to handle the shop. I told him we had an interview scheduled and it sounded promising and I had been in touch with JWU and we would have some applicants for a bakery chef soon."

"I'll bet he was pleased." Cari smiled. "I know I'm happy."

"I feel better about things, too." She started into the kitchen and stopped. "I forgot to tell you there are a couple of associate degree students sending in their résumés and maybe one person with a BA."

"Why does it matter if they have a two- or four-year degree?" Cari was perplexed.

"Well, the two-year candidates will have an excellent knowledge base similar to what we do here. They won't have the experience in artisan breads, wedding cakes, and chocolate and sugar showpieces. I don't think we really need to go to that extreme. I haven't used those skills since I came back. We'll be able to find the right person to handle the baking, breakfast and lunches, and with encouragement, develop specials." Kate got a faraway look. "Sounds like I might work myself out of a job. Maybe the timing would work out for me to have a baby."

Cari knew the baby topic needed to be handled with kid gloves and chose to let the subject stay closed. "When do you think we'll see those résumés?"

"By the end of the week. When I talked with the career development office, they said there was a lot of buzz surrounding this position."

The phone rang and Cari answered. "What's Perkin', how may I help you?" She beamed. "Hi, Ellie." She held up a finger to Kate. "Sure, you can come for dinner. Ray's cooking so there is always enough food. I'll ask Kate, too." She paused. "That sounds good. See you at six?"

After a short exchange, she placed the phone back on the hook. "Any interest in dinner tonight?"

"What's the occasion? I could hear Ellie talking but not what she was saying."

"She wants to talk about her future. I think she wants to see what we think before she makes any major decisions. Will you come?"

In an attempt to be funny, Kate said, "Well, I do have a very busy schedule tonight. But for Ellie, I guess I can squeeze you in."

"I'd better call Ray and let him know there will be four for dinner."

Kate went into the kitchen, grateful it wouldn't be another lonely night. She hadn't wanted to tell her mom, but she didn't like being alone. She wasn't afraid, but having never lived by herself, she'd discovered it wasn't for her.

The remainder of the day flew by. "Mom, are you ready to close?" Kate finished cleaning and organizing the kitchen.

"I put the CLOSED sign up and I noticed a man coming down the sidewalk. I think it's our candidate." Cari peered out the door, trying to look without being obvious. "Shoot, he caught me." Her cheeks grew pink. She pulled open the door. "Hello, you must be Mr. Ford?"

A sharp-dressed man in his early thirties, wearing an untucked light-yellow button-down and crisp, dark blue jeans, stepped into the shop. He was average height with a slim athletic build, and his dirty-blond hair was stylishly cut. His eyes were gray and he had deep dimples in both cheeks. He stuck out his hand and gave Cari and then Kate a firm handshake.

"I'm Lucas Ford, but please call me Luke." His voice was a rich baritone.

"Luke, it is a pleasure to meet you. I'm Cari Davis and this is my daughter Kate Price. Together we run What's Perkin'."

Luke surveyed the room, nodding as he took in the layout and flow. "I like the vibe of your shop. Your menu has enough variety to appeal to a diverse clientele but not so many choices to be overwhelming."

"You're familiar with our menu. I'm impressed." Cari gestured to a small table. "Shall we sit?"

Kate walked over, and Luke waited half a moment until her mom was seated before he sat down. Not wanting to beat around the bush, he opened the conversation. "I'm sure you're wondering why I have applied to work in your shop. I want to assure you I have excellent references. I was in a car accident, and I've been left with a back issue. It's difficult to carry the heavy dinner trays at the White Inn. I took a lot of pride being a top-notch waiter, and I love the food industry. I have to find something that is less taxing on my back but keeps me in food."

Cari began, "Thank you for your direct approach. We had wondered why you were interested in our little shop."

Kate interjected, "Have you been in before today?"

"Yes, occasionally. While I was recovering from the accident, other than physical therapy, I had a lot of free time. Your shop has an excellent reputation for using the finest ingredients and for top-notch customer service. When I saw your advertisement, I thought I might be a good fit."

"Well, let me tell you what is required." Cari ran down the list of day-to-day tasks and expectations. Luke nodded and smiled throughout her list.

"Cari, I can assure you I am up to all that would be required, and regarding the trays, if something is too heavy I would be happy to purchase a wheeled cart out of my own money to transport them. I don't expect any special accommodations; if you offer me the job, that is."

Kate liked his demeanor. "Luke, if we hire you and a trolley cart was needed, we wouldn't expect you to pay for it."

Cari quickly agreed.

The trio sat quietly for a few moments. "Do you have any questions for me or Kate?"

Luke paused. "No, I think you've covered

everything. Is there anything else you'd like to ask me?"

Her mom looked at Kate. "No, we have all we need to make a decision."

"Alright, well, thank you for your time, and if you decide to offer me the job, I am happy with the starting pay listed. However, I have one small request. After I prove myself to be an asset to your business, could we talk about an increase? I am confident I will boost your sales and increase the bottom line."

Cari seemed surprised with his approach. "If things go as you predict, we would certainly talk about an increase. Kate and I have a few more interviews, and then we will be in touch."

Luke stood up and extended his hand. He thanked them one last time before leaving.

After the door closed firmly behind him, her mom said, "Well, Kate, what did you think?"

"If he is half as good as he seems, we'd be

foolish not to hire him. Can we offer him the job with a sixty-day trial?"

"I'll call Charlie Bell and see if that's legal. I'd feel better with a trial period and I'm sure Luke would, too."

"If we do that for this position, we'll need to do the same thing with the pastry chef."

"Absolutely." Cari dialed Grace's number, who answered within a few short rings.

"Hi, Grace, is Charlie available?"

After waiting a few minutes, Cari said, "Hi, Charlie. I'm sorry to bother you at home but I had a quick question. Kate and I are going to hire some help for the shop. Can we hire someone with the stipulation that there is a trial period?" She listened to her old friend and nodded. "I was thinking sixty days."

Kate wondered if sixty was too long.

As if reading Kate's mind, her mother said to Charlie, "Well, thirty isn't long enough to relax their company manners so I think if we do sixty, we'll see the real person."

Cari made a couple of notes. "So, when I

have them fill out their tax paperwork, I can give them the sixty-day agreement, we'll both sign it, and then we're covered?"

She paused and said, "Great, thanks, Charlie, and tell Grace to stop by the shop tomorrow. Bye."

Cari hung up.

"I guess you heard, basically, after we offer Luke the job, we have him sign a simple contract, which Charlie will drop off tomorrow. Once we have that, he can start. If all goes well, maybe next week at this time we'll have our first nonfamily employee."

"Sounds like we're on the verge of a new beginning, Mom." Kate stood up. "I'm going to take off, but I'll see you at the house later."

Cari watched her daughter leave and wondered what the heck had gotten into her. She pulled a loaf of bread from the case and finished locking up. She thought that tonight was going to be interesting. With the change from a romantic dinner for two, she'd make it up to Ray later. After the girls were gone, she'd properly thank him for being such a sweet husband.

9

"Hello." Kate was greeted by tantalizing aromas of dinner simmering.

"We're in the sunroom!" Ellie shouted.

Kate dropped her keys on the counter and stepped out of her flip-flops, leaving them by the back door. Walking into the cool depths of the house, she was reminded of her childhood. She would cuddle up with a mystery book, avoiding the midday heat until Abby would show up and drag her outside for a bike ride. Then the two girls would race down to Scoops and wander over to the park, licking their cones before the ice cream could run down their arms. Life was so easy back then, she thought.

"Hello, family!" Kate tugged Ellie's blond hair before flopping on the couch. "What's for dinner? It smells amazing."

A pleased smile flitted over Ray's face. "Arroz con pollo. And before you ask, it's an old family recipe that I can share with you since we're family. But," he joked, "you'll need to take a blood oath never to reveal the secret ingredient."

With mock seriousness, Kate crossed her heart. "I promise to commit the recipe to memory and never share it with a soul." She leaned forward to pour a glass of wine, offering to top off anyone in need. Settling back in the comfort of overstuffed cushions, she wondered when Ellie was going to share her news.

Instead, Cari finished telling Ellie and Ray about the interview with Luke and announced she was going to offer him the job tomorrow.

"Honey, I'm thrilled you found someone you like and are comfortable bringing him into the business. As with everything, you're like a mother lion protecting her cub."

Ellie grinned. "Does this mean I'm not on kitchen duty anymore?"

"I didn't say that, Pixie," Cari teased. "There will always be an apron with your name on it."

"Well, I might not have much time to work in the shop since I plan on opening a gallery named The Looking Glass." Ellie's gaze traveled to the three sets of eyes locked on hers. "You look surprised I would start a business. Isn't that what we do in this family? Besides, it won't open until next year."

Cari spoke first. "I had no idea you were thinking about a gallery. What will you showcase? Paintings?"

"Maybe 'gallery' isn't the best term. Since I have been working for Karlene, I've had the opportunity to study what she carries in her gallery, which are primarily paintings. I'm amazed at the many forms of art—pottery, sculpture, photography, textiles, and of course paintings and illustrations—and each one has its own beauty. What I'd like to do is have mini exhibits going on simultaneously. I'm still playing with the idea, but as an example, in one section a pottery display, another photography, and another woodcarving. Art in whatever form is how the individual interprets what they see, hence the name."

Ray beamed. "I had a feeling you would come up with something creative to channel your energy. I'm sure you've thought this out thoroughly, but do you know where?"

"That is the second part of my announcement." Ellie focused her attention on Ray. "But I'll need your help. I've talked to Abby about her house. It's been empty since she and Devin moved into the lake house with Shane, and it's a great location, right on Main Street. I can rent the house from Abby, offsetting the cost of her upkeep and give her income as well. I thought that with some modifications, I could have the gallery on the first floor and live upstairs. Abby thinks it's a good plan, too."

"Have you developed a business plan and done a cost analysis?" Cari quizzed.

"I've taken lots of business classes, and when I had to create a plan for school, I used this as my hypothetical business—well, something similar. I'm hoping you'll let me use some of my inheritance from Dad as seed money." Ellie was ready for any questions the family had. Talking about the plan helped quiet her butterflies.

"Kate, you haven't said much. What do you think?" Desperate to get her sister's approval, Ellie pulled out a file folder and passed it to Kate. "Take a look. I've tried to think of everything."

Kate flipped open the folder. She nodded as she scanned the detailed lists on each page.

"You've put a lot of effort into this plan." Kate rifled through the last few pages. "This looks like it's ready to go, so why wait?"

"I want to have more money in the bank and help Ray do the renovations. The more I can save doing some of the work, the less I have to take out of the bank, and I want to immerse myself in the changes. It needs to be perfect," Ellie stated logically.

Her mom said, "Ellie, it seems you're ready to make your dream a reality."

Before she could respond, Ray spoke up. "I would be happy to help and if you really want to save money, move home with your mom and me until we can finish the renovations. You can put your rent money in the bank and you'll have more to put into the business."

"I don't want to intrude on you guys, but I appreciate the offer." Ellie was touched.

Her mom said, "El, Ray has a point, and it would save you quite a bit over the next several months, so move home. And selfishly I'd like to have you under my roof a little longer."

"You should take Mom and Ray up on their offer and move in. Put all your free time into the business and you'll be set up for success. Don't let anything get in your way." She paused, then added, "I'm really happy for you, Pixie."

"Kate, your support means so much to me. Ray, I'll get the keys from Abby and we can take a look this weekend?"

"Sure." Ray glanced at his watch. "I'm going to check on dinner." Ray left the girls to talk.

Her mom had been fairly quiet while Ellie unveiled her plan. Ever practical, she got down to basics. "Ellie, have you worked out the details with Abby, regarding rent and other mundane details with the town, like a business license and permits for renovations?"

"I have been to the town hall and talked with Charlie about setting up my business. Now that I understand the laws around handicapped access, Ray and I can outline the changes and I'll talk with Abby. I won't do anything that makes her uncomfortable. I know it's where she grew up." Ellie looked puzzled. "What happens if the gallery takes off? I wouldn't want to rent the space forever, but I can't see Abby selling the house. Even to a family member. I know what the house means to her."

Ray couldn't help but chuckle as he entered the room. "Don't get ahead of yourself, kiddo, worrying about things down the road. You need to concentrate on the next twelve to eighteen months and turn a profit. Then you can worry about expansion."

"I guess you're right. Remember, Mom bought the building her shop is in after her first year and your woodworking shop is on the property. All I'm saying is, I don't want to be a renter forever."

Kate had been silent, listening to her parents and sister. Finally, she interrupted. "It is certainly exciting, Ellie.

I can't believe my little sister is going to open a gallery. I love the concept and the idea of small intimate exhibits of different types of art being on display. Will you entertain the idea of a larger exhibit?" Kate's earlier enthusiasm was waning. There was risk involved with this type of business. It depended upon people's disposable income more than a coffee shop.

"It's my place so I can be flexible. But I really like the idea of giving unknown artists exposure. Obviously, summer and fall will be the busiest seasons, but I'd like to promote a holiday theme and capitalize on people shopping for gifts. Maybe I'll focus on jewelry and wall art. Honestly, I haven't thought that far ahead in that much detail." Sporting a huge grin, Ellie looked at her mother and sister. "I'm sure I can count on each of you to do all your gift buying at The Looking Glass."

Her mom got up and messed Ellie's carefully styled hair. "Only if there is a family discount," she teased.

"What," Ellie sputtered, "I have to make the rent."

"I'll remember that the next time you come in looking for lunch." Cari hid a smile as she strolled into the adjoining room. "Ray, I'm assuming dinner's ready?"

"Mom, I think Ellie believes you're serious," Kate continued. "Ellie, now that you're going to be a business owner, I hope you don't lose your sense of humor."

Ray leaned down to whisper in Ellie's ear. "Don't let their teasing bother you. Your mom is very proud of you, forging your way in the world, and so am I."

"Thanks, Ray. I knew I could count on both of you for support. I'm hoping Kate is, too. If I don't challenge myself now, I'll end up working hard to build someone else's business. And I don't want to do that."

"Eleanor, I've known you most of your life. You've succeeded at everything you've done, college courses in high school and graduating from college early. I think you've been on the fast track to adulthood your entire life. I wish you'd slow down occasionally and enjoy it. It goes by far too quickly. However, if you want to open The Looking Glass, I don't have any doubt that it will be a smashing success."

Cari didn't jump into Ray's conversation with her daughter. He loved her kids and had their best interest at heart.

Ellie gave her stepfather a quick squeeze. "Don't worry, Ray. I promise I'll take time to stop and smell the roses. Occasionally." Flashing her megawatt smile, she plopped down at the table. "Dinner smells great, Ray. Thanks for letting us crash your romantic evening."

He shook his head. "Nothing gets by these girls, does it?"

Kate pointed to the table as evidence. "Candles, wineglasses. It doesn't take a genius to see where this night was headed. We'll get out of your hair as soon as we finish dessert."

Ellie bobbed her head while heaping salad on her plate. A shared look passed between

Ray and her mom. His willingness to change their plans and make it look effortless made Kate's heart almost sigh. Dinner conversation turned to Don's new job and his first week away from home.

"When is Don due back, Kate?" Ellie looked at her sister, fork in midair.

"Late tomorrow. He sent me some pictures of the cottage and it's coming along nicely. He has to go back to the winery in two weeks so I'm going with him to see for myself. I need to do a little more furniture shopping and start stocking the kitchen with pots, pans, dishes, you know, the essentials."

"Are you guys going to start spending more time in Crescent Lake?"

Oblivious to the eyes focused on her, she said, "I'll go out from time to time, but most of my time will be here. I do have a job, Pixie."

Silence hovered over the dinner table before her mom spoke. "Did you tell Ellie about the bistro?"

"What bistro?" she demanded. "Why am I always the last to know stuff?"

Nonchalantly, Kate answered, "When Sam and Sherry held the family meeting and announced how responsibility of the winery was going to be divvied up, they informed me their accountant said a bistro was a good investment. It is a logical way to grow their business. But I told them my career was here with Mom at What's Perkin'."

"You did what?" Ellie sputtered. "You turned down your own restaurant, something most chefs of your caliber would give their eyeteeth to have. Are you insane?"

Kate glared at her sister. "I'm not insane, but I won't be bribed into leaving Mom high and dry either."

"Didn't Mom say she placed ads for help?"

"Yes. Luke is perfect for the front and we have a couple of potential people for baking. But it is only to lighten the hours we put in, not to replace either of us. And it will allow me some time off to travel with Don. But I am the head baker for What's Perkin'," Kate stated with finality, scraping her chair as she stood up. "Mom, I think I'm going to forego dessert. Dinner was delicious but I need to get home."

After saying goodbye, she made a hasty exit out the back door.

Ellie looked from her mother to Ray. "What the heck is going on with Kate? Don's parents offered her a dream gig and she isn't even going to consider it? Mom, it's official—Kate's crazy."

Putting her fork down, her mom said, "I wouldn't go that far, Ellie, but I think there's a lot going on in Kate's head and she has some difficult decisions to make. Hopefully, she and Don will find the solution that works best for them."

Ray remained silent as Ellie and her mom discussed Kate and the shop. He moved around the kitchen cleaning up but waiting for an opportunity to interject. Finally, there was a lull. "El, not everyone has the strength to step out of their comfort zone."

"Well, I know that, Ray, but let's face it. We've grown up with a woman who didn't have any choice but to take chances. I thought Mom had instilled that quality in all of us. Look at Shane. As a teenager he laid the foundation for McKenna Landscaping. Before Kate graduated, she wanted to move to the city or work for a luxury resort, but that didn't happen. She came home and never left. I'll admit Kate has done great things at the shop, and no offense, but What's Perkin' is Mom's, not hers. When did she turn into one of those people afraid to take a chance? I always envied Kate—she was fearless, going to college in Providence, and where did I go, an hour away."

"Eleanor." Her mom spoke more harshly than intended.

Stunned, Ellie said, "What I said is the truth."

"Just because we're related doesn't mean

we should all strike out in our own business. I was scared to death before opening the shop. Before your dad died, we had been talking about it for a long time. You have to remember that people move at a pace that is comfortable for them, even if we don't agree with it. I'm not taking Kate's side, but be patient with her. There may come a time when she needs to talk to you, so don't alienate her, but rather help her feel comfortable coming to you."

Sufficiently chastised, Ellie dropped her eyes. "I'm sorry, Mom. You're right. I won't give her a hard time. If she wants to live in Loudon and work for you, then I'll be supportive. However, I wish someone wanted to bankroll my business. I sure as heck wouldn't turn it down."

Letting go of her temper, her mom said, "I always said you had a good head for finance. Let's hope that serves you well in your new adventure." She smiled. "Dessert?"

Ellie rubbed her hands in anticipation. "Of course. I never turn down sweets. The benefit of running is that I get to enjoy them without guilt."

Ray scooped up berries and cream and placed a cookie on the side. "As requested, my ladies." With a flourish, he placed the bowls on the table. "Enjoy!"

10

The weeks crept by for Kate and Don, never under the same roof for more than a couple of days strung together. Don immersed himself in the wine business and Kate was dragging her feet hiring an assistant. Luke had turned into an asset for her mom. She had several long conversations with her mom regarding the growing tension between her and Don. But there was nothing that could be done. It was up to them to keep the lines of communication open.

Kate walked into her house and silence

enveloped her. She ached for Don. She switched on the lights to push back the lengthening shadows. Pausing to study herself in the hall mirror, she asked her reflection, "Why am I still mad at Ellie?" Not getting a response, Kate flicked on the television, surfing channels to find something that might capture her interest. Finding nothing, she turned it to a music channel. "At least there's noise."

"Kate?"

Startled, she looked around. "Daddy, is that you?"

In the kitchen shadows, her father stood next to the counter. Quickly, she crossed the room. "I didn't expect to see you tonight."

"I told you I'd be back. I just never know when. I'm guessing you must need me tonight."

Her dad's loving gaze bathed her in a warm glow. "I'm really annoyed. Ellie is talking about opening a store next year and I think it's a bad idea."

"My little Eleanor, how is she? Feisty as ever?"

"You have no idea. She is impulsive and pigheaded." Kate sank onto a stool. "She has a really good job and she's going to quit and open a gallery, of all things."

"You don't approve?"

She looked at her dad. "She is so young and has been out of college less than a year. What does she know about starting a business and making it a success? She needs more experience, and at this point in her life, she should be having fun, doing other things like dating. She shouldn't be saddled with the stress of a business."

"So, you feel she is being impulsive. Is she hanging up a sign tomorrow?"

"Well, no. Maybe 'impulsive' isn't the right word."

"Do you think Ellie should be living her life the way you have lived yours? Up to this point, you've gone to college, married, work for your mom, and down the road there'll be a baby and then a business?"

"That's what Mom did," she muttered.

"Yes, that is what your mother did, but that doesn't have to be Ellie's path or yours. Everyone needs to discover and walk their own road, taking the twists and turns as they come, and if necessary, readjust or even take a different direction." Her dad paused. "Remember the Robert Frost quote. 'Two roads diverged in the wood, And I— I took the one less traveled by, and that has made all the difference.'"

He let the words hang in the air. "That is a very powerful message. Maybe you should think about the two roads in the wood. Katie, my sweet girl, do you need to adjust your path to take the less traveled road?"

She rubbed a hand across tired, burning eyes, and when she looked up, all that remained were the shadows. "Dad?" she cried out.

She heard his voice say softly, "I'll be back. Until then, remember, I love you."

"No, wait! Daddy!" Alone again, she hung her head and sobbed.

After another long day, Kate arrived home anxious to freshen up before Don arrived. He had spent a few extra days at the winery on this trip and promised to be home by dinner. As the garage door slowly opened, she discovered her car tucked inside. She threw the truck in park and jumped out, scarcely able to contain her joy.

She raced into the kitchen and discovered her husband was waiting for her inside the doorway. "Don!" Throwing her arms around his neck, she showered him with kisses. "You're here early!"

Don picked Kate up and swung her around the room. "Once the clock struck noon, I had to hit the road and get home. I missed you so much."

"I missed you more." Kate swallowed the lump in her throat and snuggled close to his chest.

He kissed the top of her head, unwilling to let go. The couple stood motionless for a long time. Kate pulled back slightly and gazed into Don's soft-brown eyes. "Dinner?"

"Let's grab a pizza at Slices. If we stay home, I can't guarantee we'll eat and I want to hear how this Luke person is doing and if you've had any promising applicants for the kitchen."

Kate gave him a saucy smile. "That's what I was thinking, too. Oh, and I have to give you the update on Ellie's remodeling project."

"If you drive, I'll buy." Don held the door open.

"It's the least I can do since you just drove three hours." Kate slipped behind the wheel and deftly maneuvered Main Street to park. Hand in hand, the couple strolled to the pizzeria. "It is a beautiful night, isn't it? The humidity broke and it's perfect, just for us." Kate squeezed Don's hand. "I'm thrilled you're home."

"Me too, and I plan on showing you very soon, but first, I need sustenance."

Don held open the door, allowing Kate to step inside. She shivered at the cool air and waited for her eyes to adjust from the bright evening sun. She led the way to a booth in the back. Don was happy to sit away from the busy crowd, acknowledging a few friends as they passed.

"It feels like I've been gone for forever." He glanced at the menu. "Let's share a pizza and salad." He pushed it aside and gazed into Kate's eyes. "This reminds me of when we started dating."

She chuckled. "Maybe that old saying is true: absence makes the heart grow fonder."

Don leaned back. "I don't think I can get any more 'fonder' of you. But maybe it's more about appreciating what you have when there is a little distance." He dropped his voice. "I missed you like crazy. I don't like sleeping without you and I miss talking to you over dinner and breakfast; the phone isn't enough for me."

She reached for his hand. "Next trip I'm going with you. Luke is doing great with Mom and I'll do all the prep work before we go. I was thinking maybe we could leave early on a Monday. Since the shop is closed, that would help Mom."

"I'm relieved to hear about the change of your plans. And it's easy to arrange. We'll go this Monday and come home Thursday night."

She withdrew her hand. "I didn't think you'd have to go back so soon."

"With so many changes, I have a lot of meetings, and for the next several months, the pace will be brutal. Most of this must be handled in person." He waited.

"I guess if Mom gets into a real bind, she can ask Ellie or Abby," she said slowly.

Their dinner was delivered, thereby halting the tense conversation.

"So tell me, what else happened while I was gone?"

Relieved to change the subject, she said, "Ellie is still insistent on opening The Looking Glass. She and Ray are working on plans to transform the first floor into sections for different types of art, and she'll live upstairs."

"I can't say I'm surprised. That sounds just like her, combining all her talents to make it happen. Good for her."

She scooped salad onto her plate. "You think Ellie jumping into a business, at her age, is a good idea?"

"What does age have to do with anything, Kate? If anyone can do it, it will be your sister."

"Huh. I thought for sure you'd agree with me."

"What do you mean, 'agree with' you? This isn't about what you think Ellie should do with her life; it's about what she wants to do." Irritation flashed across his face. "If you can't be supportive, fake it."

Annoyed, she turned her attention to her salad. "Why does everyone keep telling me to be supportive? As her sister, I owe it to Ellie to be honest."

For several long minutes, he held his tongue. "Kate, you need to think about what your real motivation is, and until you do, I would suggest you keep your opinion to yourself."

In a flash, irritation went to a full temper. "I'm done talking about this. The family can pick her up from financial ruin two years from now." Kate ignored the curious looks she was getting from the other diners and pushed her plate away, having lost her appetite.

"Hon, all I was trying to say is you should think about this from her point of view. Ellie is detail-oriented and wouldn't go into a business venture without running scenarios and analytics to back her up."

Silence answered him. Under his breath, he muttered, "So much for a romantic evening."

The couple finished their meal in a strained silence and drove home.

Don stated, "I'm going to check email and then take a shower."

Absentmindedly, she wandered into the den. Looking for a distraction, she flipped on the television, doing her best to keep her thoughts from swirling. What was wrong with her? Why was she so adamant Ellie was making a mistake? She stared at the moving images, completely unaware of the story line. Could it be possible she was jealous of her little sister, who was not afraid to take a chance on her dream?

A familiar voice spoke, "Kate, do you want talk about what's troubling you?"

She could feel her father's comforting presence. "Daddy, what's wrong with me? I feel like a jerk, poking at Ellie, and I wonder, am I jealous because I'm unwilling to take a leap of faith and step outside my comfort zone?"

"What do you want out of life?"

"I don't know. Don's parents offered to

build a restaurant at the winery. That has been my dream since culinary school. But I love working with Mom and I don't know if I'd be happy living someplace other than Loudon."

"Ah, now we're getting somewhere."

"What if I agreed and all that money was spent, and I failed? That would hurt Don's family. I couldn't take that risk."

"Did you ask Don's family for the capital?"

"Of course I didn't! I'm shocked you would even say something like that. I would never ask anyone to put up that kind of money."

"Do you think Don's father is a good businessman?"

"He's brilliant. Sam took a very small operation and turned it into a winery that rivals the top Californian wineries. Don is taking over a great company, and with his drive, there's no telling where it could go."

"It seems you admire your father-in-law, so maybe you should trust his instincts. Part of their vision may need your bistro to take the winery to the next level. If you decide to forego this opportunity, maybe they will still open it but hire an outsider. Did you stop to think of that possibility?"

She was stunned. "Daddy, thank you!" She jumped up, standing in front of her dad. "I wish I could hug you."

"Princess, I remember what it felt like. Each hug and kiss you gave me is burned into my memory. Even now, I can feel your sweet butterfly kisses on my cheek."

She closed her eyes, remembering. When she opened them, she was alone but basking in the warmth of her father's love. She stood for a few more minutes, committing that feeling to memory before going to find Don. She had to apologize first and then share her epiphany.

Kate entered the office. "Honey, before you say anything, I need to apologize."

He looked up from his computer and waited.

She slid back his chair and perched on his lap. Slipping her arms around his neck, she pecked his lips. "I am so sorry I've been cranky the last couple of months. I should have been more supportive about the winery and, well, everything."

He hesitated. "Thank you for the apology."

"And when we go to Crescent Lake, I am going to do some scouting around about area restaurants and I'll look at the information your dad pulled together. I'm not saying yes, that we're going to open a bistro, but I want to take a good look at everything, including the proposed location."

"Why the change of heart?" He pulled her closer.

"I realized the offer isn't a bribe, more than likely it's based on good sound business information. I'll admit I'm scared to think about making such a big change, but I don't want this to drive a wedge in our marriage, and I don't like being away from you for extended periods of time."

"All good points."

She continued to explain. "If we, you and me, decide this is the right or wrong decision, then we'll talk to your parents. I just have one favor to ask you."

"I'm listening."

"If we do move to Crescent Lake and open the bistro, I want your promise we will come back to Loudon often. Not just for holidays and special occasions."

Don hugged her tight. "If we move, we're only a short car ride away, and we'll make sure there is plenty of room for our family in Crescent Lake. Kate, please don't worry. I know how important family is to you. I would never want to be more than a couple of hours from either of our families. Put that out of your head."

Kate kissed him hard and long. "I love you, Donovan Price."

In answer to her declaration, Don scooped her up in his arms and she giggled. "Is this where we get to make up and have a welcome home celebration?"

"If you'd like."

Words didn't need to be spoken. Kate

pulled his mouth down and slowly ran her lips over his. Caressing them lightly and then increasing the heat and pressure, without losing their rhythm, Don walked into their bedroom and slid Kate to a standing position. With one gentle tug, her hair tumbled down her back. His fingers caressed each lock. "So silky."

They stood toe to toe. She fit perfectly in the curve of his long, hard body, touching hers in all the right places.

*D*on groaned as her hands slid down the length of his back and up under the tails of his shirt. Her fingers tickled and caressed his warm flesh, creating exquisite torture. He mirrored her, caress for caress, stroke for stroke. After all these years, the physical relationship between the couple felt exciting and fresh. How did she do it? he wondered.

Dismissing his thoughts, he focused entirely on his wife. She burned with passion. Impatient, she ripped his shirt from his back, demanding access for her hands to roam. Don did the same. Clothing lay forgotten at the foot of their bed. She walked him backward, never letting their bodies part, lips fused together, her body urging him to lie back on the soft, plump blankets. She ran her toes up his leg, over his calf, and returned to rest on his foot. She shifted slightly, allowing them to come together in perfect union. Joined together, emotions raw, riding to the peak until she shuddered. Waiting for her to be spent, Don let go to join her in a state of release. Skin slick and hearts slowing to a normal beat, Kate snuggled in the crook of his arm.

"Honey, what made you change your mind about Crescent Lake?"

"I'm not sure you'd believe me if I told you."

"Try me," he urged.

"The first night you were gone, I was feeling lost and alone. For a moment I thought I was hallucinating but... I talked with my father."

He was at a loss for words. "Your father? Here?"

"Actually, I've talked to him a couple of times. My mother talked to him for years after he died. But when she married Ray, the visits stopped. I guess it's my turn."

"I wonder why now?" Caressing her arm, he said, "Did he tell you to give it a try, the bistro?"

"No, it wasn't like that exactly. I was mulling over Ellie's life plan. Bottom line, I'm jealous. At first, I thought I was being her big sister, wanting to protect her from failing. But the more I've thought about it, the more I realized I long for her courage and to have more faith in my ability. The truth is, I am afraid to take your parents up on their offer. What if I can't cut it running my own place? Mom did all the hard work before I joined What's Perkin'. She built the business from the ground up. It was only years later that I started working with her and it's been wonderful. She let me take control of the menu, but essentially, it's always been her business."

He remained quiet, stroking her arm.

"I need to do my own research, see what is in and around Crescent Lake." She sat upright. "You have to promise me you won't say anything to them. I would prefer they think I'm working on the cottage."

He pulled her into the warmth of his arms. Smoothing long locks away from her face, he gave her a tender kiss. "You have my word. I will keep your true mission a secret. However, I hope we'll keep the lines of communication open between us. You are the most important thing in my life, but I need for you to understand this job is very important to me, too. I want this opportunity to work for both of us."

She pecked his lips. "Be patient with me while I work through my issues. I had thought we'd have a baby by now and since that hasn't happened, I feel like I failed you." Tears escaped and slid unchecked down her cheeks.

He felt the wet warmth on his chest, and

his heart constricted. "Oh, honey, we will have a baby even if we have to adopt. I can assure you our family will grow and you're going to be a terrific mother. You have to take some of this pressure off yourself. Maybe it's time we go to a specialist and see if there is something out of whack."

She sniffed. "Dr. Thomas said he didn't see anything when he ran some tests."

"Maybe I need to be tested, too. We haven't done that yet. Ask your doctor for a referral and then, if you can, make me an appointment. We'll start crossing things off the list." Don kissed her brow. "One step at a time, sweetheart."

"If you're sure, I'll call first thing tomorrow."

"Katie, I love you. Don't doubt that, not for a single second."

The couple fell silent, each lost in their own thoughts. Don listened as Kate's deep breathing reached his ears. She surprised him by admitting she was afraid to fail. He wondered when that had cropped up. He always held fast to the belief that his wife was fearless; at least that was how she projected herself to the world. He let a few other ideas roll around in his head and vowed to keep his eyes open in everything that had to do with her. Pulling the comforter over them both, he closed his eyes. Tomorrow was a fresh start and he planned on making the most of it.

11

After a few hectic days, the car was packed and Kate was ready for Crescent Lake. Luke was working out better than she had hoped, and there were three interviews for kitchen staff scheduled for when she returned. Her mom had reviewed the résumés and was confident they would find a baker. Kate had mixed feelings about letting another person in her kitchen but it was the right move for her future.

The phone rang, and her breath caught;

Don's doctor's office was listed on the caller ID.

Forcing herself to remain calm, she said, "Hello?"

"Hello. I'm calling for Donovan Price. Is he available?" The voice on the other end of the phone was pleasant.

"Just a moment, please." She put her hand over the receiver. "Don! Phone!"

Kate prayed for good news and handed him the phone.

"Hello, this is Don Price."

She watched his expressionless face, wishing she could hear what the woman was saying.

"Thank you for calling." He disconnected and grinned. "Good news! Everything is in perfect working order. But the doctor suggested I wear boxers. Something about cooler temperatures."

She went from elation to devastation.

"Honey, I thought you'd be happy with the news."

She wiped away a lone tear. "I'm happy you're okay, but that means there has to be something wrong with me, and the doctor had said I was fine. Oh, Don." She dissolved into tears. "Now what are we going to do?"

He wrapped his arms around Kate and steered her to the sofa, making soothing sounds while she cried, until all that was left were gentle hiccups.

"Sweetheart. I know you're upset but we must stay positive. We both have a clean bill of health and that tells me it's just a matter of time until we get pregnant."

She stared at her hands. "Do you really think so?"

"Of course I do. We just need to be patient a little longer." Putting his hand under Kate's chin, he gently raised her mouth to his lips and whispered, "Can you try to be positive, my love?"

Through dark, tear-dampened lashes, she mustered a tentative smile. "I'll try."

"We're in this together for the long haul." Tenderly, he kissed her lips.

Kate looked at her husband. She didn't want to dwell on a painful topic. "We should get on the road; your parents will be expecting us."

Don walked with her into the sparkling sun. He pulled the door tight behind him, making sure it was secured. "Let's try to stay in the vicinity of the speed limit, lead foot."

With a toss of her hair, she fastened her seat belt. "You'd better buckle up. I don't guarantee anything." Feigning lightheartedness, she pulled out of the driveway.

She marveled at the landscape and how it had changed; the corn was turning brown, ready for harvest, and the tall grass danced from side to side in the light westerly winds. She glanced at her copilot, reclined with eyes closed. "Isn't it gorgeous today?"

"Hmm." He sat up in the seat and glanced around. "Sorry about that. If I'm not behind the wheel, riding makes me sleepy."

Kate chuckled. "So, I've noticed."

"Point taken. When do you think we'll get to Mom's?"

She looked at the dashboard clock. "Another hour. We've made good time; traffic has been light."

"Do you want to stop in town for dinner, just the two of us? It would give you an opportunity to see what is typical this time of year."

"That sounds nice. Do you have some place specific in mind?"

"I was thinking Sawyers. It has good food and the best feature: very romantic." Don's grin said more than his words.

"Perfect, you should call your mom and let her know."

Don was dialing the phone before she could finish her sentence. After a short exchange, he slipped the phone into his pocket. "You'll want to take the downtown exit."

"The exit after ours?" She couldn't believe she had just used the word *ours*.

Don nodded. "Are you excited to see the cottage?"

"I am. I'm hoping the colors are as pretty in person as in the pictures. I'm worried about the kitchen. I am hoping to make it functional without a need to expand." Kate fell silent. It hadn't been that long since she'd finished the kitchen in Loudon. To start over again was disheartening, but not willing to let on she was having doubts, she continued. "Maybe I just need to have faith the vision I have will work."

Don saw the look Kate tried to mask behind her smile. "Honey, if we need to add on to any part of the cottage to make it comfortable, then we will. With the salary I'm making, money isn't an issue."

He peered through the windshield. "We'll be getting off the highway in twenty-seven miles."

"These exits sure are far apart," she murmured.

The couple remained quiet, each reflecting on what lay before them. Inwardly, Kate was determined to scrutinize the opportunity for a bistro before making a hasty decision. Don's phone rang and he glanced at the number.

"Sorry, hon, this is one of the sales guys. I need to take it."

She let her mind wander as the miles ticked away. He wrapped up his conversation as she was exiting the highway. "Where is Sawyers?"

He gave her the directions and indicated a parking space.

Don pointed to a two-story building across the street. "Here we are." There were a few small tables outside under a blue-striped awning. "Hungry?"

"When am I not?" Dropping the keys in her bag, she stepped from the car and waited for Don. The couple crossed the street holding hands, enjoying the lingering warmth of the evening. He ushered her inside the dusky interior. They walked through the bar area to the hostess stand. Kate was surprised to see Peyton Brien behind the podium.

Clearly taken off guard, Peyton said, "Welcome to Sawyers."

"Hello, Peyton. I didn't know you worked here, too." Don's voice boomed.

"I never turn down an opportunity to earn extra money. Being a single parent means it's just my income." As if reading Kate's thoughts, she said quickly, "Owen is with my parents tonight. Basically, they spoil him when I work."

She didn't know what to say and was surprised by the sharp tone in Don's voice as he greeted the young mother.

"If you'd follow me…" They followed Peyton to a cozy booth. "Your waiter will be with you shortly." She handed them menus and excused herself.

"I guess you didn't know Peyton worked here," she stated the obvious.

He shook his head. "I don't know why I never considered she might not make enough money to support her son. It must be tough, being a single parent."

"I'm sure it is. Has she ever said where Owen's father is?"

"No one seems to know. But I'm going to ask Peyton. A boy deserves to have his father as a part of his life."

She quickly thought of her father. "Don, sometimes there are extenuating circumstances and you might be invading Peyton's personal life a little too much as her boss."

He thought about her comment. "I consider her my friend. I won't push too hard. Maybe no one has tried to talk to her about the situation."

Kate was happy to hear he wouldn't do his usual thing—push so hard until someone was forced to reveal every detail. It was a double-edged sword as far as she was concerned. "Why don't we spend the rest of our meal enjoying each other's company and forget about the world, at least for a little while?"

He caressed her outstretched hand. "With pleasure."

The waiter placed their salads on the table before discreetly slipping away. She speared a sample of the roasted mixed vegetables on Don's plate, savoring the sweet and spicy dressing they were tossed with before dipping into her Caesar salad. "Both salads are excellent, fresh and bursting with flavor. I'm really looking forward to the rest of our meal."

Surreptitiously, she pulled a small notebook from her handbag and jotted down a few notes about the food and ambiance. "Research," she informed Don.

"I wouldn't expect anything less." He grinned.

The remainder of the evening passed with a little note-taking and a lot of pleasant conversation. After a shared dessert of fresh blackberry cobbler and cream, Don paid the check and held out his hand. "Let's take a stroll around town before we drive out to the folks' house."

She slipped her hand in his. "I could use some exercise. I'm stuffed."

As they were leaving, they bumped into Peyton again. "I trust you enjoyed your meal."

"Everything was very good, thank you," Kate reassured her.

Peyton smiled. "I'm sure Harry will take it as high praise coming from you."

"We're going for a walk. But maybe we'll run into each other while I'm here." She wanted to be friends with Peyton.

Peyton nodded. "I hope we do. I'll be working this weekend. Stop by the tasting room anytime as I'll be setting up for lots of visitors."

"Definitely. I'm sure I'll need to prod my husband out of the office for lunch." Kate winked. "I'll be sure to stop in. Have a good night."

"You, too," Peyton called after them.

• • •

She watched the couple stroll down the street arm in arm and sighed. What she wouldn't give to have someone special. But she was blessed with Owen and he was the only man in her life for the foreseeable future. Dismissing thoughts of romance, she returned to work.

Don gave Kate a quick peck on the cheek. "Thanks for being nice to Peyton."

"Why wouldn't I be? She's a nice girl."

"You know the last time I hung out with her, we were taking a break. You had moved back to your mom's after graduation. One night she really wanted to go to a party at the lake. Usually, she and Tessa went everywhere together, but for some reason my sister didn't want to go. So Peyton asked if I'd tag along.

I'm guessing she didn't want to show up by herself."

"I thought you said you felt lost when we broke up and spent all your time trying to think of ways to win me back," Kate said, half joking and half serious.

"I did, but I didn't want her to miss the party, so I agreed to drive. It really wasn't my scene. The kids were a lot younger, and there was a lot of booze flowing. I stayed for a while. By the time I was ready to leave, Peyton had met up with some friends and said she'd catch a ride home. The next day I drove to Loudon fully committed to convincing you to let me back in your life. That party made it glaringly obvious you were the only woman for me."

"Maybe I should thank Peyton. If it wasn't for the party, maybe you wouldn't have come to your senses." She caught a flash of something unreadable on Don's face.

"You know, it was the following spring she had Owen."

"Do you think the father was someone she met at the party?"

"I'm not sure, but the timing makes sense." Don grew quiet. "I think I'll reminisce with her about that night and thank her for helping me see where I belonged. Maybe then she'll open up about her son's father."

She admonished, "Or maybe Peyton will tell you to mind your own business and you'll have to drop the subject once and for all. Don, I swear you are worse than a dog that doesn't want to let go of a bone."

He gave a hearty chuckle. "Only my wife could know me so well." Pulling her close, he whispered, "So what am I thinking now?"

She laughed. "You're wishing we weren't sleeping at your parents'. Because sleep is all we'll be doing."

"I know what I'm going to do before the office tomorrow."

"What's that?"

Sporting a wicked grin, he informed Kate, "I'm going by the cottage to offer overtime to all the workers to get our house finished. Our next trip, we will be doing things couples do."

"Well, Mr. Price, I agree that will be money well spent."

Don's phone rang. "It's Mom." He punched the button and had a short conversation. "I hate for this to end, but I told her we'd be out soon."

She turned in the direction where the car was parked. "I'm sure your parents are anxious to see you."

"Not only do you know me well, but those were Mom's words, too." He allowed himself to be led to the car. He vowed silently that this would be the last visit they spent at his parents'. He was a married man, and it was time he and Kate lived in their own home in Crescent Lake.

They had scarcely gotten out of the car when the front door opened. Sam and Sherry stood on the top step. "Hello," they called.

Kate waved and Don grabbed their bags and they climbed the steps to the porch.

"Hi, Mom. Hi, Dad." Don hugged his parents warmly. Kate stood to one side, waiting.

Sherry turned and greeted her only daughter-in-law. "We're so happy to see you. I can't wait to show you the cottage. I hope you'll be pleased."

Kate murmured that she was sure it would be perfect before Sam pulled her in for a bear hug.

"How are you, young lady?"

"I'm fine, Sam. How are you feeling?"

"Semiretirement agrees with me, and I never thought those words would come out of my mouth. Having Don at the helm gives me peace that my company is in good hands."

"Thanks, Dad. I had a great teacher."

"Well, of course you did!" Sam gave a hearty chuckle and swatted at the air. "Let's get inside before these darn mosquitos eat us alive."

He dropped their bags at the bottom of the

stairs and joined Kate and his parents in the kitchen.

Sherry finished pouring decaf into the waiting mugs and had a plate of cookies waiting.

"Did you bake, Mom?"

"No, I bought these from the farmers' market the other day. They're delicious; you should try one."

He munched on a piece of chocolate-dipped shortbread. "This is good."

Mildly curious, Sherry asked, "Where did you have dinner?"

"Kate wanted to check out a local restaurant, so we ate at Sawyers."

"That's one of the best in town." Sherry kept her face neutral; after all, Don knew she had made dinner for them. "Do you plan on trying more restaurants this trip?"

She nodded. "I'd like to. We'd be happy if you would join us one night."

Sam and Sherry exchanged a quick look. "No, dear. We don't want to barge in on your romantic evenings. But I'm happy to give you some recommendations."

"That would be great. I'd like to try several." Don knew she didn't want to share that their dining out was in fact research, and she hoped they wouldn't read between the lines and draw their own conclusions.

"I'll put together a list for you tomorrow," Sherry continued. "If you'd like, I'm happy to go with you to the cottage and town, too."

"Thank you, Sherry. I might take you up on the offer another time. I'd like to explore on my own, if that's okay."

"Of course." Sherry and Sam shared an unreadable expression. "So, how is your family?"

Grateful for the shift, Kate filled them in on news of Loudon until it was time for everyone to retire.

Lying in the moon-drenched bed, Kate leaned over to kiss Don goodnight. "I'm really glad we're here."

Don smiled in the darkness. "Me too, Katie. Good night."

12

Kate looked up from her notepad as Don entered the bedroom.

He glanced at her papers. They were filled with lists. "What do you have planned for to-day?" From past experience, Don knew her to-do list was in a specific order.

"I thought I'd drop you off and then go to the cottage. Depending upon how long I'm there, I'll either bring you an early lunch or wander around Main Street. After lunch, I'm going to shop for kitchen supplies, dishes, pots, and pans. You get the idea." Kate chewed on the pen cap. "I may end up ordering what I need online and have it shipped to the winery, if that's okay?"

"Of course, it is. Remember, our family owns the place—lock, stock, and all shipments."

He kissed the top of her head. "Are you ready for breakfast? I'd like to get into the office early. I need to look over a couple of supplier contracts before lunch."

She picked up her bag and followed him down the stairs. "I smell coffee and it's making me hungry."

He ushered her through the kitchen doorway. "Morning, Mom."

His mom glanced up from the paper. "There's fresh coffee. I left the cereal on the counter, and if you want a muffin, they're under the tea towel. Help yourself."

Don glanced out the back door, looking for his father. "Where's Dad?"

"He's taken to sleeping in most days but is

usually up by eight." She glanced at the clock and smiled. "You two are up early."

Kate placed a coffee mug and bowl on the table and pulled out the chair. "I made a list of everything I want to get done this week. I may be overly ambitious, but I hope to get at least half done by dinner."

"Speaking of dinner, last night I wrote down a list of good restaurants. It's on the counter."

"Thanks, Sherry. While I'm in town, I'll see if any menus are posted. Then I'll surprise Don." Kate flashed him a loving smile. "He'll eat anything."

Not speaking directly to either of the women at the table, he said, "You know me so well."

"Don, would you like to use my car this week since Kate will be busy?" His mom pointed to the hooks on the wall. "Nowadays Dad and I go places together. He even likes going to the market with me."

"I can't picture Dad strolling up and down the aisles while you shop." He chuckled.

"Believe it or not, your father is quite the bargain hunter—better than me."

"Did I hear someone talking about me?" His dad walked into the kitchen sporting jeans, a T-shirt, and sneakers, looking relaxed and happy.

"Good morning, dear. Don't you look handsome." Sherry offered her cheek for a kiss.

Sam obliged before crossing the kitchen to retrieve a mug.

"I was just telling the kids you've become quite the bargain hunter. Oh, and I offered Don the use of my car since Kate has lots of errands planned."

"That's fine. We don't have anything going on." Sam sat down at the table and studied the change in his son's appearance. Pleased, he said, "Do you need my help today at the office?"

"No. I'm reviewing the vendor contracts

for bottles and corks. With the natural supply of cork dwindling, I need to check out suitable alternatives."

His dad's eyebrows shot up. "We talked about cork last week and I thought you understood my position. We have to stay the course."

"For our fine wines, yes, but I am thinking that if we expand into a less expensive line, an alternative to cork will be needed," Don said firmly.

"Humph." His dad grew quiet.

Sherry watched the two men, one taking control, and the other having a difficult time letting go.

The tension ebbed as the minute hand moved on the clock.

Sam broke the silence. "That sounds reasonable. I'll look forward to hearing what you decide."

He relaxed. He expected his father to react in exactly that manner. There would be other skirmishes coming, but he was confident they would be able to discuss the changes as businessmen and not as father and son.

Don glanced at his watch. "Kate, are you almost ready?"

"Give me a minute to load the dishwasher."

"Leave those and run along with Donovan." Jokingly, his mom added, "Sam has taken over dishwasher duty."

"No, I haven't. I tried but you told me the dishes didn't get clean enough."

Don and Kate laughed as the older couple continued to banter as they left the room.

"Do you think that'll be us in thirty years?" Kate asked.

"Darling, I hate to tell you but we bicker like that now. I can't imagine what we'll be like in ten years, let alone thirty."

"My gosh, I never thought about it, but you're right, we do bicker just like your folks." Laughing, Kate got behind the wheel and within minutes she had pulled up to the side door at the winery and waited while Don gathered his backpack and cell phone. "I'll be back later, and I promise to bring lunch fit for a king."

Don leaned in for a kiss. "I'm going to hold you to that. Have fun."

He shut the door and blew her another kiss. "Be careful driving."

"I will. Promise." Giving a jaunty wave through the sunroof, Kate turned up the radio and took off down the road, her tires kicking up dust.

She drove up the long driveway, savoring the gentle twists and turns until she caught sight of the cottage. She sat inside the car for several minutes, holding her breath and taking in each detail. It was more beautiful than the pictures. Sherry had done a wonderful job with the landscape company. The house looked just as she imagined it would. The exterior color flawlessly complimented the flower bed. Kate got out of the car and walked to the door. Hesitating before she entered, her hand rested on the doorknob.

"Here I go." She pushed open the door and stepped into the foyer. The smell of fresh paint wafted to her nose. She looked at the floor and walls. "So far so good." She entered the living room, taking in the view around her. The house was coming together, right down to the pergola off the back. Kate wandered into the master bedroom, saving the kitchen for last. Reverently, she stood on the threshold. "This is where we will start our family."

"Mrs. Price, is that you?" A man in painter's whites approached her. "How do you do? I'm Serg."

She thought she was alone.

"From Manzelli Painters."

"Of course. My mother-in-law hired you." Kate extended her hand. "You have done a wonderful job, and so quickly. Thank you."

"Painting is an art, ma'am." He shifted between one foot and then the other. He cleared his throat. "Sherry said the second floor isn't to be painted, but if you would come with me, I'd like to show you something."

Mildly irritated, she followed Serg into the living room.

"Look up." Her gaze followed to where he pointed.

"Oh." Dismayed, Kate could see the issue.

"Can you see how there is a line between old and new? It makes the old look dingy."

"I had no idea that it would look that awful. I take it you are suggesting we paint the upstairs, too." Worried that this was going to go over budget, she thought first to call Don to discuss finances. Before dialing, she remembered their conversation about getting the house done as quickly as possible.

"Serg, would you be able to stay on and get it done?" If necessary, she was ready to offer a bonus.

"I was hoping you would say that." He grinned. Serg produced some cards from his back pocket. "I've taken the liberty of gathering some paint swatches for you to look at.

Nothing that can't be easily changed either now or later, but it will blend nicely with the color scheme on the main floor."

Kate suppressed a grin and accepted the swatches. "I'm guessing you've encountered this dilemma before. Let me hang on to these for a bit and I'll let you know before I leave."

"Excellent. I'll be outside. We're putting a protective coating on the deck." Serg left Kate to continue her tour.

"Well, this is all part of getting the house done, I suppose. Onward to the kitchen." She walked through the large expanse and discovered most of the work was complete and without having to add on to the room. She wasn't sure if Sherry had hired workmen or magicians.

"Hello," she called out. Without getting an answer, she walked to the side door. Peering out the window, she saw several men sitting around enjoying their coffee break. She glanced at her watch. "I guess it doesn't matter; the kitchen is almost done." Kate opened the door in search of who was in charge.

Conversation halted when she stepped into their midst. One man separated himself from the group. "Mrs. Price? Hal Baker at your service."

She gave him a warm smile. "Please call me Kate. Mrs. Price is my mother-in-law."

"Okay then. Kate, what do you think of your cottage?"

"I'll have to admit I'm pleasantly surprised. It seems to be almost finished. You've done a beautiful job." Kate's smile included the guys standing around gawking at her. She pretended not to be aware of the open-mouthed stares. It was like they hadn't seen a girl before. "When do you think you'll be done?"

Hal seemed pleased. "Today. We're cleaning up, inside and out, going through our punch list, and turning the house over to Serg for the last of the interior painting. Sherry said you were here all week so I thought you and

Don could do a walk-through with me and make sure you're satisfied. Then I'm done."

"Excellent."

"Sherry asked me to bring my entire crew and get the job done fast."

She gave him a warm smile. "Well, thank you. Everyone. The cottage is lovely. It should be in a magazine or on a television show." Kate looked at her watch. "I need to run, but I'll call and we can set up a meeting with Don."

Hal pulled a business card from his shirt pocket. "If you call this number, leave a message when it's convenient and I'll make it work."

She waved to the crew and jogged around to the front of the house. Before she turned the corner, she heard someone say, "Wow, how did Price get lucky and marry a girl who looks like that? And those green eyes."

Kate snickered before starting the car. She needed to pick up lunch and get to the winery before her husband perished from hunger.

She grabbed the paper bag from the hatchback. Kate entered the tasting room and glanced around, allowing her eyes to adjust. The space was vacant. She wandered around, absorbing the feel of the room. Various types of glassware lined the shelves behind the over-size wood bar. A few stools were scattered around. Kate was pleased to see the attention to detail on display, from paper napkins to small bowls with the winery's logo embossed. It was a good way to subtly reinforce the brand. Whoever had laid out the space did an excellent job. She found her way to the office area. With everyone at lunch, it was strangely silent. She walked down the hallway, which led to Don's office. Hearing voices, she stopped short of the open door. Something in Don's tone caused her to freeze.

"Peyton, are you saying you got pregnant the night of the party at the lake?"

She strained to hear the response.

"Yes. That was the night Owen was conceived."

Horrified, heart hammering in her chest,

she turned and quietly ran back down the way she had come, unsure where to go. She burst into the sunlight, leaned against the car, and processed what she had just heard. Peyton got pregnant the night Don took her to a party, while they were broken up. Was Don Owen's father? Kate drew deep ragged breaths. All the joy drained from the day.

She wanted to get in the car and drive as far and fast as she could, but Don was expecting her. Kate had to go back inside.

"Pull yourself together." She made several laps around the car, pacing. Straightening her shoulders, she took a deep breath and pulled open the door, determined to talk to her husband and get to the bottom of this mess. Whatever it was, they would deal with it together.

She retraced her steps, but this time in an attempt to make her presence known, she called out, "Hello. Where is everyone?"

Don stood in the doorway of his office. "We're in here, Kate." The physical distance between them lessened. He welcomed her with a chaste kiss. "Well, look at you. Your face is flushed. I'll bet you enjoyed shopping!" He reached out and took the bag. "Lunch. I'm hungry. It looks like you brought enough for an army."

He looked at Peyton. "Care to join us?"

Peyton rose from the chair. "No, thank you. I have supplies to order and I need to re-stock the wine cooler before I leave. I'm sure Kate has a lot to tell you about your new home. I hear it is quite lovely." She gave Kate a warm smile, which Kate forced herself to return while avoiding Peyton's red-rimmed eyes.

Taking the bag from Don, she said, "Yes, we have a great deal to discuss. It has been an enlightening morning." Kate set cartons on the conference table.

"Well, I will leave you to enjoy your lunch." Peyton pulled the door closed behind her.

Don had been paying close attention to the exchange between the two women and rubbed his hand over his chin, wondering what had just happened.

"So, how was your morning?"

"Good," she snapped. "We need to do a walk-through with Hal in the next couple of days and I met Serg Manzelli. He is going to paint the upstairs so we won't be moving furniture in this trip. But overall, I am happy with the results."

Don nodded, unsure what he should say next.

"How are things here? What were you and Peyton working on?"

Don noticed a frosty edge to Kate's voice. "We were going over how things run in the tasting room. She seems to have a good handle on the operation. It's important I understand every facet of the business. If I want to make any changes, I should understand how they might affect other areas of the business," he explained. "Lunch is excellent. Where did you get it?"

Surprised by how smoothly Don covered

up the conversation, she had to recover quickly. "Um, I'm not sure."

Don glanced at the plain paper bags. "You'll have to show me tonight. Have you picked out where we are having dinner?" He grinned. "You always find the best places to eat."

Distracted, Kate murmured, "I'm sorry, Don, what did you say?"

"I asked where we were having dinner."

"I spent the morning at the cottage and grabbed lunch. I haven't walked around town yet. I'll do that this afternoon." Kate's voice was tight.

"Did something happen at the cottage? Was a worker rude to you?" His radar was on alert, something was definitely wrong. Was there a chance Kate could have overheard his conversation with Peyton?

"No, nothing happened. I am feeling a bit overwhelmed." Kate patted his arm. "I'm fine."

He leaned back in the chair. He knew Kate;

if she had overheard the exchange with Peyton, she would be asking questions. He steered the conversation to specific updates on the house.

Following his lead, their banter revolved around easy topics. After putting the leftovers in the break room, Don walked Kate outside. She kissed him goodbye and stated she'd be back by six. He stood in the parking lot watching Kate drive away.

"Something is bothering you, Katelyn, and I am going to get to the bottom of it tonight. One way or another."

Kate's car was on the side of the road and her tears fell unchecked. Heartbroken, she wondered, how could Don have lied to her? They had just spent an hour together and he couldn't tell her he had fathered a child? Unsure how long she'd been sitting in the hot car, she glanced in the rearview mirror. Her mascara was smudged and her face was blotchy. Digging to the bottom of her handbag, she found a compact. Peering into the tiny mirror, she dried her tears and repaired the damage. Satisfied with the results, she stated to her reflection, "He'll tell you tonight at dinner. The office wasn't the place for a serious talk." Feeling better, she drove toward town.

She slid into a parking space on the south end. Kate noted there were a few shops worth exploring that might hold treasures for the cottage. Wandering around, checking menus posted outside of a few establishments, she decided on an Italian place for dinner. Parched, she wandered into a small bakery. She looked around, pleased to discover it was quaint and reminiscent of her mom's shop.

Two girls about her age were having coffee. Kate couldn't help but overhear their conversation.

The blonde spoke, "Have you heard Donovan Price is back and taking over the winery?"

The redhead leaned in. "This may break up his marriage. I've heard she doesn't want to leave her family."

The blonde sighed. "Maybe he'll be back on the market. He is *so* good-looking."

"Don't hold your breath, Winona. I'm sure there is a line of women a mile long to date him. Looks, money, and he's a nice guy. The triple threat."

Kate turned to leave but instead detoured in the direction of the two girls. Heat flushing her cheeks, she addressed the pair. "Allow me to introduce myself. I'm Katelyn Price, Donovan's wife. Feel free to spread the word: Don isn't now, nor will he be in the future, on the market. We are happily married and intend to stay that way." Leaving the girls speechless, Kate marched out the front door and walked straight to her car, shaking from a variety of emotions and vowing to herself that no matter the obstacles, her marriage would survive.

Don walked out of the office at six on the dot and found Kate leaning against the car. It was obvious she had stopped and freshened up. Her dress flowed over her curves perfectly and her long dark hair hung in loose waves around her heart-shaped face.

He gave a low whistle. "You look pretty." He pulled Kate to his chest and nuzzled her neck.

"Does a girl need a special occasion to wear a dress for dinner?" she teased.

"Absolutely not. We should dine out more often if you're going to look this hot. Wowzer!" Don twirled her around and opened the passenger side door, helping her inside. He slipped behind the wheel and eased the car down the drive. Where are we having dinner?"

"I'm in the mood for Italian tonight. So I reserved a cozy table at La Trattoria." Kate brushed a stray lock from her cheek. "I'm happy to say I got some things for the house today and I think I'll need one more day of shopping for furniture, but then the house will be ready, although we have to wait for the deliveries. We should bring clothes that we can leave here so we're not dragging so much between houses."

He struggled to contain his excitement. "Does this mean you're going to spend more time here?"

"Of course, I am. I still have responsibilities at What's Perkin', but I'm sure we can work it out."

"Oh." Don was riding a roller coaster on this topic. "I was hoping you were ready to open your place here."

"Don, this is a process for me. The first major project is our home and I'm still looking around, trying to figure out if a place would even be profitable." She turned to watch the passing landscape. "This afternoon I stopped in a coffee shop downtown."

"And what did you think?"

"I overheard some girls talking about you." Kate studied her husband's profile. "There is speculation our marriage is over and you'll be available soon."

He let out a sound she hadn't heard before,

something between a snort and a laugh. "I guess no one asked my opinion or I would have told them that when I married you, it was for keeps."

Reassured, she continued. "Well, I hope you get a chuckle out of this. I introduced myself and told them in no uncertain terms that I planned on staying married to you and to spread the word. Then I left before I took their heads off."

"Bravo, my darling. I wouldn't expect anything less from you. Do you have any idea who they were?"

"I think the blonde was named Winona but I'm not sure." Putting her hand lightly on Don's, she said, "I hope you're not mad, but it irked me and I wasn't going to stand there and let anyone gossip about us or the state of our marriage!"

"I probably would have done the same thing if I had been in your shoes." Don squeezed her hand. "Let's forget about people who have nothing better to do than gossip about others and enjoy our evening."

"Wonderful idea, but if there's anything you want to talk about, I'm here to listen." Kate prayed he would bring up the subject of Peyton and her son.

He expertly tucked the car into a tight spot and turned off the engine. "Have no fear, I'm sure I'll bore you with so many details of my day you'll regret that last comment." He hopped from the car and sprang around to the passenger side to help her.

They strolled hand in hand, taking in the bustle of people enjoying the wonderful weather. They walked into the courtyard and Don greeted the host. "We have reservations. Price."

The host did a double take. "Don Price!" Grabbing Don's hand, he pulled him into a brotherly hug. "How the heck are you?"

"Al, good to see you. I didn't know you worked here." Don pulled Kate close. "This is my wife, Kate."

Letting out a whistle, he grinned. "How did you get so lucky, and Kate, my apologies."

"Is it safe to assume you two know each other?" Kate looked from one grin to the other.

"This is Alan Waters. We hung out together as kids. Mom would tell you Al is an honorary Price." He smiled. "So, what's going on with you?"

"I keep busy. For starters, I own this place and Sawyers, and I've started to build a house out on Route Nine. A log cabin." Pride filled his voice.

"Good for you. I'm sure you heard I took over the winery from my dad. It was time for him to retire, so here we are. Kate and I have fixed up our cottage and next trip we'll start living there."

"Full-time? That's great. We'll have to get the old gang together." Alan picked up a couple of menus.

"Don't get ahead of yourself, Al. We're not living here full-time. At least not yet. At the moment, Kate runs her mom's kitchen in a café in Loudon."

Alan nodded. "I heard you're a chef."

"That's right." Kate wondered where this conversation was going and how much Don was going to reveal.

"Impressive. Looks and a chef. Don you really lucked out, but then you always did have the luck of the Irish. Well, you came for dinner, not to stand around shooting the breeze with me. If you'd like to come this way, I have a very romantic table just for you." Alan held a chair for Kate. Laying the menus on the table, he said, "Enjoy your dinner."

"You didn't tell me your friend owned this place." Kate surveyed the menu.

"I had no idea. Alan was never interested in working for anyone. And he loves food but can't cook to save his soul. I guess owning is the next best thing for him." Don studied the menu. "If the food is as good as it sounds, we're going to have a great meal." He glanced over the top. "Do you know what you want to order?"

"Yes, I'm going to have a salad with the cioppino and a glass of white wine."

Don looked at the wine menu. "Hmm, he's not carrying Crescent Lake. I wonder why. I'll give him a call in a couple of days and see if he'd like to have a tasting and maybe he'll start."

He set the menu aside as the waiter approached their table carrying a bottle of wine. "Compliments of Mr. Waters." He showed Don the bottle and poured him a taste. He sipped, then nodded, and the waiter poured a glass for Kate and then Don. He looked at Kate with expectancy.

"Are you ready to order, Miss?"

The waiter listened carefully and withdrew, leaving the couple to enjoy the wine.

Don studied the label. "This is from a small local winery, Sand Creek, and it has only been producing for a couple of years." Don took a small sip, rolling the beverage around his mouth before swallowing. "It's nice, light, slightly sweet with a hint of pear. Try it."

Kate lifted her glass and did the same. "I usually prefer a dry white, but this is very nice. A little competition, Mr. CEO?" she teased.

"I can assure you, nothing we can't handle." He exuded confidence. "Our brand is well established and there is room for the little guys, too."

Their conversation drifted to the cottage and arrangements for the walk-through the following day. She kept wishing Don would talk about Peyton, but short of her asking him directly, it didn't seem likely it would be addressed. They were enjoying coffee when Alan stopped at the table and asked if he could join them. The restaurant was buzzing with activity, but all seemed to be running smoothly.

"So, Kate, tell me, did you enjoy your meal? If you did, maybe you'd write a review for the website." He looked from Kate to Don and then back to Kate.

"Alan, everything was excellent. You have a very nice restaurant and I'd be happy to write a review. I can tell your chef is focused on accentuating the flavors of the ingredients and not trying to cover them up by over-seasoning. The presentation was lovely and the service was impeccable."

Alan beamed like a proud papa. "Thanks, Kate. I hope that if you were dissatisfied, you'd be honest."

She grinned. "Just ask my husband, I never hold back the truth. Sometimes that isn't popular but it's who I am."

Don chimed in, "Thank you for the wine. It wasn't necessary but it was appreciated."

"It's the least I can do for an old friend. I hope I'm not being presumptuous, but since you're going to be around more, you should come back often."

"We'll be back; you can count on it." He stood up. "We've had a busy day so we're going to head out." Don gave Alan a firm handshake.

"Kate, it was a pleasure to meet you. Hopefully this becomes your favorite haunt." He grinned. "I'll even give you access to the kitchen, the grand tour so to speak."

"Your chef might have other ideas. We are a territorial bunch." Kate laughed.

They walked into the crisp evening air. "Don, would you mind if we went for a short walk before going home?"

He helped Kate wrap a pashmina scarf around her shoulders and then tucked her hand through his arm. The couple strolled in silence, doing a bit of window-shopping before coming to a bench.

"Shall we sit?" he asked.

She nodded and shivered slightly. Don slipped his arm around Kate as she snuggled into his side, and a deep sigh slipped out.

"This is nice," she said softly.

He was quiet, soaking in the moment. "I'm really glad you're here."

"This is where I want to be, Don. I know we still have some things to work through, but I'm confident we will. The key is open and honest communication." Kate looked at him out of the corner of her eye, expecting him to say something.

"Honey, I think being here is a wonderful first step. I'm relieved you're willing to look at the possibility of moving permanently."

"I think it's more than us moving. We still have to deal with some issues of the past."

He kissed the top of her head. "Don't worry, we'll work out how to increase our family. It really is just a matter of time."

Kate was dumbfounded. She was trying to get Don to open up and he was still tap-dancing around the topic. "Is there anything else you'd like to talk about tonight?"

"No, I don't want to bore you with work stuff. This is our time." Don smiled. "Is there something you want to talk about?"

Her thoughts raced. "Have you had an opportunity to talk with Peyton yet, about her son?"

"I talked to her today. She won't tell me who Owen's father is. I get the feeling she is protecting the guy, but for the life of me I don't know why. He needs to step up; if he doesn't want to be a father to the boy, at least pay child support. I hate the idea that she is shouldering the financial burden." Exasperated, he continued. "Owen is a great kid. I'll bet his father would be jazzed to know him. I'd want to know if I was his father."

What the hell? Couldn't he put one and one together and get three? "So, when you talked with Peyton, she didn't tell you anything? Don't you find that odd?"

"All she would say was she got pregnant around the time I was living here."

"Hmm," was all Kate could respond with.

"Why do you think she is being so secretive?"

She sat up and pulled from Don's arms. "I'm sure she has her reasons. Maybe she thinks Owen's biological father would try and take him away from her. Maybe he's married or something."

"Huh, I didn't think of that," Don said thoughtfully. "I guess that would be enough to scare her into silence. You know, maybe you could talk to her. I know you just met, but she might be more inclined to open up to someone who doesn't really know her and won't judge her."

She was shocked. "You want me to talk to Peyton and ask her who the boy's father is? Are you nuts?"

"Well, I wouldn't suggest that during the first conversation you say, 'Hey, who's Owen's dad?' But maybe you could ask her some questions about the area and over the course of the conversation bring it around to Owen."

"Don, you really don't know?"

"She won't tell me and she said no one knows but her and she plans on keeping it that way."

She pulled her wrap closer and stood up. "I'm cold. Do you mind if we go home?"

"Of course." Don wasn't sure what had happened. They were having a nice conversation and then a chill definitely fell over them, but it wasn't from the weather. He took her hand and they walked back to the car in silence.

The drive home was strained. He tried to strike up a conversation but Kate stayed uncharacteristically silent. "Are you feeling okay?"

"I'm tired. Everything has caught up with me." She forced a smile. "Don't worry. I'll be fine after a good night's sleep."

He wasn't as sure but took her explanation at face value. "So, tomorrow you're going furniture shopping in Anderson?"

"Yes, and then dinner with your parents." She stared into the dark night. "I'll try and bump into Peyton before we go home. But I'm not making any promises."

"Thanks, Kate. I bet she'll open up to you. You're easy to talk to."

He pulled up his parents' driveway and turned off the car. The couple sat in darkness.

"Don. If Peyton decides to keep her secret, will you stop pushing?" She held her breath.

"I won't have a choice. If Peyton doesn't want anyone to know, I'll let it go and find another way to help her and the boy."

"What exactly does that mean?"

Curious, he studied his wife. "I'll give her more responsibility and a raise. What did you think I meant?"

"Honestly, I'm not sure. You've become consumed with invading her private life and I think you should have more respect for her." Kate pushed the door open, amazed that he couldn't read between the lines. It was as plain as the nose on his face—Owen was his son and Peyton didn't have the courage to tell him. She would ferret out the truth. It was only right that Don should know his son.

"Are you coming inside?"

Confused, Don nodded. "Right behind you."

One thing was for sure, she decided, Peyton would get the help she deserved.

14

Kate lay awake for most of the night with one question weighing on her mind. Why hadn't Peyton told Don she was pregnant? It would have changed things for all of them, but at least Owen would have grown up with a father. She was finally drifting off to sleep but the nagging question invaded her dreams.

"Kate, hush, it's just a bad dream. Everything is going to be fine."

Her eyes flew open and found Don's deep brown eyes filled with concern. "Don!" she cried.

He pulled her to his chest, smoothing her hair. "You were thrashing and crying out, 'no,' over and over. Do you want to talk about it?"

She shook her head.

"It's over now."

She couldn't tell him that in her dream he had left her because Peyton had given him the son she couldn't. Maybe it was time to let sleeping dogs lie, she thought. Kate gazed into Don's eyes. "I love you with all my heart."

He kissed her, allowing heat to slowly build. Kate responded with an intensity he hadn't expected. His hands roamed down her back, tentatively at first, unsure how far things would progress. To his delight, she tossed her nightgown aside.

"Are you sure?" he whispered.

In a hushed tone, she said, "Yes. It doesn't matter where we are. I'm yours always."

Before she could change her mind, he eased

her back, never letting her skin cool. He teased and tantalized each nerve ending, holding her just at the peak when she pulled him into her. They came together in a quiet rush, holding each other until the world stopped spinning. With a soft laugh, Kate brushed her hair away.

"I guess we bent that rule," she whispered.

"Some rules are made to be broken. Maybe it's a good thing we waited until our last time under this roof. Otherwise, I'd never keep my hands off you," he growled.

"Sweet nothings are very romantic at sunrise, love."

"Ah, but when the sun is up so are we. Do you want to shower first?"

She pulled the sheet over her, blocking the first rays of morning. "You go ahead. I'm going to savor the last few minutes under the covers."

He gave her a quick kiss before going into the adjoining bathroom. "Kate," he called, "do you want to drive me to the winery, or should I take Mom's car?"

"I'll drive you. Maybe I'll bump into Peyton when I swing by later."

Kate stretched her arms over her head before she got up from the bed. Clothes were strewn around and she took a few moments to straighten the room. Pausing in front of the full-length mirror, she turned sideways. Sticking her tummy out, she imagined what she would look like when they were expecting a baby. Maybe this morning was the start of their family. Lightly, she ran a hand over her flat midsection and smiled. Hearing the water turn off brought her back to the present. Gathering her clothes, she tucked all thoughts of a baby into the recess of her mind. For now, she was going to focus on kitchen supplies and furniture.

Kate was cruising down the road while she made a mental list of what she'd need tonight for the cookout she and Don decided to host at the cottage. She was well within the speed limit when she drove past a sign for Sand Creek Winery. On impulse, she turned up the narrow dirt road to check it out and report back to Don. She parked in front of an old white farmhouse. A modern structure jutted off the back, going in both directions and making a large T. With a sharp eye, she took in the perfectly manicured lawn and flower gardens. They were classic rambling roses that looked like they had been there long before the expansion. Kate meandered up the flagstone path towards a door marked ENTRANCE.

She pulled the door open and stepped inside, surprised to discover the interior was decorated like someone's home rather than a tasting room. She walked around, picking up bottles and assessing the depth of inventory.

"May I help you?"

Startled, Kate turned. A tall spare woman dressed in a tailored black suit, with almost-blue black hair pulled back into a severe bun, stood before her, her facial expression nonexistent.

"Yes, I had some of your white wine last night at La Trattoria and I wanted to purchase a bottle."

"How did you get in? We're not open for business today."

"I'm sorry, the door was unlocked. I'll come back another time," Kate stammered, feeling like she had been caught red-handed with her hand in the cookie jar.

"I don't know when or if we'll be open again." The woman passed Kate a business card. "I suggest you call before you come back."

She slipped it into her pocket. "If I may ask, why?"

Glancing around to make sure they were alone, the woman whispered, "Not that this is for public knowledge, but we're struggling and the owner can't keep investing, despite the wines being excellent. Unless he can raise additional capital, he'll be forced to sell."

"I'm sorry to hear that. The wine I had was very good." She looked at the bottle in her hand. "Will you sell me a half case?"

Momentarily, the woman hesitated. "I guess so. It certainly couldn't hurt. Is that all you want?"

Kate surveyed the shelves and selected a variety of whites and reds for a total of six bottles. "This will be all. Can you take a card or do you need cash?"

"Cash, please."

Kate hastily left the building, wondering if this would be good news for CLW. Setting the box in the back seat, she headed toward Anderson.

⚭

The back of her car was overflowing while the larger items were scheduled for delivery in the next few days. She called the winery from the car. After the third ring, Peyton answered.

"Crescent Lake Winery. How may I help you?"

"Hi, Peyton, it's Kate." She paused. "How are you?"

"I'm great. Thanks. I assume you're looking for Don."

"Well, yes. Do you know if he's free?"

"He and Jack went over to the aging room. Would you like me to track him down?" Peyton offered.

"No, that's not necessary. I'd appreciate it if you let him know I should be there in about an hour."

"I'm not sure when he'll be back. But I'll be here for a couple more hours. I'm arranging a private tasting party and we're having the event catered, complete with a jazz duo."

"That sounds nice. If you'd like, I'm happy to look at the menu and offer pairing ideas." Kate hoped she wouldn't offend Peyton.

"I would welcome your input. See you soon."

"Okay, and remember, if you do see Don, please give him my message."

Peyton reassured Kate before hanging up.

Well, that worked out perfectly, she thought, and she might have the opportunity to ask some tough questions that needed answers.

Kate zipped along, rehearsing her approach. Based on experience, the best way to get someone to open up was a casual conversation about family and work. She was ready by the time she parked the car.

"Hello. Peyton?" Kate called into the empty room. She heard a mumbled response but was unsure where it came from. She walked over to the sink to get a glass of water. Her mind began to wander. Kate could picture the south wall replaced with a set of French doors giving access to a restaurant. Not a lot of tables, she thought, maybe a seating capacity of forty. She was so lost in thought she didn't notice Peyton studying her until she cleared her throat.

Flashing the girl a warm smile, Kate set the

glass down. "Here, let me help." She took a case of glassware and set it on the bar. She peered inside and was delighted to see painted glasses for red and white wine. "These are pretty. I didn't know the winery stocked something like this."

"We don't. Stacey Miller, the woman hosting the party, brought them in. She painted them as a party favor for her guests and asked that we use them for the tasting." Peyton held one up and twirled it, showing off the intricate design.

"I wonder if you could stock something similar but with the winery logo. The hand-painted versions would sell better than something mass produced," Kate suggested.

"That's an interesting idea. I'll talk to Stacey—she may be interested in doing a small order on a trial basis. If not, she might know someone who is." Peyton walked behind the bar. "Would you like a glass of wine? I have a red open."

She hesitated for a fraction of a second.

"After the busy day I've had, that sounds wonderful. Will you join me?"

Peyton glanced at her watch. "I guess I can call it a day. We can go out to the gazebo and relax until Don's back." She poured. "This is a blend we serve chilled for the summer. It's a fun, unpretentious beverage. It won't ever be a Cab but it's refreshing." Passing a glass to Kate, she said, "After you."

The ladies walked through a shaded pathway to an oversize gazebo. Kate took in her surroundings. "Is this used for weddings?"

"Occasionally, but it's complicated. For events, we only permit our wines to be served. Most wineries in the area have a similar policy but they offer catering." Peyton placed a hand on her arm. "I'm sorry, Kate. I wasn't trying to sway your decision about the bistro."

Kate glanced up. "I guess there aren't many secrets around here."

"Secrets, yes, but not well kept." Peyton laughed. "I'm sorry I shouldn't have said anything."

"It's okay, really. I've spent the last few days wandering around town and the surrounding area, checking out the competition, and I think we may have an opportunity. I'm still mulling it over, so please don't say anything. I need to talk to Don first."

Grinning, Peyton held up her hand. "Owen and I do a pinky promise. It's sacred. So, I'm prepared to offer you my most sacred promise."

Kate did likewise. The two linked pinkies and laughed until tears streamed down their cheeks. "I don't know why that struck me as funny." She wiped her face with the back of her hand. "But I haven't had a good laugh in a long time."

"Me either. Being a single parent is tough, and some days I forget life should include silliness." Peyton sipped her wine. "Tell me a little about Kate, the girl, not Don's wife."

"Well, I'm afraid there isn't much of a story: small-town girl, one sister, two brothers, two sisters-in-law, and three nephews and one niece.

I cook for a living and have terrific parents and an amazing husband." Kate peered over the rim of her glass. "And what's your story?"

"Smaller nutshell than you. Local girl, got my degree in business, had a baby, and take care of both of us with help from my parents. I don't have any siblings, so we're all my parents have."

This was the opening Kate had been hoping for. "It is admirable, raising your son alone. His father didn't want to be a part of his son's life?"

A flash of something passed over Peyton's face and she spoke very softly. "His father isn't a part of our lives. In fact, I never told him."

"Why not? I'm not trying to pry but I would think most guys would want to know something like that." Kate's eyes were glued on the girl's face.

"He isn't available to help me and he's not the man I had hoped would father my child. It's better this way." She wiped a small tear from the corner of her eye. "Kate, if you don't mind, I'd like to change the subject."

Stunned at the raw emotions Peyton struggled to contain, she fell silent. "I'm sorry, Peyton, of course."

Peyton composed herself and carried on the conversation in a breezy tone. "I hear the cottage is coming along. Don said you should be ready to move in soon."

She nodded. "If you're free tonight, you should stop over. The family is getting together for an impromptu barbeque." Kate glanced to the sky. "Hopefully, it won't rain."

"The weatherman said there wasn't a drop in sight for the next week. Would you mind if I brought Owen?"

"Of course not. The more the merrier." At that moment, Don and Jack came striding around the corner of the building. Peyton was quick to hide her delight as the men approached, but not before Kate took notice and her heart sank.

Don bent to kiss Kate. "Look at the two of you, enjoying the afternoon."

Peyton blushed. "I'll admit I knocked off early. Having a glass of wine in the gazebo was too tempting. I'd like to say Kate twisted my arm, but I think the reverse is true."

Jack sat down and propped his feet up. "Your husband is a slave driver, Kate. Since he took over, I've had to work harder than ever."

She laughed. "You can't fool me, Jackson Price. You are just like your brother, and you thrive on staying busy."

Peyton joined in the teasing. "You're on an energy high all day, running when most people walk. So don't be spinning any tall tales, Jack."

Don let the girls put Jack in his place before suggesting, "Jack, how about you and Peyton join us at the cottage for dinner tonight?"

"Oh, I've already asked Peyton and told her to bring Owen. By the way, did you call your parents and tell your sisters and Leo?"

"Yup, I did. Mom is going to bring dessert

and salad. I'll throw some burgers and dogs on the grill. Easy and good food."

"I think you're forgetting one thing, Don." Kate suddenly realized they were missing a crucial component. "We don't have a grill. I can cook inside but it won't be very picnic-like."

"Now, Kate, what do you think I did today—well, besides running a winery?" He grinned. "I had one delivered—actually the same model we have in Loudon."

"This is why I married you, always thinking ahead." Kate leaned back and soaked up the moment. She couldn't remember the last time she was this relaxed in the middle of the week.

"What time should we come by?" Peyton asked.

Don glanced at his watch. "About an hour?" He looked at Kate. "Will that be enough time to get ready?"

"I think so. I'll finish my wine and we can go. Jack, will you bring the wine for tonight?"

"Yeah, no prob. Peyton, I can swing by and pick up you and Owen. This way you can have another glass of wine if you'd like." Jack did his best to act nonchalant. "I'll be your DD."

*D*on knew his brother and wondered what was going on between the couple. He raised one eyebrow in Jack's direction, who skillfully avoided the intense gaze.

"That would be nice. I never drive Owen if I've had anything to drink." She held up the partially empty glass. "So now I can join everyone for your first barbeque—hopefully the first of many." Peyton smiled. "It's been a while since all the Price kids have been together for a midweek cookout. This will be a lot of fun."

"Well, I can't guarantee fun, but I can assure you there will be plenty of food." Kate stood up. "Ready to go?"

Don took her hand and helped her step

over Jack's feet. "See you in a while, Jack, and don't forget the wine."

"Hey, no worries, big brother."

Jack watched his brother and sister-in-law stroll through the grass holding hands. "Guess I'd better get the wine." Jack waited for Peyton. "Do you want me to follow you home?"

Peyton was still focused on Kate and Don. "Do you wonder what their secret is?" she said wistfully.

"I don't think it's a secret." Jack looked at her. "It's love, Peyton, pure and simple. Someday I hope to have a woman look at me the way Kate looks at Don."

Involuntarily, Peyton sighed.

"Peyton?" Jack touched her arm. "Am I following you?"

She looked at Jack. "Sorry. Can you pick me up? Owen is a typical little boy, covered with dirt by the end of the day, so I want to give him a quick bath and a change of clothes first."

"You've got it. I'll give you a thirty-minute head start."

"Sounds good, see you then." Peyton jogged to the building. She still needed to close up.

Jack watched her, wondering how long before Peyton would be ready to let a man in her life besides the memory of Owen's father. With slumped shoulders, he slowly walked into the warehouse. One bright spot—tonight, he would get to spend time with Peyton and Owen. Suddenly Jack had a great idea. Kate could talk to Peyton and see if she ever thought about dating. Feeling optimistic, he hurried inside. He'd find a clean shirt in Don's office and change, silently vowing to wait as long as it took to ask Peyton on a proper date.

ate peeked out the window just in time to see Jack and Peyton arrive. She was holding the back door open, waiting for Owen to jump out. The boy studied the pebbles in the driveway before taking off at a run. Kate hurried to the front door where muffled sounds of a little hand were knocking.

Owen stood on the top step grinning. "Hello, Mrs. Price," he said as soon as he saw her.

"Hello, Owen. You can call me Kate." She glanced at Peyton. "If that's okay with your mom."

"Is it, Mommy? I like Kate a lot better than Mrs. Price cuz she's not old."

Peyton swallowed a laugh. "Since Kate suggested it, then yes. But remember your manners," she called after Owen as he dashed through the house to the back deck.

"He was in a hurry."

"Owen has a one-track mind where Anna is

concerned."

"Does someone have a crush on Anna?" Kate grinned.

Jack stepped around the girls. "That's an understatement." He walked into the house.

Peyton playfully jabbed his arm. "Owen thinks Anna hung the moon, and thankfully, she doesn't mind him scampering after her. He told me Anna's cool because she works with fruit in a lab. I'm not sure if he understands what she is doing. But if he's happy, I'm happy."

Kate could see love shining in the young mother's eyes. "You're welcome to join everyone on the deck. I have a few more things to do in the kitchen."

"Would you like some help?" Peyton didn't hide her curiosity as she looked around the large room. "You've done a wonderful job in here. I love the way you used colors to create defined spaces."

Kate paused in the living area. "Thanks. It came together nicely. If you'd like to help, I could use an extra set of hands bringing out the trays."

Peyton stopped short. "Wow." She gasped. "This is a professional kitchen! I'd kill for that stove, six burners, double ovens."

She laughed. "It comes with the territory of being a chef—once you get used to it, it's hard to use a typical stove. It's my one indulgence in the house." She dropped her voice to a conspiratorial whisper. "At least that's what I told my husband."

Peyton crossed her heart and chuckled. "The less he knows the better."

She passed her a tray. "If you'll take this out and ask Don to turn on the grill, I think we're ready."

"Sure." Peyton passed Jack on his way into the kitchen.

"Hey, Kate." He turned to make sure they were alone. "Can I ask you a favor?"

"What's up?"

"Could you find out if Peyton is dating?"

The question piqued Kate's interest and she

gave Jack her full attention. "Who wants to know? You?"

Jack shifted uncomfortably. "Yeah, I was thinking I'd ask her to a movie or something. I don't think she dates much, but well, you know, we're both single… maybe we could hang out."

Kate wiped her hands on the towel. "We're leaving tomorrow, and I don't know if I'll get a chance tonight, but next time I'll see what I can do. Jack, she is a nice girl. I like her." She realized she genuinely liked her. Despite that she had neglected to tell Don that he was a father.

"Thanks. I'd really appreciate it." He grabbed the last tray and made a beeline for the deck.

"Well, that certainly changes a few things," Kate mused. "If Jack is interested in Peyton, what does that mean for Owen and Don?" Reluctant to worry about the problem, she pushed it to the back of her mind. "Tomorrow I can decide what to do about everything."

Don attempted to get Kate's attention, but

she was lost in thought. At last, their eyes met and he relaxed as she smiled and walked toward him.

They passed out burgers as they came off the fire. One by one, people found seats and sat in small groups on the deck. "We're going to need a bigger table if we plan on hosting family parties."

He slipped his arm around her waist. "I like how that sounds." Giving her a peck on the cheek, he handed her a burger. "Let's eat. I'm starving."

The evening passed quickly, and after cleaning up the kitchen and promising to host another event, their guests departed.

"I hope it's okay but we need to stay at your parents' tonight. I forgot to buy linens for the bed."

Don took one look at his wife and realized how hard she had worked over the last few days. Sweeping her into his arms, he said, "Of course, sweetheart. When we come out in a few weeks, we'll come straight to the cottage and have a romantic evening, and that will be our first official night in our home."

Kate laid her head on Don's chest and held him close. "I don't want this to ever end."

Confused, Don asked, "Tonight?"

"No, silly." She gazed deep into his eyes. "Us."

"Well then, that's easy. We will always be us."

He kissed her. His voice low and husky, he said, "You are the love of my life and nothing will pull us apart."

Kate held on even tighter, wishing that were true. Their marriage was about to be pushed to the limit. She didn't have the illusion it was going to be easy.

Don pulled back. "Let's lock up and go home."

Kate walked around securing windows and doors, took one last look around the charming home, and prayed she'd be back. Tomorrow was going to be a difficult day for both of them.

15

Don was loading the car as Kate surveyed the bedroom one last time. She planned to drive back to Loudon. Having the steering wheel in her hands would steady her jangling nerves as she broached the subject of Owen's paternity. Satisfied they hadn't forgotten anything, she walked downstairs.

"Good morning, you two." She poured cereal into a bowl and splashed some milk on top. "Don should be finished loading the car. Do you know if he had breakfast?"

"Not yet." Sherry looked up when Don came in. "And here he is now. Breakfast, son?"

"Thanks, Mom. Kate, I grabbed our travel mugs from the car." Don slathered jam on a slice of toast and devoured it.

Nervously, Kate finished her cereal and washed out the bowl. She held up a mug after adding cream and sugar.

"Coffee?"

"That'd be great." He stood up. "We need to hit the road. I'll give you a call tomorrow, Dad, and we'll touch base."

Sam nodded. "Drive careful," he said gruffly.

"Not to worry, Kate drives most of the time. It keeps her from getting car sick."

"Oh, don't tell them my secret." Kate felt her cheeks flush bright pink. "It's something most people outgrow by adulthood."

"Don't worry, Kate, it's safe with us. Some people never outgrow it and it's nothing to be ashamed of," Sherry said, trying to comfort her.

"Thanks, Sherry."

Don held the door open. "Ready?"

Waving, Kate slid behind the wheel and buckled up. "See you soon," she called.

With Don's seat belt fastened, she drove down the driveway. After they merged onto the highway, Don asked, "Kate, what's on your mind?"

Her stomach flipped over. "What are you talking about?"

"Your mind has been elsewhere for days, and you're distracted and distant. Did something happen that we need to talk about?"

She struggled to find the right words. "I wasn't going to bring this up until we got more distance between us and the winery, but yes, something is bothering me." Kate took a calming breath. "How long were you going to wait before you tell me you are Owen's father?"

"What? That's insane!" Don bellowed.

"Is it? The timeline fits. You were living at your parents'. You took Peyton to a party, and nine months later she had a baby." Kate spoke quietly but deliberately. "Do you deny you went with her to the party?"

"Of course not. I drove her to the party, but Peyton stayed and I came home. Alone."

"Then how is it that nine months after that night she had a baby and won't name the father? I think she is protecting someone and everyone knows right after that night you moved to Loudon. Maybe she never told you either."

He turned in the seat to watch her. "Did Peyton say I was Owen's biological father?" Don demanded.

"Well, no. But I put one and one together and got three." She sulked.

"Kate, I can assure you if I was Owen's father, I would take responsibility and I would be a part of his life. If it makes you feel better, turn the car around and let's go see her and we can clear this up now. I don't want this to drive a wedge between us."

"Are you serious? Turn around and show

up demanding what, exactly? If she hasn't told you by now, maybe she doesn't want you to know."

"Pull into the next rest area, Kate. It's impossible to talk about something this serious while you're driving."

She saw a sign up ahead, put her blinker on, and slowed the car to a grinding halt. She turned off the car and bolted. Don ran after her.

"Wait!" In a few strides, he caught up to Kate. "Do you really believe I would have cheated on you, fathered a child, and walked away?"

"Don," she wailed and the tears flowed. "I don't know what to think. The little boy looks like you, with brown eyes and blond hair and he's tall for his age."

"So that is what caused you to jump to conclusions? Owen could look like a lot of guys." Don drew Kate into his arms. "Kate, I promise you from the moment I saw you on Fed Hill, I haven't looked at another woman. You are the only girl for me. Despite what was going on at that time in our lives, I knew it was temporary. We were going to be husband and wife and have a family."

Desperate to believe him, she stammered, "Don. I know you have always loved me but if something did happen, too much beer or you got caught up in a moment, I need to know for sure." She looked into Don's deep brown eyes and saw the hurt smoldering. "Please understand, if I don't ask, I'll always wonder. Were you serious about going back to talk with Peyton?"

"If that is what you need, then yes, let's go now. I don't want this crazy notion to fester for one more minute." Don kissed her lightly. "Katie, I promise you, Owen is not my son."

Don draped his arm loosely around her shoulders as they returned to the car.

She took the next exit and reversed direction. tion. The next stop: Peyton.

*P*eyton's car was parked in her usual spot. Kate glanced at Don, who wore an expression she had never seen before. Had she made a mistake demanding to confront the situation?

"Well, at least this will accomplish something," she muttered.

Don turned to his wife. "What's that?"

"You said you wanted to find out who Owen's father is. By the end of this conversation, maybe we'll both know the truth."

"This isn't exactly what I had in mind, and I never dreamed you'd think I was his father." He pushed open the car door. "Let's get this over with."

Peyton glanced up from the laptop when the door opened. "Hey, guys. I'm surprised to see you here. Weren't you going home today?"

"Do you have a couple of minutes? Kate needs to talk to you about something."

"Of course." With a hand shaking, Peyton

tucked a stray lock of hair behind her ear. "Do you want to sit?"

She noticed the gesture and pulled out a chair.

Tension hung heavy in the air. She looked from Don to Kate and back again. "I'm afraid you have me at a disadvantage. What do you need to talk to me about? Have I done something wrong?"

He hung his head and waited for Kate.

"Peyton, I don't know how to say this so I'll be blunt." Kate glanced at Don and swallowed hard. "Is Don your son's father?"

A look of disbelief flashed over the young woman's face. "Are you serious?"

Neither Kate nor Don spoke, waiting for Peyton to say something of substance.

"Kate, why would you think Don was Owen's father? Since we were kids, we've been only friends. I've looked up to him like an older brother. It has never been anything more. I promise you, Don is definitely not my son's father."

"Based on the timeline, you got pregnant when he was living here and you implied it was around the time of the party. I put two and two together. I understand you didn't want to burden Don so you kept it a secret. But if Owen is Don's son, they both have a right to know."

"Don!" Peyton cried. "Tell her we've never been together that way."

"Believe me, I tried. But I am curious. Why haven't you said who the father is? If nothing else, he should take financial responsibility for the boy's welfare."

Peyton stood up and her temper flared. "It is none of anybody's business but mine. Frankly, I'm disappointed in both of you. You thought you could come in here and accuse me of withholding my son from his father, when my son's father wants nothing to do with him!"

Kate could see Peyton was distressed and was instantly apologetic. "Peyton, I'm sorry. I didn't mean to cause you pain."

Peyton's eyes were brimming with tears. "You wouldn't understand. I would appreciate it if we could just forget this conversation. Kate, if it would put your mind to rest, we can do a paternity test and you'll have proof Owen isn't a Price."

Don watched Kate's reaction. He knew what it had taken for Peyton to make the offer. How would Kate respond? Their marriage needed Kate to put this aside and move forward.

"You would do that, agree to a test?"

"Kate, I know what the result will be. Don took me to the party and when he was ready to go home, I stayed. I've never even thought of Don in that way, and even if I had, it wasn't a secret you were, and are, his one and only. So, doing a cheek swab isn't going to make one iota of difference. I know in my heart Don is not Owen's biological father. It's not possible; we've never slept together."

Kate pushed back from the table and bolted for the door. Don started after her. Kate turned midstep. "No. I need time."

Don mumbled, "I'll be waiting for you."

Peyton was uncomfortable. "What happened here?"

"This has been a very difficult time for Kate. Deep down she knew Owen wasn't my son. But what you don't know is that we have been unsuccessful in getting pregnant. I think somewhere Kate got twisted up, thinking if I had already fathered a child and if we weren't blessed with a child of our own, I would have a son. And if I were Owen's father, then she is the reason we're not able to conceive. There is the added stress about my parents retiring and Kate caught between working for her mother and striking out on her own."

"I could see how a bit of information could get misconstrued. My heart goes out to her." Peyton sat watching the clock hands creep around the dial. "Do you think it would be alright if I talked to her?"

Surprised, Don said, "Do you think it will help Kate?"

"Honestly, I think it might help us both." She bowed her head.

"Peyton, you're a good person. If you think it will help, I'll be in my office."

*D*on left the room and Peyton walked into the bright sunshine. It didn't take long to find Kate in the gazebo where the girls had shared a glass of wine the day before.

"Kate," she said softly, "may I sit down?" Getting a nod, Peyton took a seat. "Can we talk?"

"I'm not sure what else there is to say, except I'm sorry. I hope someday you'll forgive me for being a horrible person and butting into your personal life."

Without answering, Peyton looked out over the rolling acres of vines. "Do you know what I love about this spot?"

Kate shook her head.

"Those vines were planted on this land long before either of us were born. Mother Nature is unpredictable, and when she sends a hard winter our way, the vines always spring back to life. They don't give up. Instead, they unfurl their greenery; they soak in the warmth and rain she sends. They forgive the bad days because there are always good days ahead."

"I'm not sure what you mean."

"What I am trying to say is we're human, and when I was dealt a tough hand, I sprang back and flourished. If I was in your shoes, I might have jumped to the same conclusion. I guess I've gotten used to people gossiping about Owen's dad, why he isn't in the picture. But I am telling you the truth. Don is not Owen's father."

"I still don't understand," Kate said. "Why didn't you tell him? Couldn't you use the support?"

"I'm sorry but this isn't something I want to discuss. I have my reasons and I would appreciate it if we could just drop the subject."

Peyton struggled to keep her voice controlled. She was on the verge of losing the battle with her tears and desperately wanted to change the subject.

*K*ate sat with her hands folded in her lap and stared at the rolling landscape. She wished the silence would be filled with Peyton telling the truth, but at the same time, she wondered, did she have the right to expect this girl to confess her deepest secret to a virtual stranger? Kate was at war inside her head. Logically, she knew Don wasn't the boy's father, but why hadn't they been able to conceive? It was time to admit they would have to go further in their quest to have a baby.

Kate's voice was thick with tears as she said, "Peyton, I really do need to apologize. Your personal business is just that, your business. Can you forgive me for being an insecure, overly emotional woman?"

Peyton gave her a tiny smile. "Nothing to forgive. I kind of understand."

"Maybe we can start over. Hopefully I haven't destroyed a chance for us to be friends? Other than family, I don't know anyone here."

Peyton gave Kate a fierce hug. "I'd like that. Now what do you say we find your husband and you can get back on the road? You still have a long drive."

*D*on was staring at a jumble of words on the computer screen when Kate walked in. He wasn't sure what had happened and didn't want to ask. "Are you ready to go home?"

Kate nodded and picked up her handbag. "Yes."

"Just let me grab my laptop."

Peyton was waiting next to the car when the couple came outside. After a short goodbye, Don and Kate drove off once again down the long driveway toward the highway. He was prepared to wait until Kate was ready to talk about the morning, but he hoped it wouldn't be a silent ride.

"Are you hungry?" Kate asked. "How about we get a bite of lunch before we get on the highway? I'd like to sit and talk."

"Sure, any place special you want to try?"

"The Shack. I'm in the mood for a juicy veggie burger and I've heard good things from your family about this place."

Relieved, his shoulders dropped, and Don said, "They have the best onion rings."

Kate flashed a tentative smile. "The Shack it is."

Don started to give her directions, and Kate giggled. "I've been doing a lot of driving around lately and I just might know this town better than you do."

"I'll bet a lot has changed since I lived here. You might be right." The miles slipped away. "Ah, there it is."

The couple placed an order and took a ticket. Don pointed to a table in the shade. "How about over there?"

Kate laid napkins on the picnic table and put straws into cups of lemonade. "It's too nice to be inside, don't you think?"

Don nodded in agreement. Before he could say anything, their number was called over the loudspeaker. "Wow, that was fast!" He sprang up. "Be right back."

Kate looked around, trying to figure out the best way to apologize, practicing the words over and over in her head. She watched Don balance an overflowing tray in one hand and a bag in the other.

"They took pity on me and put the burgers in here." Don handed her the bag and placed the tray on the table.

"I guess it's good we're sharing fries and onion rings. There's enough to feed four people."

. . .

*D*on was happy to hear the lighthearted tone in Kate's voice; it had been missing for far too long. Realization hit him—the burden she'd been carrying, worrying about Owen's paternity, not to mention the move.

Kate squeezed ketchup on a paper plate and placed it in the middle of the table. It took several long minutes before she found her opening. "Don, first I want to say I'm sorry. I should have believed you about that night."

Don put his burger down and chomped on an onion ring. "I'm guessing whatever you and Peyton talked about helped."

"It helps that she doesn't hate me for being a jerk." Kate took a deep breath, then said, her voice ragged, "Will you leave me if I can't have a baby?"

Stunned, Don watched tears slide down Kate's cheeks. "Of course not. I love you and that isn't conditional on you giving birth. There are a lot of ways for us to have a family."

Using his thumb, Don caressed her tears away. "Is that what has been worrying you?"

Kate's head bobbed, unable to speak.

"Katie, how many times do I have to remind you I love you, and if our family is two or ten, you have been and always will be its nucleus."

She rested her cheek in Don's hand. "I'm so sorry I've been acting crazy."

"Well, I feel bad you haven't been able to talk to me. We're supposed to share our hopes and dreams as well as stress and worries." He grew serious. "Will you promise me something? The next time something is bothering you, talk to me before you get carried away."

"I love you more at this moment than ever."

Don leaned in for a kiss. "Is there anything else we should talk? I have a strong suspicion there is a lot going on behind those emerald eyes."

She cocked her head and smiled. "Well, now that you mention it, I did have an interesting observation this week. Jack likes Peyton."

"How do you know that?"

"Last night he asked if I would find out if Peyton was seeing anyone. And if you were more observant, you'd see he keeps an eye on her, very casually. I think he is interested in more than a friendship, and he enjoys playing with Owen." Kate picked up her burger and bit into it, juice dripping off her chin. "Don? Jack isn't the only one who should take a step toward the future. It's time to move forward and face our fears."

Don looked up and studied Kate. "What are you saying?"

"I'm ready to move to Crescent Lake, and if CLW is ready to expand, I'd like to open up some type of eatery." She held up her hand. "Before you get ahead of yourself, it will take time to make sure What's Perkin' is running smoothly, but I think by this time next year, we can be living here full-time. Can you be patient with me?"

Relief coursed through Don. "Kate, this is fantastic news. I would have continued to do the long-distance thing, but this will be better for us, you'll see."

She brought his hand to her lips. "My love, our future is in Crescent Lake."

16

*K*ate was happy to be driving down Main Street, soaking up the vibe in her hometown. Loudon would always be Kate's safe haven, but she was excited about the impending move to Crescent Lake. Although she had talked with her mother over the last few days, their conversations were about the shop and Luke. From all reports, he seemed to be fitting in, which helped Kate feel less anxious about breaking the news to the rest of her family.

Kate slipped in the back door and savored

the sight and smell of the What's Perkin' kitchen. She slowly walked around the room, fingers trailing over the counters, wondering how she could recreate this space in a new location. Maybe Ray still had the plans from when he designed and built her mom's kitchen. It was hard to believe it had been almost twenty years. So much had changed and yet so much had remained the same.

"When you're deep in thought, you look just like your mother."

Kate recognized the voice and turned. "Hi, Daddy. I'm surprised you're here."

"Why, did you think you weren't going to see me again?"

Kate could see her father leaning against the refrigerator, a soft glow surrounding him.

"I didn't think you'd come to me anywhere but my house."

"I've never gotten the hang of this popping in and out thing I do. Besides, I go where needed. But let's not waste our time talking about where I can go. How are things going for you and Don?"

"Much better. Don and I are going to move. He'll run the winery, and I will open my restaurant."

"Well, that is good news. What changed your mind?" Her dad gave her an encouraging smile to continue.

"After our last conversation, I realized Don had given up what he loved to be with me, here. How could I deny him the opportunity to live his dream when my dream is to cook and be his wife? In reality, I can cook anywhere, but he can only run the family business from Crescent Lake. I never intended to work for Mom long term, but it's comfortable. What's Perkin' was Mom's dream. When Don's parents talked about retiring and whether to pass on the business to their kids or to sell, I wondered if Mom was holding on to this place for me. For years, she's worked hard. Now that she and Ray are married, maybe she wants to sell or lease it to have fun with Ray... and I don't want to hold her back. I could insist on living in Loudon, and Don would travel between here and the winery, but at what price? I am not willing to risk our marriage just so I can keep my feet firmly planted in Loudon."

Her dad smiled. He was pleased. "You have grown a lot these past months. And you're right, being pigheaded can damage even the best relationship beyond repair. Have you thought about how you're going to tell your mother?"

"That's the toughest part. I know she'll be happy for us and never say otherwise. After we close today, I'll tell her the plan and timeline and reassure her I will hire a great chef. That won't be easy as I have high standards, but I'm confident we can make it work."

The front door jingled and Kate heard Lucas call out to her. When she looked at her father he was gone, but she heard him say very softly, "Bye, Katie." Kate tied on her apron; it was time to get ready for the busy day ahead.

"Good morning, Luke." Kate gave him a

warm smile. "How have things been with my mom?"

He beamed. "Great. Your mother is easy to work for, and the café is busy, so the day is over before it has begun. I thought I would miss the pace of the evening crowd, but this has a charm all its own, and I don't need to deal with people who overindulge, if you know what I mean."

Kate nodded as he talked. She vividly remembered one incident when she was an intern when a customer got out of hand and had to be escorted from the restaurant. "Been there, done that." Kate grinned over the shared experience.

"Did you and your husband have a good trip?" Luke did side work while they chatted.

"We did, but I worried about this place while we were gone." A pang of guilt danced through Kate. "Mom has been running What's Perkin' for a long time and can work circles around me, but we enhanced the lunch menu after I came back. I've never thought about all the changes we've made."

Luke's face looked pained. "Hey, I'm sorry. I guess I shouldn't have brought it up. For what it's worth, I think Cari liked taking control of the kitchen. She made these triple chocolate cookies that were to die for; I think she called them Romeos. Have you ever had one?"

Kate laughed. "Not only have I had them, but I'll confess I made them up when I was about eleven. Mom had to tweak the recipe a bit to make them actually taste good, but the basic idea was mine."

"Cari made them on two different days and they sold out before lunch. I had to save one from the second batch just so I would get a sample. Sounds like you've always had a knack for being in the kitchen."

"I guess you don't know Mom started the business out of our home. Her first orders were at Thanksgiving; my brother, sister, and I were her helpers. After the first success, she took orders for Christmas. I think she always believed people placed orders to be nice, but the orders for Christmas cookies and pies really gave her something to think about. After mulling it over for a few weeks, she leased this space, hired Ray to do the renovation work, opened that spring, and the rest is history."

"Isn't she married to Ray?" Luke was clearly confused.

"Yes, they've been married for a couple of years, but it took them a long time to figure out they had fallen in love. Once they did, it was a seven-day engagement and they have been inseparable ever since."

Just then, her mom walked in and squealed, interrupting the conversation. "You're here!" She hugged Kate tightly.

"Hi, Mom. Did you forget I was coming home?" she teased.

"No, I didn't, but seeing you is completely different. How are Don's parents?"

"Good. Sam and Sherry are really getting into the retirement groove. He doesn't go into the office as much and they're talking about all the trips they want to take. As much as they didn't want to retire, now they are embracing it. It's really pretty funny."

"Sounds like things are good then? Anything else important transpire over the last week?"

"Things are very good, but we need to get busy. We open in fifteen minutes, and I need to get something in the oven." Kate rushed through the swinging door.

"Cari, I've got the front covered if you want to help Kate."

"I think she could use a hand. Thanks. If you get busy, give me a shout and I'll come out." Cari tied on her apron as she disappeared into the kitchen.

"Last night I got some things prepped to make this morning go smoothly." Cari pulled some covered containers off the shelf and said, "Grab four large bowls."

Kate did as requested and retrieved eggs, butter, and milk from the refrigerator. Kate pointed to the first container. "What is this?"

Cari looked up, glanced at the other three, and stated, "Muffin base. You can choose whatever fruit strikes you and it needs spices, too."

Kate went to work mixing in apples, coconut, pineapple, and nuts along with the balance of wet ingredients. Whisking it all together, she made short work and slid trays of muffins into the convection oven. Turning to the next tub, she repeated the same procedure and finished all four batches while Cari started the scones. Then she turned to load trays and passed them out to Luke, who promptly filled the display case.

"I'll keep baking if you want to handle the breakfast orders. I just saw a couple come in and take a seat."

Kate peeked into the dining room and discovered several tables were full. Luke placed the slip down on the window and called out the order. Kate whipped up omelets, toast, and sausage, along with home fries before calling out, "Order up."

The morning hummed along, not leaving time for idle chitchat as the front and back of the house worked together like a well-oiled machine. Lunch was over and Kate wiped her hands for the umpteenth time. "Who's ready for something to eat besides me?" Not waiting for an answer, she made up plates with sandwiches and salad. Passing one plate to her mother, Kate carried the other two out front. "Luke, let's eat before we fade away." She smiled. "You're quite the asset to our little business."

"Thanks, I try." Pleased with the compliment, he joined the ladies. "I had no idea a coffee shop could be so busy, and it's like this every day. Well, at least so far."

Cari bit into a tangy egg salad sandwich, enjoying the mixture of crunch and creaminess. "Business increased after Kate started cooking. She brought an entirely new element to the place. Gave it a shot of sass, I think."

Kate blushed. "Mom, stop. You always did a solid business. The burst isn't because of me; your reputation proceeds you, and as our menu grows, so does the business."

"You're right; you had nothing to do with the increase," Cari teased.

"Fill me in on everyone. How are Abby and Shane, and Jake and Sara? I haven't had an opportunity to call them. And what about Ellie, is she still determined to open a business of her own?"

Cari wiped her mouth with a napkin. "Everyone is doing great, but you can see for yourself on Saturday. I thought we'd barbeque, and Shane wants us to go out to the lake."

"Sounds good. I'll give Abby a call to see what I can bring."

"If you have some time, we should talk this afternoon about the applications for kitchen staff." Cari watched her daughter, unable to put her finger on what exactly it was that was different.

"How many résumés did we get? I plan on staying around after we close, to do inventory and plan out the next few daily specials. We could go over what you received before I start."

"Five. Three referrals from JWU and the other two are somewhat local. But let's finish lunch, clean up, and you can look later."

The door jingled and Luke jumped up. "Hi, Ray, can I get you something?"

"I'm hoping Kate made blueberry muffins and there are some left."

"She sure did and I put two aside for you. Coffee?"

"Luke, thanks for saving me a couple. You're having lunch, go sit and finish. Besides, you don't need to wait on me."

"It's no trouble, I insist." Luke steered Ray toward his wife and stepdaughter.

"Hey, Ray, did you miss me?" Kate teased.

"I missed your muffins; your mothers are

good, but yours? Superb." He leaned over to place a fatherly kiss on the top of Kate's head before kissing his wife hello.

"Hello, dear. Did you have a busy day?"

Cari chuckled. "How could you tell?" She glanced around the room. "Other than the place being in shambles."

"The front display case is just about empty, so that is always a good sign of brisk business."

"It was a good day and Kate got back just in time." Cari beamed.

Inwardly, Kate cringed. How would she ever be able to tell her mother she was leaving What's Perkin'? It had to be done. She wondered if it would be easier if Ray were there too, quickly dismissing the thought.

"Ray, Mom tells me there is a cookout Saturday at Shane's. Do you think Jake and Sara will be there with the triplets? I haven't seen them in, what seems like, forever."

"They're planning on it. The kids are changing every day. Kaylee started to walk and Brad is right behind her, but Zach is still holding on to everything. He is a little more cautious." He beamed. "I couldn't be happier; our family is growing, and everyone is healthy."

"That's good. I bet when Zach starts walking, he'll run, just to make up for taking his time. He seems to be a thinker and lets his sister and brother take the lumps. Smart kid, if you ask me."

Cari stood up. "If I want to get out of here today, we should clean up. Ray, I'll see you at home?"

He kissed Cari full on the mouth. "I still need to go quote a job so I'm going to take off." With a salute, he called to Luke, "See you later." He turned to Kate. "See you tomorrow, kiddo."

Kate gave him a wave and picked up the empty dishes. A few customers had come in and Luke was waiting on them. Pushing the broom, her mom made short work of the front, leaving everything sparkling in her wake. Kate had retreated to the kitchen and was perched on a stool, lost in her own thoughts while adding items to the order sheet. Cari walked in, delighted everything was tidy and ready for a new day.

"Luke finished closing up and left for the day." Cari pulled out the companion stool and dropped onto it. "Another good day this month. If this keeps up, it will be a record year."

"Hmm," Kate murmured. "Mom, can we talk?"

"Always." Her mom waited.

"Don's new job is quite a responsibility, and it has always been his dream to run the winery." Kate paused, waiting for her mom to interject. "You remember his parents gave us the cottage as a wedding gift and at the time I dismissed the idea of ever living in Crescent

Lake." Kate got up and stood in front of the sink, grabbing a towel and twisting it in her hands. "The last time we were there, I agreed to hire some people to get it remodeled to suit our taste. Originally, I thought Don could stay there every other week instead of staying with his parents. And when I went out there, we'd have a place that was ours."

"And now?" her mom prodded.

"Don and Sherry will provide me with the capital to open a bistro at the winery. There is also the possibility to have catered events such as weddings, too." Kate still didn't want to look at her mom. "I know I should have talked to you before I made a final decision, but after giving it a lot of thought, I've decided it's time we move to Crescent Lake."

Cari walked to where her daughter was intent on staring at the floor. "Kate, look at me." Gently, Cari pulled her chin up. "This is a wonderful opportunity."

"You're not mad at me?" Her voice quivered.

"Absolutely not! Why would I be? This has been your dream. What made you decide to move forward, if you don't mind me asking?"

Kate hesitated, weighing her answer carefully. "Daddy."

"What did your dad have to do with the decision to move?"

"You know he came to see me… well, it has been a few times, not just once."

"That's interesting."

"After talking with him, I realized I was being selfish, expecting Don to commute six hours, round trip, every couple of weeks. He walked away from the winery to marry me. If he would do that for me, shouldn't I be willing to do the same for him?"

Her mom nodded. Encouraged, Kate continued.

"Don can't be effective if he's at the winery part-time. He needs to be there to show his family he is capable of not just running the winery, but putting ideas in action and growing the business for the next generation. I love him and I'm not willing to lose him over what amounts to me having a temper tantrum."

Cari hugged her daughter. "I'm proud of you, Kate. You're finally ready to begin the next stage in life."

"I don't want you to worry. Well see each other a lot, I promise, and you and Ray have an open door at our house. We'll have a spare room all set up."

"Kate, three hours isn't like going to the moon. We'll see each other, just not every day."

Kate jumped in, "You don't need to worry about What's Perkin' either. Don agreed we wouldn't move until you have a full staff. We'll find a replacement for me and I still think we need to add one more kitchen person and maybe even another counter person. That way you'll have time to come out and visit."

Cari laughed. "When you get ready to put a plan in motion, you go for it. How about we start with kitchen help and worry about re-placing me later."

"Mom, I didn't mean, well, I just thought you and Ray might like to have some free time to enjoy your life together. You both have worked hard your entire lives and maybe it's time to have some fun."

"I'll give that some thought." Cari moved to the counter and picked up the stack of ré-sumés. "First, we need to set up interviews for next week. I assume you'll be going back to the winery soon?"

"In two weeks, we'll drive out with both vehicles and Don can stay for the week. I'll be gone a few days. I need to move some clothes and such."

"When do you plan on telling the rest of the family?"

"Saturday, at the lake. I want Don to be with me." Kate chewed on her bottom lip. "Do you think anyone will be mad at us for leaving?"

"Kate, stop putting so much pressure on

yourself. Everyone in the family will be thrilled. We will miss having you both around. You may want to think about adding on to your cottage, in case we all come to visit at the same time for the holidays or something." Her mom grinned.

"Hmm, I hadn't thought about that. I should talk to Don." Relieved, Kate took the résumés from her mother and scanned them, separating them into piles.

"Katie?" Her mom hesitated before she said, "Do you think you'll talk to your father again?"

"I don't know, but I hope so. Why?"

"If you do, tell him I'm happy." Tears hovered in her mom's deep-emerald eyes. "Ray and I have a good life together and he doesn't need to worry about me."

"I'll tell him, Mom. I promise." Kate drew her mother in close and held on like she used to as a child.

After a few minutes, her mom cleared her throat. "We'd better pick out a couple of candidates. I put the most promising ones on the top."

"I see that." Kate wiped her eyes and concentrated on the task at hand. After she finished sorting, they chose three to interview. She pulled out her laptop and sent emails, offering dates and times. She also asked each one to be prepared to bake a sample cookie, muffin, or scone. In Kate's opinion, the best way to judge a cook's work was to taste it.

Before Kate had finished the final email, the first person responded. "We're off to a good start." She smiled. "One confirmed, two to go."

She closed the laptop. "Are you sure you're okay with me leaving?"

"Honestly, I never expected you to stay as long as you have. You wanted to conquer the world, Kate. You aren't meant to be in the shadows of my business. What's Perkin' is comfortable for you. You don't have to take any chances. Most people never get an opportunity like this. If you didn't take it, I would be very disappointed and I might have even fired you, just to push you out of the nest."

"You'd have fired me?" Kate was shocked. "Really?"

"If I thought you were giving up on your dream, yes, I think I would have. Now we don't have to find out. Just promise me you'll have a table for us on opening night."

She grinned. "You can count on it, the best table in the house!" She frowned.

"Kate, what's wrong?"

The emotional dam burst. "Don and I have been trying to have a baby for a long time," she croaked. "I feel like I've failed my husband."

"Oh Kate, come here." Her mom wrapped her arms around her child, ran a hand over her hair, and held her while the tears flowed.

A gentle hiccup filled the silence of the shop. Cari waited for Kate to talk.

"Each month I get my hopes up, that this will be the month I don't need to go to the drugstore for supplies, but each month my dreams are dashed."

"Have you seen the doctor?"

"Yes, and supposedly there isn't anything wrong. Dr. Thomas says I need to be patient and it will happen. Don has been tested too, and he has a clean bill of health. So, it has to be something going on with me. I've been tracking my temperatures, taking vitamins. What else am I supposed to do?" she cried.

"Are you going to start fertility treatments? I understand there are a lot of options to help."

"We're considering it, but I want to conceive naturally." Kate wiped her eyes. "Don and I have talked about it, and he says we will have a family. If necessary, we can explore adoption. But I'm not ready to give up yet."

Cari wiped her face with a tea towel. "Is there anything I can do to help?"

Kate shook her head, fresh tears hovering on her dark lashes. "No, but I don't feel as alone now. It helps to say it out loud to someone other than Don. I wish I had talked to you long ago." Kate gave her mother a hug. "I'd like to avoid this topic for a while. You understand, right, Mom?"

Her mom touched her cheek. "Of course, but I'm here when you need me. You're never alone, Katie. I'm only a phone call away."

"Thanks, Mom." With shoulders slumped, Kate slipped out the back door.

17

Saturday evening had arrived and Shane's backyard buzzed with activity. Cari watched over her growing family with joy. Kate and Don had arrived lugging a cooler between them, and Don carried a large baking pan in the other hand. Cari couldn't help but see Kate's face glow with happiness and she hoped everyone would support the couple on their new adventure.

Don set the cooler down and Cari tried to peek into the covered container. "What's for dessert?"

"Vanilla ice cream and triple chocolate brownies." Grinning, Kate said, "I don't remember the last time we made ice cream and I thought it would be fun taking turns at the crank."

Don came carrying two large bags of ice.

"Mom, do you think we can put these in the coolers on the porch?"

Cari shook her head and redirected Don to the laundry room. "They're full of beverages. Let's put it in the freezer."

Don followed Cari and waited while she made space for the bags. Laying them on a shelf, he shut the freezer door. "Cari, can I talk to you a minute?"

Surprised, Cari closed the laundry room door and gave Don her full attention. "What's on your mind?"

He shifted uncomfortably. "I'm aware Kate told you we are moving to Crescent Lake and she's going to open a restaurant. I know her contribution to What's Perkin' and it means a great deal to both of us that you understand this is part of our journey. As a kid, I dreamed of taking over for my father. When I met Kate, she became my world, and I thought I could leave it behind. And as much as I love her and our life here, I've started to feel like I was missing something critical. I didn't know how much until Dad got sick and asked me to step in." Don leaned against the washer and looked out the small window. He watched Kate rearranging the grill area. "I discovered what had been missing: my passion for my family's business. I wouldn't have risked my marriage to take it over. I was prepared to commute between here and the winery if that's what it took. I can promise you I didn't pressure her in any way. She decided it was time to strike out and make her mark in the world." Don searched his mother-in-law's eyes for approval. "You and the family are welcome anytime, and I promise we'll be back as often as possible."

"Don, if I had any doubts about you, your love for Kate, or the future, rest assured I would speak up. But the time has come for you both to make a change, and we'll come out to visit and we will expect to see you here, too." Cari gave him a reassuring smile and touched his arm. "All I ask is for you to not lose sight of what is truly important, and that is your marriage. Be patient with Kate as she adjusts to a new life."

He wrapped Cari in a bear hug. "You don't have to worry. I know there is a lot of change for both of us over the next few months. Together we can conquer the world!"

Cari gave him a final squeeze. "Let's rejoin the family."

*D*on stepped out the back door. Catching Kate's eye, he smiled and gave her a slight nod—the signal everything was fine.

Kate relaxed. She knew Don was nervous her mom would be angry they were moving and leaving What's Perkin' without a chef. The sound of slamming car doors reached her ears. The rest of the family had arrived, and it was time to unload baby gear. She looked around, savoring the chaos. So much had changed for the McKenna family in a few short years—two weddings, a pending adoption, the birth of the triplets, and a college graduation. It was fitting another change was on the horizon.

Ray and Cari were playing with four rambunctious toddlers as Ellie approached her mother.

"Hey, Mom, what time are we eating? I'm starving!" Ellie grinned, trying to mask feeling out of place among the couples surrounding her. It was a new experience to have a large family. She loved everyone and wanted them to be happy, but she was starting to miss something she had never had.

"I'll bet you went for a long run this morning with the intent of working up an appetite?"

"Yeah, I didn't eat much after my run as there is always so much food at these family picnics." In a conspiratorial whisper, she said, "I heard a rumor that Kate made brownies."

Cari winked. "And ice cream. Your sister brought all the fixings."

"She did? Really? Even better." Ellie whipped around. "Kate!"

Kate smiled, knowing Ellie had just heard about dessert. "What, El?"

"When are we going to start the ice cream? It should be soon so it's ready for dessert; otherwise, it might not be hard enough. You know ice cream is serious business." Taking matters into her own hands, Ellie started toward the house, with Kate trailing behind her. Once the sisters were out of earshot, Ellie got straight to the point. "When are you going to tell the family?"

"About?" Kate was unsure what Ellie was referring to. "Do you mean the ice cream?"

"Kate, I'm not stupid. You and Don are moving to Crescent Lake, aren't you?"

"Why do you ask?" Kate paused. "Did you hear something?"

"No, but I've been paying attention. Don has been trying to run a huge business from here and you've been going back and forth—I assume to get the house ready. You're finally smiling, which tells me a decision has been made about your future, and lastly, Don is grinning from ear to ear, which confirms my suspicions."

Kate stopped fussing with the ice cream freezer and looked at her sister. "You always amaze me; you are so in tune with everyone."

"I'm not sure I understand what you mean," Ellie retorted.

"You've been watching from the sidelines and somehow you cut through all the nonsense to put everything into perspective. So, to answer your question, Don and I are moving to Crescent Lake. We have a lot to sort out, including my work, and lastly, we want to have a baby. Since that isn't happening, we may need to get medical help for infertility."

Ellie opened the back door and they went inside. "I wish you had talked to me about all this stuff. I might have been able to help you through it all."

"Well, I have talked to someone and it helped." Kate stopped short.

"Who? You haven't talked with Mom, Abby, or Sara. And you and Don haven't been communicating that great lately."

"No, things have been strained between us. I didn't want him to give up the winery, but I wasn't ready to leave Loudon. I felt like his parents were trying to coerce me, and then there is the issue with a girl from his hometown—she has a son and I was convinced Don was the father." Seeing the look of anger flash in Ellie's eye's, Kate quickly chirped, "But he's not. I was so wound up about everything, I jumped to conclusions."

Ellie's eyebrow arched. "Wow, that was a lot for you to handle. So, if you didn't talk to any of us, who did you talk with to figure out what you wanted?"

Kate hesitated before she spoke. "You might think this is wacky, but Dad."

"Huh? You talked to Dad? How?" Ellie peppered Kate with questions.

"I know it sounds crazy, but one night when Don was at his parents', I came home from work and I was sitting in the living room and he just... appeared." Kate struggled to logically relay the events to Ellie. "At first, I didn't believe it was him, but he told me a story only I knew and I felt safe, just like when I was a kid and had a bad day and Daddy would come to my room and talk to me. I told Mom about it, and she said Dad always came when she needed him the most. She thinks that was why he did. I was struggling, at a crossroads. Was I letting my marriage fall apart because I was being pigheaded? I never doubted I loved Don, but I didn't feel I was ready to change." Kate shrugged. "So, after spending time in Crescent Lake and scouting the restaurant community, I thought I could bring something special to the winery. I guess Dad had something to do with me finally realizing that I had so far given up nothing and Don had given up everything so we could have a life together. How could I keep Don from something he had always dreamed of doing, running the winery? Once I figured that out, the rest was easy." Kate pushed a lock of hair from Ellie's eyes. "Pixie, you know our door is always open for you."

Ellie choked back the lump in her throat. "You know I'll visit; it's not like you're moving to the Mars," she teased. Pointing to the family, she said, "So when are you going to tell everyone?"

"That's funny. Mom said the same thing."

"Kate, I don't think it will come as a big surprise; I'm sure everyone figured something like this was brewing."

"You think?" Kate picked up the box of salt. "I haven't heard a peep from anyone."

"Well, maybe…"

Kate straightened her shoulders. "No time like the present. We'll make our announcement and get it over with." She took a deep breath and walked outside, calling to her husband, "Don, can I see you a minute?"

Don crossed the lawn. Grasping her hand, Don cleared his throat. "Can we have everyone's attention?"

A hush fell over the family and everyone looked at the couple, waiting expectantly.

Taking a deep breath, Kate said, "Don and I have an announcement. As everyone knows, we've been spending time in Crescent Lake and Don has taken over CLW. What you don't know is Don's parents have suggested I open a bistro at the winery, six months a year, from April through October. They hired an architect and had some preliminary designs created for me. After giving it a great deal of thought, we've decided to make Crescent Lake our home."

Shane was first to congratulate his twin and her husband. "Wow, this is awesome."

Don interjected, "It won't be immediate. Kate wants to make sure Cari has a reliable cook. We're not going to put the house up for sale right away." He gave Kate a gentle smile. "It has to be when the time is right."

Abby and Sara hugged Kate, and everyone started talking about the wonderful opportunity and how many bedrooms were in the new house.

Kate laughed. "Don, we may need to add on or have people stay at your parents' if everyone comes to town."

Don assured the family that everyone was welcome at any time. "Between my parents and Liza, there is plenty of room."

After the conversations died down, Kate and Ellie brought out the ice cream freezers and everyone pitched in, churning cream into a sweet icy confection, while Shane flipped burgers and hot dogs on the grill. It was a perfect day spent with the family. And it was over too quickly.

On the drive home, Don asked, "Kate, is something bothering you?"

"Hmm? No, I was just thinking about how fast the kids are growing. It's amazing how the triplets each have a distinct personality and Devin acts like the big brother. It made my heart ache, just a little." Kate flashed Don a look. "Before you start worrying about me obsessing over a baby, I wasn't. I just don't want to miss the important milestones of their lives."

"I understand, really. We will make it a point to stay connected. And you don't plan on opening the bistro until next spring, and even after you open, I thought you had decided the days will be Thursday through Sunday."

With a slight quiver in her voice, Kate said, "You're right. It will just be different." Then she brightened. "But we will be able to spend time with Liza's boys and of course everyone in the Price family."

Don pulled into their driveway and turned off the car, clasping her hand as he spoke softly. "Honey, have you changed your mind?"

"No, of course not. I'm excited about the bistro and your new job, and I love our cottage. It's just going to be different."

"I will be as patient as you need." Don cupped her cheek. With a whisper, he said, "I love you, Katie." His lips brushed hers with a tender kiss. "We'll take the move at your speed, no worries."

Kate's lips warmed under Don's. She reveled in the depth of his love and silently thanked her dad; without his guidance she might have lost the most precious gift in her life. "I love you, too. How did I find you?"

With a low chuckle, Don said, "All it took was iced tea, a bright-white chef coat, a terrible temper, and here we are today."

18

Over the next few weeks, Cari and Kate held interviews for kitchen help. Kate thought it would be better to have a breakfast and lunch cook as well as a pastry chef to do the baking, who could then expand to special occasion cakes. It was taking longer than Kate expected. There were several good candidates, but small-town life wasn't for everyone, and so far, they were coming up empty.

Every couple of weeks Don traveled between the winery and Loudon. He understood plans for the bistro were on hold until Kate could spend time with the architect. She pondered names that would draw people into the restaurant and complement the winery. The last thing Kate wanted to do was harm the reputation of the family business. Hence, she was putting a lot of pressure on herself to find the perfect name.

Early one morning Cari walked into the shop and found Kate sitting at the counter with a blank pad of paper in front of her. "What are you working on?"

"I can't think of a suitable name for the bistro. I was trying to find a play on words for Crescent Lake, something about a pond or river, maybe a stream, but my mind is blank."

"Maybe you're trying too hard. Did you consider just letting ideas flow into your head?"

"How did you decide on What's Perkin'?"

Her mom's face softened. "Funny story. It was the first morning after your dad and I got home from our honeymoon. I had never made coffee before and I misread the directions on the coffeepot we had gotten as a gift. You know how I love a good cup of coffee. Well, it was perking and as I'm watching the pot fill, it got darker and darker—more so than I had ever seen. Your dad walked into our tiny kitchen, lured by the aroma. He inhaled deeply and asked me what was perkin'. He wondered if I had a secret blend or something. I told him it was regular coffee while he poured two mugs. I'll never forget—it was the color of black onyx, and the smell was overwhelming. Ben blew on it before taking the first sip." She laughed. "The look on his face was priceless. Without saying a word, he carefully poured half down the drain, took cream out of the refrigerator, and poured until it became a normal coffee color."

"Are you saying it was too strong?" Kate chuckled.

"Not only was it too strong, but I swear if we had stirred it with a spoon, it would have melted. I don't know how, but your dad drank the entire cup. Of course, I was horrified. I reread the directions and discovered my mistake; I used four times the amount required. After that, every morning your dad would come into the kitchen and ask 'what's perkin', good lookin',' and it stuck. When I decided to open the shop, I wanted your dad to be a part of it, hence, What's Perkin' was the only logical choice."

Kate's eyes glistened. "I don't think you ever told me that story. It's a great way to honor Daddy."

"Well, you kids don't know all our stories. I have to keep some to share at just the right moment. When I tell you to stop thinking so hard and the name will come to you, it will." Cari kissed Kate's cheek as she left the room. "Luke is coming in the front door; time to start our day."

"Thanks, Mom. You're right. I'm going to just let my mind go and see what pops in." Kate gave a wave to Luke and retied her apron. "Luke, when you get a minute, come on back and I'll give you today's specials."

. . .

*L*uke was refilling the napkin dispenser when he heard a tentative tap on the door. He glanced at the clock, thinking he forgot to unlock it, and saw there was still fifteen minutes until opening. Wondering who was so anxious to get coffee, he went to investigate. He was surprised to see a girl with a large satchel slung over her shoulder peering through the glass. She looked about twelve years old. Luke flipped the lock and swung it open. "Good morning. We're not quite ready to open yet, but please come in."

The girl peered at Luke with pale-blue eyes through large round wire-rimmed glasses. Brown fringe bangs graced the rims. "I'm not here as a customer. I'd like to apply for the pastry chef job."

Clearly taken off guard, he let the door slam shut. "If you'd take a seat, I'll get the owner."

The girl nodded and Luke went in search of

Kate and Cari. "Ladies, there is a young girl out front who said she wants to apply for the job."

Kate wiped her hands and glanced out front. Cari stood beside her. "Does she look familiar?" Cari asked.

"No, I don't recognize her. Do you?"

She shook her head. "I'm going to talk to her. Care to join me?"

"Absolutely."

The McKenna women walked through the swinging door. Cari extended her hand and smiled warmly. "Good morning. I'm Cari Davis, and this is my daughter Kate Price. We understand you'd like to apply for the pastry job."

"Hello." The girl shook Cari's outstretched hand with a firm grip. "I'm Danielle Michaels, but please call me Dani. And yes, I saw the posting on the internet. I believe I have the necessary skills."

Cari pulled out a chair and gestured to Dani. "Please have a seat."

Kate sat down and noticed Dani chewed on her lower lip.

"Do you have a recent résumé?" Kate inquired. Dani handed her a sheet of paper. Kate scanned the typewritten document. "I notice you don't have formal training. It seems to be primarily on-the-job experience." Kate looked at Dani.

"I never had the opportunity to attend culinary school. After high school, I had to help support my family." She glanced uncertainly from Kate back to Cari, sensing this woman could relate more to her situation. Dani had done her research on What's Perkin' before she came to Loudon. She learned Cari Davis had been a single parent when she opened the shop and ran it flawlessly while raising three children. "When I was a teenager, my father was hurt in a car accident. My mother worked in an office but what she made didn't cover the bills, so I went to work at a local bakery to help out. Eventually, my parents moved to Arizona and my dad found work in the technology field. I stayed behind. The bakery owner and his wife took me under their wing, teaching me everything they knew. After they retired, I couldn't afford to buy the bakery, and finding myself jobless and homeless, I was forced to move. I've had a few jobs, but basically, I haven't found a place that feels right, where I can put down roots."

"What makes you think Loudon is the place you'd like to call home?" Cari quizzed. She understood Dani's need to find a place where she felt a sense of belonging.

"Honestly, I'm not sure. But this week, after spending some time around town, I can tell it has a good vibe and the people seem nice."

"How long have you been here?" Kate wondered.

"Since Friday. I spent the weekend wandering around and I've looked at a few apartments. I've also eaten a couple of meals here to see if I liked your menu and style of cooking."

"And do you?" Cari was amused with Dani's candor.

For the first time, Dani's smile reached her blue eyes. "I do like it, very much. I know there is a lot for me to learn, especially working with Kate. What she puts out of this kitchen is incredible, but I have a few tricks up my sleeve, too."

Cari wasn't swayed by flattery but quickly came up with an idea. "I'd like to propose an unusual opportunity. Pieces of paper don't mean as much to me as how you handle yourself in the kitchen. Would you like to work for us for one week, with pay? And if at the end of that time we feel you're a good addition to the team, we can talk salary and hours. If either of us thinks it's not a good fit, we can part ways and at least you'll have some extra money in your pocket."

. . .

*D*ani couldn't believe her good fortune. She could showcase her talent *and* get paid. If this worked out, she just might have found a place to hang her hat, at least for a while. "I think that sounds like a great idea, and rest assured, I'm prepared to work hard." Excited, Dani stood and the chair toppled backward. "When can I start?"

Cari looked at Kate. "It's your kitchen."

"Can you start tomorrow at six? We bake all items fresh each day."

"What time do you get in, Kate? I can start at the same time."

"I come at five, but tomorrow you should come in at six. I'll have things ready for you. After the lunch rush, we can talk about changing your hours."

Dani pumped first Cari's and then Kate's hand. "Thank you very much. I promise, you won't be sorry." After gathering her oversize bag, Dani left the shop with a bounce in her step and a jaunty wave.

"Kate, I'm pleased you're willing to give Danielle a trial. There's no way to check her references and she seems awfully young to have that much experience. Do you think she stretched the truth?"

"Honestly, I don't know. She has no formal education, not that it was a requirement, but there is something about her I like, and to use her word, I got a good 'vibe' she might be just what we're looking for. But falling back to my sensible side, I'll know very quickly if she's all talk; the proof will literally be in the pudding." Kate's chair scraped the wood floor. "I have a great deal to get organized if I'm going to share my kitchen tomorrow."

Cari lingered at the small bistro table while her daughter went into the kitchen. There was change in the wind; she hoped it would be a good steady breeze and not a storm brewing.

.   .   .

*A*rriving a little before five, Kate parked in her usual spot, anxious to see Dani Michaels in action in her kitchen. She had given it a great deal of thought and decided that if Dani couldn't handle the grill but knew how to bake, they would hire a grill person. The two sets of skills weren't necessarily interchangeable. She unlocked the doors and flipped on the overhead lights. It was the same thrill each time she entered the kitchen. It was where she had fallen in love with baking, and every moment spent measuring, mixing, and creating new recipes had been pure heaven. It was going to be hard turning it over to the care of another person.

Kate enjoyed the solitude, moving through the usual routine: starting coffee, turning on the ovens, and filling out the specials board. While pouring a mug of fresh coffee, she heard a soft rapping on the front door. Chuckling to herself, she unbolted the door and pulled it open. "Good morning, Dani. You're a little early."

Dani stood on the step, hesitant to go inside. "I was too excited to sleep so I figured it's better to be early than late." She shrugged and gave Kate a lopsided grin. "So here I am. You don't have to pay extra."

Kate swung the door wide. "Come on in. There is coffee behind the counter. Feel free to get a cup, and then I'll give you the tour. There is a coatrack in back."

Dani followed, taking in the shadows of the shop, enjoying the silence. "I've always loved early morning in a bakery. It's like the world is waiting for us to wake up just to start their day."

"I've never thought of it in that context, but I guess you're right." Kate held the swinging door and Dani got her first glimpse of Kate's inner sanctum.

She gave a low whistle of appreciation. "What a great kitchen. Everything sparkles like new."

"I can assure you nothing is new. We have high standards for both the front and back of the house."

Dani nodded, understanding the industry terms for the kitchen and dining room.

"Where can I stash my things?" Kate pointed to a closet, and Dani quickly tucked her bag, coat, and hat inside. She ran her fingers through closely cropped curls. "Do you have a cap for me?"

Kate handed over a deep-purple hat, T-shirt, and apron all bearing the What's Perkin' logo. "There is a restroom out front; you can change in there. I'll send you home with a few extra shirts and you can toss the apron in the laundry bag each day. You'll be responsible for laundering the T-shirts." Kate was all business.

Dani returned to the kitchen, sporting the hat and apron tied in the front. Kate gestured for Dani to join her. She pointed to a large loose-leaf binder. "This is my mother's recipe book. Over the last few years, I've added additional items, but our standard offering is what my mother built this business on, from the ground up, and we will always serve them as is." Kate glanced at Dani to convey a strong message.

Dani's head bobbed. "Got it. We don't mess with tried and true and especially success."

Kate laughed. "Besides, I think she'd kill us both if we fooled with her recipes too much." Kate placed a handwritten page in front of Dani. "Each night I make a baking schedule; this is my attempt to get as much baked as possible before we open. I don't make huge batches of any one item. We have a lot of regulars so on weekdays we have a good idea how many muffins are needed depending on the season. I try to use fresh fruits and vegetables whenever possible, which we purchase from a local farm. They deliver to us daily, typically after lunch." Dani nodded and studied the plan. "I think to start I'm going to have you get familiar with the pantry. Once you're comfortable, see where I am in the baking lineup, and

I'll give you something to work on. Does that sound fair?"

"Totally. Just one question, do you want me on the grill today?"

Her brow arched in surprise, Kate shook her head. "No, today we're going to concentrate on baking, maybe tomorrow we'll talk about the grill."

"Alright then, let's get started." Dani studied the open pantry and noticed it was lined up alphabetically. "This is different," she muttered to herself. She moved to the baking center, where all the pans were stored, once again noticing the detailed organization by type and size. This too struck Dani as interesting.

"Ah, Kate?" Dani asked. "Everything is super organized, was that by accident?"

Kate laughed loudly despite Dani's expression. "It's all Cari, she thrives on order."

"Good to know. Well, since I know the alphabet, I'm ready to bake." Dani grinned.

"How do you feel about coffee cake? We

need six." Kate slid the baking binder to her new assistant.

Anxious to impress, Dani carefully read the recipe and gathered the items she needed along with the baking pans. "Which ovens are free?"

Kate pointed to the second bank of convection ovens and Dani went to adjust the temperatures before mixing up the batter. Kate observed out of the corner of her eye, watching as Dani made short work of the task, and then slid the pans into the ovens. Kate hadn't bothered to remind her that convection takes less time and was pleased when she adjusted the timer before cleaning up the work center. Kate opened the binder to the next page and said, "Four each, banana and lemon poppy seed bread."

Dani found her rhythm and before another hour had passed, she was working directly from the list, filling the display case in the front as each item was ready for customers. Aware Kate was keeping an observant eye, she cleaned and baked throughout the morning until the list was complete. Surprised, she looked to Kate for guidance.

"What's next, boss?"

Kate glanced out at the full display cases. "Do you have any specialties?"

Dani went through a checklist in her head. "I like making cupcakes. One is like a s'more but in a cupcake. The bottom is crushed graham crackers with chocolate cake, then frosted with a vanilla buttercream, drizzled with chocolate ganache, and then topped with a mini toasted marshmallow. Truly decadent, and I think it will show off a few of my skills for you."

After Dani was done describing the confection, Kate said, "You've got my mouth watering. You'll find everything you need in the pantry, so why don't you get started and we'll see how they sell with the lunch crowd."

"You don't have anything to worry about, Kate. I guarantee they'll sell out before the end of the day." Confident with her choice, Dani went to work, humming mindlessly.

Cari poked her head into the kitchen and waved Kate to the front. "So, what is our newest employee whipping up?"

Kate shook her head. "You're never going to believe it but a s'more cupcake. It sounds super decadent and she promised it would show off some of her skills. Up to this point, Dani has impressed me. She navigates our kitchen like she has been doing it for years. But it is day one; we'll see how things are at the end of the week."

"What about the grill? Will you let her try breakfast or lunch?"

Kate nodded. "I'm not going to ask her to come in early tomorrow but give it another day handling the baked items. If that goes smoothly, then we'll turn her loose on the grill." As Kate talked, Luke effortlessly handled customers, greeting each with a warm smile and thanking them for stopping in without a thought as to how much they'd spent. "We did a good job hiring him," she said with a tilt of her head in Luke's direction.

Cari's eyes followed. "I wasn't sure if the pace here would be enough to keep him busy but so far he seems happy. And my stars, he can sell ice in the North Pole. He has certainly lightened my load."

Smiling, Kate said, "That was the point, Mom, to give you the opportunity to take some time off, remember?"

Cari placed a hand on Kate's shoulder. "I won't be taking much time off until your replacement is up to speed and I feel comfortable leaving the shop. I've put too much heart and soul into it to start goofing off."

"Mom, I know that; this shop means a lot to all of us. But you've worked hard, and you should have an opportunity to enjoy life. But not too much, as I might need you to come to Crescent Lake and help me. You started a business and it's been very successful. I'm afraid I'll make expensive mistakes."

Cari laughed out loud. "Making mistakes is part of starting a business, but I can give you some pointers, things to avoid, but you'll make plenty of your own."

"Great, I have something to look forward to." Kate glanced in the kitchen where Dani was sliding a tray of cupcakes into the oven.

"I have an order." Luke wiggled a piece of paper in the air.

"I think that's my cue. On my way." Straightening her apron, Kate walked to the swinging door. "Break's over, Mom," she joked.

"Yes, ma'am." Cari tidied the tables before going behind the counter to give Luke a break. "You might want to eat a light snack. Kate told me Dani is making a specialty cupcake and we're all going to want one."

"Thanks for the tip, Cari, but I'm a bottomless pit when it comes to sweets." Luke turned to go into the kitchen.

She was surprised he was allowed to putter in Kate's domain. "Would you mind bringing me a cup of whatever today's special is? I think Kate made chili."

"Sure thing, boss," Luke called over the sound of the front door jingling. He marveled at how many customers came to What's Perkin' each day. It was great to see a small business thrive, and he was surprised that it was locals and tourists alike. Luke could hear Cari talking with one of her regular lunch customers and he knew luck shined on him when Cari offered him this job. Especially now that another newbie had come along, and if his nose wasn't deceiving him, she was one heck of a baker, too.

Dani finished arranging the cupcakes on a tray, reserving four. She walked through the swinging door backside first. Luke stepped aside, giving Dani room to slide the tray into the case. A customer was standing in front of the display, trying to decide between brownies and cookies when he asked, "What are those?" He pointed toward Dani's creation.

"It is today's special cupcake, a s'more. Would you like a taste?" Dani took one off the tray and cut it into small pieces, offering the man a sample. He reached out, took the largest piece, and popped it in his mouth.

Kate and Cari stood watching the reaction, not sure what would transpire. This particular customer was notoriously picky.

"Oh, this is amazing. Can you box up a dozen? I'm supposed to bring dessert to a cookout tonight and this will make me look like a superstar." He reached out and plucked another piece off the plate. "You don't mind, right? Actually, make that a dozen and a half. I'm going to want some left over."

Dani beamed. "Luke will ring you up." She filled a large bakery box and passed it over the counter. "Thank you for stopping in; be sure to come again." She gave him a wink. "Each day we'll feature a different flavor, guaranteed to be just as decadent."

"I'll be back for sure. Thanks a lot." The customer took the box and was already opening it before he stepped onto the sidewalk.

"How many do you think will make it to the cookout?" Luke wondered.

"Hmm, Dani, I think you had better let us have a sample. After seeing his reaction, I don't think they're going to last long and Luke will be tempted to sell mine," Cari joked.

Dani sailed into the kitchen, quickly returning. "Here we go." She extended the plate. Luke took the first bite and pretended to stagger back while he clutched his chest.

"Kate, you just might have some competition," he teased.

Kate and Cari bit into the moist cake with a marshmallow filling eking out on the sides. In unison, the women sighed and said, "Delicious."

Dani took tiny bites of the heavenly cake, hiding a modest smile. "I'm glad you like it. I have several more twists on cupcakes, and if you'd like, I can make a different one each day."

Without hesitation, Kate said, "I'm looking forward to it, but I had better make sure I exercise this week because I know these are not calorie-free. Besides, you did promise that customer there would be more."

The group was interrupted by more customers and, as Dani had promised, the tray was sold out before close of business, but not before a couple were tucked away for family members. Cari and Kate wanted their husbands to sample the goods from what might be the newest employee of What's Perkin'.

19

For the remainder of the week, Dani impressed Kate and Cari. Not only could she handle the baking, despite lack of training, the grill came second nature to her. Cari and Kate talked it over, weighing the pros and cons. They came to an agreement and Cari offered Dani a permanent position. She was thrilled and quickly accepted the job.

"Cari, I'll work harder than anyone and take my job seriously. Kate has big shoes to fill, but I promise I'll do my best." Dani beamed. In her excitement, it hadn't occurred to her if she should ask about the salary. "I do have one question. Do you know where I can find a decent rental, not overly expensive and close to the shop?"

Kate cocked her head. "We assumed you had a place. Where have you been staying?"

"I have a tent, and the state forest has hot showers. If this job didn't work out, it would have made it easier to move on. For now, I'm comfortable, but soon the weather is going to turn cold and I need to find a place. I don't need anything big, just warm and dry."

Cari's mouth dropped open and she quickly closed it. "Let me talk to Ray and see what we can come up with. Do you think you could camp for a few more nights?"

"Of course, I love camping. I just need to plan ahead, that's all." Dani's enthusiasm was contagious and she certainly didn't want her new bosses to think she was a charity case. She had learned long ago that traveling light usually worked out for the best.

• • •

Kate smiled. "We should get back to work. Hopefully we'll have some time to go over ordering and vendors in the next day or so. It's another part of this job you haven't seen yet."

She saw the look in her mother's eyes and knew her mom had a soft spot for people in need. Each year the shop sponsored a drive for items to fill holiday baskets for families. The number of families continued to grow and her mom found businesses willing to donate and help deliver the baskets. Her mom's compassion was one of the traits Kate admired the most. Their family had their share of sorrow, and Shane, Ellie, and Kate had learned first-hand it was a blessing to repay kindness with kindness. Besides, it was a lot of fun helping to create a little magic for families who needed a helping hand.

The front door opened and Abby strolled in with Devin in tow. "Hey, everyone. We thought we'd stop in. Devin was missing one of his favorite aunties, so here we are!"

Devin clutched his toy truck until he spied Kate. "Kiki!"

Abby let go of his hand and the little boy made a beeline into Kate's outstretched arms. She scooped the little guy into a bear hug, tickling him until giggles erupted. "How's my little buddy today? Auntie Kate made cookies. Would you like one?"

Devin strained to be set down so he could go into the kitchen. He knew exactly where the goodies were hiding. "Devin, Auntie has to carry you. Dani is cooking." Devin nodded very seriously as if he understood exactly what Kate had said. He didn't care how he got to the kitchen as long as there was a cookie when they arrived. The two disappeared behind the swinging door and Abby poured herself some iced tea.

"Mom, can I get you a glass?" Abby stopped mid-pour. Cari shook her head. "So how are things here? Shane said Dani is doing great things in the kitchen. Have you made a decision yet?"

"We offered her the job and she accepted. Kate started training her. Soon they'll be free to move." Cari released a deep sigh, not realizing how it must have sounded.

Abby crossed the room and took a stool at the counter. "Mom, are you okay?" She glanced around and didn't see Luke. "Do you want to talk about Kate leaving?"

With a shake of her head, Cari said, "No, it's a great opportunity, but I'm really going to miss her."

Abby laid her hand on Cari's. "It will be different but I was thinking we'll make sure to get out there often, even if it's a trip we make a few times without our men."

Cari squeezed her daughter-in-law's hand. "Thanks, Abby. I may take you up on that. When Kate was in college, she talked about moving away, but since she's been back, I got used to having all my kids close by."

Abby listened, letting Cari ramble, nodding at the appropriate moments.

After Cari stopped, she smiled. "Well, aren't you clever? Helping me realize everything will work out."

"You're giving me too much credit. All I did was sit down and have something to drink. You took care of the rest. But I'm happy you think I helped." Abby grinned. "I'll go find Devin before Kate gives him too many cookies." Abby picked up her empty glass and smiled at Cari. "Mom, Kate is going to do great things in Crescent Lake."

Cari's head bobbed. "I'm pretty lucky. All my kids are doing great things."

Leaving Cari alone with her thoughts, she pushed open the swinging door. "Kate, how many cookies has Devin charmed out of you?"

She grinned. "Don't look at me. He's cast his spell over a new victim. Dani is totally smitten with the little man." She gestured toward the pair studying the cupcake platter. "I think she baked magic into them."

"Huh, you're right, Kate, that little devil has done it again. And I thought it was just the McKenna women who fell for his charms."

Dani didn't look up. "You know I'm in the room and I can hear you." She chuckled. "And for the record, there is magic in everything I do. But you don't need to worry; we're just looking at them. Devin said he wanted one to go."

"I'm sure he did. We'd better wrap up a few. Shane would love to sample them. What is the flavor today?"

Dani rubbed her hands together. "Well, I was out at Blake's Farmers' Market and they had the most amazing peaches. I couldn't resist, and after playing around with a few ideas, this is the result: a caramelized peach cupcake with a light cinnamon buttercream frosting. It reminds me of when I was growing up and my mom made the best peach cobbler. The cinnamon and peach combination was to die for. Hopefully they'll sell."

"You're making me drool. I'd better take

six. These aren't going to last at my house or out front!"

"That is really sweet of you to say, but you haven't tried them yet." Dani filled a small box and tucked two sugar cookies inside for Devin. "Make sure to let me know what your husband thinks of them."

"I will. Thanks." Abby picked up the box and Devin took her free hand. "We had better go. I have plenty of work to finish before Shane gets home."

Kate followed Abby out front. "Abs, I think Don and I need to go out to the winery next week for a couple of days. If Mom gets in a bind, can you help out?"

"Sure, but I think with Luke handling the front and Dani in back, she'll be fine."

Cari walked over to give Devin a hug. "What's this I hear? Kate, are you still worried about me? In the last couple of months, we've hired good people. You need to stop fretting."

"I'm not really worried, per se, but I guess I've got feet planted in both places. It's hard to let go after running the kitchen. Mom, I am sure the same thing happened to you when I came back."

"When I started the shop, I had limited hours and closed a couple of days a week so I could work behind the scenes, and your grandparents came to help during the busy times. When you started working here, your goal was to grow the business. Now it's time to focus that energy into your dream."

Kate tossed a towel over her shoulder and retied her apron. "I know what you're saying and I'm excited to get started, but for as long as I've been cooking professionally, it's been your kitchen. In a way I'm reinventing myself."

Abby reassured her best friend. "Kate, you're not quietly going into business with your personality and skill. Your business will be booming within weeks of the doors being opened. People will buy the wines you pair with food. It's a win-win for the Price family." Abby paused on the threshold. "I need to run, but I'll see you both soon. If you want, stop by the house; the lake is very refreshing. Soon it's going to be too cold to swim or boat."

"Thanks for the invite, Abs. I'll talk to you soon."

Cari watched her daughter grab the inventory sheet and go back into the kitchen. She knew Kate would have a hard time adjusting to the physical distance. But the family would always be very close. She grabbed a cloth and spray bottle and moved to wipe down the already clean tables. She needed something mundane while she mulled over an idea. Maybe it was time to rent the efficiency apartment above the shop. When she got home later, she'd talk to Ray.

Ray listened as Cari outlined her plan. "It wouldn't take much to get it livable—a deep clean, fresh paint, and a new rug in the bedroom. The wood floors in the kitchen and living room will be fine. If she wants to add an area rug, she can, but for now she'll be out of the elements. And it's affordable."

After all these years, he knew when his wife set her mind to something, even a national disaster would have a hard time slowing her down. "Are you sure you want an employee living above the shop? We really don't know much about her, do we? Our last tenant was perfect. Shane was either working or sleeping."

"I know enough about her to have offered her a job. I'm sure she doesn't have a large bank account to rent something else, which would be a huge cash outlay with first, last, and security, and you know it wouldn't be half as nice as our apartment." She crossed her arms over her chest. "Besides, if she had money to spare, would she be living in a tent?"

"Have you mentioned the apartment to

Dani? What if she has other plans?" Ray asked gently.

"Now, Ray Davis, are you saying we shouldn't rent to this girl?"

He could tell Cari's temper had started to simmer, especially since she sensed a few roadblocks ahead.

"Cari, that isn't what I'm saying. Before we paint and carpet, it would be nice to know if she'd like to be our tenant *and* employee." Ray cocked one eyebrow, wondering why his bride was so insistent on renting the long-vacant apartment.

"That settles it. I'll ask Dani first thing tomorrow. When you stop in for coffee, we can take her up and Dani can decide." She plopped into his lap, lavishing him with kisses all over his face. "Your reward for being the best husband around."

Ray chuckled and wrapped his arms around her. "If I had known this would be your reaction, I would have agreed sooner."

"If you had, this might not have been your

reward." She giggled. "Seriously. You're in agreement we should help this girl, right?"

"Of course, I am, but I wanted to make sure you thought about it carefully. My part in this marriage is, when necessary, to play devil's advocate." He nuzzled her neck.

"Oh, Ray, you do think of my best interests first."

"I do, but you did just fine before I came along."

"I'm doing much better now that you're here and my husband. As awful as it was, the day Vanessa shot you was a blessing in disguise," Cari murmured. "I wish we hadn't wasted all the years we could have spent together. Instead, time was spent pretending we didn't have feelings for each other. But thankfully it all worked out in the end."

He swallowed the lump in his throat. "We both got lucky that day, Cari. You saved my life in more ways than one."

The couple grew silent as they sat on the

back porch in the warm setting sun, safe in each other's arms.

⁂

Dani was in the shop the next morning when Kate and Cari arrived. Luke was coming up the walk when Cari flipped over the OPEN sign. Wonderful aromas of baked goods and coffee filled the shop and it was ready for the hustle and bustle of customers. Cari secured her apron in front and went looking for Dani, finding her in the back pantry weighing flour. "Do you have a moment?"

Dani set down the bowl she was holding. "Of course. Did I do something wrong?"

"Nothing is wrong. I wanted to talk with you." Cari paused and gestured to the coffeepot. Dani shook her head. "Yesterday you mentioned you have been staying at a campground and that got me thinking. Ray and I have a small apartment over the shop, and it's vacant. It hasn't been lived in since Shane bought his house. It needs a good cleaning and paint. But we thought if you were interested, it might be ideal for you." Cari laid a piece of paper on the counter. "We think this is a fair rent, and heat, electric, and hot water are included."

Dani glanced at the paper and then stared hard at the number. "I think you've made a mistake."

Cari's laughter filled the room. "You haven't seen it yet. You might think we're asking too much. Why don't you give it some thought, and when Ray stops in, we'll run upstairs and check it out."

In disbelief, Dani slowly nodded. She didn't know what she had done to deserve a great job, with good people, and now they were offering a place to live. She went back to baking, her mind churning. She didn't notice Kate watching her.

"Everything okay, Dani?"

"Did you know your parents are offering me an apartment? I mean, you could knock me over with a feather. I'm happy to have a job, and now this?" Dani stuttered. She wasn't the kind of girl good things happened to; every break she had ever gotten took hard work.

"I figured Mom would get around to it. It's a great space—not very big but your landlord is easy to get along with. It might be good for both of you."

"We're going to check it out later. It'll either be love at first sight or oh-em-gee, no way." Dani looked at Kate. "Do you think Cari would be offended if I declined?"

Kate laughed. "If I know my mother, she would remodel it to make it work for you. She is a very determined woman."

Dani let the conversation dangle in midair while she rolled dough and cut biscuits. She was going to think about the apartment later. At the moment she had work to finish.

Dani had plated a breakfast order when Ray popped his head in the kitchen. "I've heard we've piqued your interest in the apartment?" Dani was taken aback. Ray Davis was intimidating. He was tall, well built, and had the most amazing blue eyes she had ever seen. The corners crinkled when he was joking around, but now they were looking at her expectantly.

"Just let me get this order to Luke. And Kate said she would cover me."

Ray was waiting for Dani and Cari in the rear parking lot.

Dani grinned from ear to ear as she stepped on the first stair. "I feel like a kid at Christmas, getting ready to open presents!"

"Well, I hope you're not disappointed, Dani." Ray chuckled. "It's small." Ray and Cari followed her up the stairwell through the open door.

Dani's hand flew to her mouth. "It's perfect!" she exclaimed and rushed into the bedroom before peeking into the small bathroom.

Twirling around the sunny space, she asked, "When can I move in?"

"Honey, do you think we could get it ready in a week?"

"I think so." Ray hesitated. "Is something wrong?"

"I'd love to move in as soon as possible. I'm happy to clean and paint. It's just been a long time since I've had something this nice, and I'd really like to get settled."

Before Cari could speak, Ray interjected, "I will look at the appliances and double-check the electrical and plumbing. If all is in good working order, we can pay for all the cleaning and painting supplies and you can move in to-morrow. Would that suffice?"

She had hope this really was going to work out. "It sure would, and thanks!" She gave the room a once-over and then noticed the walls were all the same off-white shade. "Do you want me to repaint the same color?" Dani hesi-tated. She hated to ask but continued. "I love color and wondered if it would be okay if I change a few walls, maybe a warm tan and a soft blue or purple in the bedroom. I would show you the swatches first, for your approval."

"I don't see why that would be a problem. When you find something you like, bring the color samples by and we'll go from there. Ray will leave your name at the hardware store so you can charge everything to his account."

Surprised at the trust, Dani gave Ray and then Cari fierce hugs. "You have no idea what this means to me—the job, apartment, and, well, everything. I don't know how I'll ever be able to thank you for all that you've done for me." Tears hovered and Dani quickly blinked them away.

Cari smiled. "Work hard and keep that smile on your face. That's all we ask."

"Alright, ladies, if we're all set here, I'll get a key made, talk to Tony about the charge account, and be back to do my part. I'm happy this apartment will get some use."

The trio went back downstairs and parted company.

Kate glanced up when Dani and Cari entered. "So, what did you think of the place?"

"It's awesome. After work I'm going to get some paint samples and start cleaning, but first I'll pack up my tent because tonight I'm going to sleep in my new apartment!" Dani was walking on air as she went back to baking.

"Wow, she sure is happy," Kate whispered to Cari. "I guess all the pieces are falling into place."

Cari nodded. "Do you know when Don is needed at the winery again?"

"We talked last night and we'll leave early Monday so Don can be in the office around nine, depending on traffic. I'll go to the house and unpack. I want to schedule a meeting with a contractor about the addition to the winery. I have a great location in mind. I think I told you, Sam talked with someone about the design, but they're giving me free rein to do what I think is best."

"That's wonderful. Stay as long as necessary and don't worry about rushing back." Cari turned her gaze to Dani. "I'm curious to see how she handles a weekend."

"Are you sure she's ready?" Kate was mildly concerned. "She might need more training."

"I didn't give you much time before you took over the kitchen. Besides, I suspect she needs challenges to excel for her personal benefit."

"Then I'll let Don know we're good to go. If you have any issues, just let me know and I'll come home. If need be, we can hire someone part-time to fill in for me."

"Katie," her mom said gently, "we will be fine and What's Perkin' will survive." Cari gave her a quick peck on the cheek. "Now, let's get back to work before Luke and Dani think we've abandoned them."

For several minutes Kate stared at an

empty pot, lost in thought. Suddenly it hit her like a ton of bricks. Her mother was very wise. Excited, she pulled her cell out of her apron pocket and hit the speed dial button. She couldn't wait to give Don the news. She might even leave early to pack a few more things. There was so much to do.

20

Kate was behind the wheel of her car and Don was following in his truck. Both were loaded with household items and small pieces of furniture Kate wanted at the cottage. Don had said he was thrilled with her newfound enthusiasm for the move and grateful things were coming together sooner than he had hoped. He thought it would be better to stop at the cottage and then go to the office, getting in at some point around noon. Their exit was just ahead and Kate pulled into the right lane. "Here we go."

Kate pulled up the tree-lined driveway that led to their new home. She was happy they weren't listing the Loudon house for sale, at least not right away. She was totally committed to the change, but wasn't quite ready to let go. Don said it would be good for them to keep the house—for visits and holidays; he felt privacy was important for happy family vacations.

Kate got out, stretching tall, working out the kinks. She waited for Don to do the same before running over to throw her arms around his neck. "Welcome home, my dear husband." She looked into his deep brown eyes and planted a kiss on his lips. "Are you going to the office first or will you unpack?"

"Well, we could do something else first." His words were laced with suggestive tones. "What would you like to do?"

"I want you to carry me over the threshold, give me a kiss, and then help me unpack. All we'd need is for someone to come looking for you and find us, well, you know." Kate chuckled. "There is plenty of time for hanky-panky after work."

"Okay, if you insist." Don swept her off her feet. "Do you have the key for the front door?'

She dangled it from her fingers. "I'm ready. Can you carry me that far?" Kate looked at the stone walkway. "Don't drop me."

Don pretended to stumble while holding her tight in his arms. "Not a chance, Mrs. Price."

Effortlessly, Don carried Kate to the front door where she slipped the key in the lock, turning it smoothly. He turned sideways as he walked through the door opening. "Welcome to our new home. I pray we have many long and wonderful years within these walls." Don tenderly kissed her lips. "I love you, Katelyn McKenna Price."

Kate's heart melted in her chest. "I love you too, Donovan Price, and we will make wonderful memories in the coming years."

Don released Kate and glanced around the

room. "You're right, as usual. Eventually someone will come looking for me."

She opened the French doors and windows before going back outside. He was already taking a small table off the truck. He grabbed a box in the other hand and made his first trip to the house in no time. Kate followed suit and the couple worked in tandem to get everything inside.

"I don't know what we have to eat but would you like a snack before going to the office?" Distracted, she surveyed the kitchen, planning where things would work best.

"No, I'm sure there is something to eat in the break room. Do you want to go out to dinner tonight, crash my parents', or cook? Your choice."

"You know, I'll cook tonight. It's the first night in our home and I want to feel like we belong." With a wave of her hand, Kate shooed Don out the door. "Off with you. I have work to do."

. . .

*H*e blew her a kiss and hurried down the path. He was anxious to see what was happening in the fields and with the crew preparing for the crush.

His brain wandered to past years when the crushing of the grapes took on a life of its own. For several weeks during the harvest, huge crates of grapes waited to be pressed into juice. Bees buzzed around the warehouse and his dad always had an EpiPen on hand in case someone had an allergic reaction to a sting. It had happened to his sister Liza, who now made herself scarce during those weeks. After the fruit was crushed and the skins, stems, and seeds were strained off, the real fun began. Crescent Lake Winery grew most of what they used in their wines but there were a few specialty varieties that CLW would purchase from other vineyards that had better success growing. Any excess grapes were sold to smaller wineries in the northeast. At any given time, small box trucks would pull up and get loaded before heading off down the road. Sam Price had always been eager to share his knowledge and excess harvest with start-up wineries. It was a source of family pride when some of his grapes were used to produce a good wine for a small family-run business, which typically produces less than one hundred gallons per year.

Don entered the warehouse amid a buzz of activity. Undetected, he observed Jack talking with some workers, clapping one on the back before glancing up to see his older brother watching.

"Hey, I didn't expect to see you until this afternoon." Jack gave his brother a hearty handshake and pounded his back in a half hug. "It's good to see you. How long are you staying this trip?"

"About a week or so. Cari told us to get out here and get settled. The new girl Kate hired, Dani, is amazing. It's all working out. Oh, and Dani rented the apartment above the shop."

"Mom and Dad will be happy to hear the news, especially since it's crush time. You know it's crazy around here right up until we get all the wine in barrels. And you know Dad will be hands-on so you'll have time to keep tabs on sales. Dad's upstairs. Wanna go see what he's working on? Did you hear he took one of the smaller offices? I don't think he's quite ready to give everything up entirely."

"Yeah, I thought he'd find a space somewhere. He's a gentleman's businessman or something like that. You know, do the fun stuff and leave the hard work to us." Don fell in step next to Jack.

"What's Kate doing today?"

"Unpacking clothes and odds and ends. She's cooking dinner for us tonight. Then she plans to work on the expansion. She has a meeting with the general contractor so she's going to be busy."

"Kate's cooking, count me in!" Jack gave Don a high five.

"Ah, hold on, Jackie boy, it's an intimate dinner for two tonight." Seeing his brother's face droop, he added, "We'll have you over soon. At least let us get settled."

"Alright, but I wanted to talk to Kate about something important. I guess it'll have to wait; I've waited this long."

"Care to share with your big brother?" Don quizzed.

"Oh look, there's Dad," Jack smoothly changed the subject.

"Good to see you, Pop. I hear you moved into a new office."

His dad held back a grin. "Yup. I moved out of the CEO's office and into a consultant's office, just in case the new bigwig needed some advice." His dad let out a deep laugh. "So, where is my lovely daughter-in-law?"

"At the cottage. She has a few things to get done today, and tomorrow she plans to start working on her business."

"Well, that is music to my ears. Anything your mother and I can do to help, just let us know."

"Kate appreciates the groundwork, but let her take it from here."

Sam nodded. "I get it. This is one of those times Mom and I need to give space to Kate. Now, let's get down to business. I have a full afternoon planned to go over sales numbers, market projections…"

"Sounds like I'm going to need a strong cup of coffee and lunch. It's going to be an intense afternoon," Don joked with an underlying seriousness.

"Good idea. Jack, are you going to stay?" Sam looked at his sons.

"Nope, I'll skip the meeting, but I will be back for lunch so order enough food—meat lover's pizza would hit the spot."

"I'll call your mother." Sam winked. "I'll invite her first and then ask if she'll pick it up." He turned to the phone and hit a few buttons, waited patiently, and then spoke in a quiet voice to his wife. After a loud laugh reached the boys' ears, he hung up. "All set. Lunch will be here in an hour."

Jack glanced at his watch. "I'll be back."

As he went out the door, Jack called over his shoulder, "Have fun, Don. I've got grapes to check on."

"Jack! We each march to our own drum," Don called after him, but he was fairly certain the comment fell on deaf ears.

Sam rubbed his hands together with anticipation. "Where to begin?"

Don became immersed in the business of wine and everything else was forgotten.

*K*ate caught a glimpse of the clock on the mantel; it was getting late. Pleased with her progress, she grabbed her bag and keys. If luck was on her side, she'd get most of what she needed at the farm stand, then a quick stop at the grocery store for milk and maybe a little ice cream.

The gravel crunched as Kate parked. She'd been determined to find a shorter route from her house, but in the end, the trip had taken longer. She closed the car door and spied a large waist-high flat planter bursting with lettuce. Delighted to discover it was still growing in soil, she pulled the knife from the side pocket and cut off enough for a couple of meals. After placing the lettuce into a wooden basket, she selected additional fruits and vegetables. All the while, the aroma of fresh bread teased her nose.

Kate stepped inside the semi-dark interior and promptly bumped into someone. "I'm so sorry. Pardon me." She reached out a steadying hand.

"Hi, Kate. Welcome back." Peyton was visibly nervous when talking to her. "Did you have a good trip?"

"Hello, Peyton. Thank you, it's good to see you. The drive was uneventful and we've gotten settled, at least what we brought this trip." She held up her basket. "But the cupboards are bare. I promised Don a home-cooked dinner. So"—she shrugged with a grin—"here I am."

"You found the best spot for just about everything, including amazing pies and ice cream." Peyton pointed to a cooler on the back wall.

Her eyes followed to where Peyton pointed. "Oh, I didn't see that the last time I was here. And it looks like they have milk, too."

She nodded. "Yes, and everything is grown or made right here. You pay a little more but it's worth every penny." Embarrassed, she mumbled, "Oh, what am I saying, I'm talking to a chef."

Kate was unsure how to respond. It was clear Peyton was uncomfortable. "Have I done something to upset you?"

"No, of course not. I'm sorry, I have a headache. I've got to get home." Peyton moved toward the cashier and turned to Kate. "It was good to see you." The girl paid for the items in her basket and scurried toward her car.

Puzzled, Kate watched her hurry out of the

building. Something was troubling Peyton and Kate wanted to help. It was obvious Peyton needed a friend.

*D*on came in the front door. "Something smells good." He whistled as he scanned the first floor. "Someone was very busy today." Kate was standing in front of the stove, and Don circled his arms around her waist and nuzzled her neck. "Did you have a good afternoon?"

She turned in his arms. "I did. All the boxes are empty and waiting to go back to Loudon. I lucked out at the farmers' market and discovered I didn't need the grocery store, at least not today. I got everything on my list. They even had local free-range chicken." Kate pecked his lips.

"Well, dinner smells positively mouthwatering." Don pointed to a covered pot. "What are we having?"

She was thinking about Peyton and didn't hear Don. "I ran into Peyton today."

"You did? How was she?"

"It was really weird; she was very nervous and couldn't wait to leave. I'm going to make it a point to stop by tomorrow and talk with her."

"That visit will have to wait. She works weekends and is off Mondays and Tuesdays." Don grabbed a radish off the plate and opened the refrigerator. "Wine?"

"Of course, there's a bottle of white in the door," Kate said offhandedly.

Don pulled the cork and poured two glasses, passing one to her. "Are we eating on the deck tonight?"

She had plated the chicken, salad, and a side dish of what looked like orzo pasta on a tray. "We are. If you carry the tray, I'll hold the door."

Happy to oblige, he placed the glasses next to the plates. Kate held the screen door open, stepping through, and then closed it after Don. "It's a beautiful night."

He looked around—flowers overflowed vases, soft music was playing, and candles were shimmering in the dusk. "Now this is dinner for two! If I had known this was waiting for me, I would have hurried home."

She gave a low husky laugh. "You haven't seen nothing yet."

Don put the tray down and swept her into his arms. "I do like the sound of that. Can we skip dinner and go straight to dessert?"

"No. You need sustenance." She playfully pushed him toward a chair. "Now sit."

"No, let me." He held the chair for his wife before joining her. The night held much promise. "Now can we eat, Kate?"

She smiled indulgently. "Of course. If I know you, you're dying of starvation." Kate passed him a plate.

With his fork in midair, Don glanced up. "There is more, right?"

Kate couldn't help but smile at her husband, the bottomless pit. "There's plenty."

The couple settled in for a relaxing meal. Once the plates were cleared, they adjourned to the overstuffed wicker chairs in front of the fire pit. Don said, "Jack was disappointed he wasn't invited to dinner. He said he needs to talk to you."

"Really? Any idea why?"

"Nope. I'm sure he'll catch up with you at some point soon. I wonder if your suspicions are correct about Peyton. I get the feeling nothing has changed since he didn't mention asking her out, and I'm sure he would have let that slip."

Kate grew thoughtful. "I wonder if that's why Peyton was so nervous around me. If there is something going on between them, maybe she would think we won't approve, considering I just got done accusing her of keeping a child from you."

"Well, thank heavens that has been resolved and we've moved on. I have to admit,

Kate, it really bothered me that you thought I had a fling with a woman while we were figuring out the next step in our relationship. That time was as hard on me as it was on you." He reached out and caressed her hand. He continued. "I loved you then, today, and always."

Kate gazed lovingly at Don. "I can't explain what happened. In case you haven't noticed I've been a little crazy. I feel like I've let you down."

He gave her hand a tug and pulled her into his strong arms, holding her tight. "Kate, I know we've talked about this before, but it bears repeating. If we can't have a child, we'll cross that bridge together, but for now we need to enjoy life. We have a rare gift some people never find."

Her hand rested on his broad chest. He was right, and there was no need for words. She felt safe and secure and for now that was all she needed.

She looked up through long dark lashes.

"I'm pretty tired. What do you say we call it a day?"

Don grinned. "I'll lock up?" Before Kate could answer, there was a knock on the front door. "If that's Jack, he really has bad timing." Don left Kate to straighten up the deck and douse the fire while he went to the door. Glancing at his watch, he wondered who could possibly be out at this hour.

Don pulled open the door, surprised to find Peyton standing on the top step.

"I'm sorry to stop by without calling and I know it's late, but could I talk to Kate for a minute? I was rude to her earlier and I want to apologize."

He pulled the door wide, welcoming her inside. "Kate! Company."

Hiding her surprise, Kate greeted Peyton warmly. "Peyton, is everything alright?"

"Hi, Kate." She bowed her head slightly. "I'm sorry to bother you, but I needed to apologize. I wasn't very nice earlier and I didn't want you to think it had anything to do with you. I've had a lot on my mind, and well, I don't have any excuse, but when I saw you, our last conversation hit me between the eyes again."

"Peyton, don't give it another thought. We all have off days." She could see the young woman was carrying the weight of the world on her shoulders. "If you need someone to talk to about anything, I'm a good listener." Anyone carrying this kind of burden would eventually crack.

"Well, I won't keep you any longer. Good night." Peyton turned on her heel, walking into the inky darkness.

Don waited until he saw taillights and then locked the door. He mused, "Do you have any idea why she really stopped over?"

She shook her head. "I don't, but I can assure you Peyton is reaching out for help even if she doesn't realize it, and I'll be ready when she needs me."

"It seems that won't be tonight. Are you still planning on giving her a few days?"

"After this visit, absolutely." She gave Don a soft, seductive smile. "Let's not talk about Peyton anymore. I have a few other things I'd like to say, if you're interested."

"You drive me crazy, woman. Lead the way, I'm all yours."

Kate turned and went down the hall, confident her husband was one step behind her.

The next few days were filled with appointments—an architect, general contractor, a consultant, and town-building officials. Kate was closing in on a final design and was anxious to show Don the plans.

She jogged to the side entrance of the warehouse, barely able to contain her excitement. Her eyes adjusted to the dim interior. Peyton was perched at the bar. Not wanting to startle her, Kate called out, "Hello."

Peyton turned. "Hi, Kate. I didn't expect to see you today. Are you looking for Don?"

Kate closed the door behind her. "Eventually, I want to show him the plans, but I think they might interest you, too. Would you like a sneak peek?" If she was caught off guard, she didn't show it.

Peyton slid the stack of papers to one side. "This is exciting. It should help increase wine sales in addition to the revenue the restaurant will bring."

"That's the idea. I've been meaning to ask you, I don't know anyone from the area so would you be available to sit in on interviews?"

Peyton beamed. "I'd be happy to help. I'll make some calls when you're ready. I know some people who would be a good fit."

Kate rolled the papers over the bar. Peyton's admiration for her continued to grow. Kate Price wasn't at all what she had expected. She was beautiful, accomplished, and from what she had heard, an amazing businesswoman. In Peyton's mind, this woman was a triple threat.

Peyton focused on the task at hand. "You'll be open Thursday through Sunday?" Studying the flow into the tasting room, she pointed to a spot on the papers. "When the people get done enjoying a meal, they'll wander through this area and, hopefully, buy a few bottles."

"That's the plan, at least during the busy season. I'm thinking in the winter we'll be open Saturday and Sunday—except for long weekends—then we might add the extra day. But we'll see how business is and play it by ear."

"When do you plan to break ground?"

"Ideally, in a couple of weeks. If we can get the exterior done before bad weather sets in, a late spring opening is feasible."

"Aggressive timetable, but I have a feeling that with you it is definitely doable."

"Ah, I see you've discovered my first flaw. I can be a tad pushy when it comes to something I want." Kate laughed. "But at least I have the best of intentions."

Peyton looked at the floor.

Kate said, "Peyton?"

Silence hung heavy in the air. For several long minutes Peyton didn't speak.

"Kate, I like you. For some reason I feel compelled to tell you the truth, something not another living soul knows. But I'm begging you, will you keep my secret, even from Don?"

"Are you sure you want to confide in me?"

Her shoulders sagged and she lifted her eyes to meet Kate's. "Truthfully, I'm not sure. I've decided the time has come to share my story with someone who won't judge my decisions or want to fix things for me."

Softly, Kate said, "If you want to talk, I will never share your secret. You have my word."

Peyton paused and asked, "Do you mind if we go for a walk?"

The girls left the building, plans forgotten. They stepped into the warm afternoon sun and strolled down a row of heavy grape-laden vines. Kate waited patiently.

Looking straight ahead, Peyton began, her voice barely above a whisper. "You were right; I got pregnant the night of the party. I really wanted to go and there was this guy I liked and he was going to be there with some of his friends. Tessa and Anna weren't going—they were never into the party scene—so I talked Don into taking me. At first, it was a lot of fun, a bonfire roared, someone brought a boom box, people were roasting hot dogs, and of course beer flowed like water. That guy I mentioned, he was there and flirting with me. When Don was ready to leave, I told him one of the girls would give me a ride home." It was hard to breathe as if the air had been sucked from her lungs. She was at a loss for words.

Kate walked next to her, and her presence gave Peyton courage to continue.

"The next thing I knew, someone was passing around small paper cups with whiskey or something. I took one and drank it down like a shot, just like everyone was doing. It tasted awful and burned my throat. It was just vile." Peyton choked back a sob. "After that, everything is blank until I woke up on the front porch at my parents' house, shivering." Heart-wrenching sobs filled the air.

Kate grabbed Peyton, wrapping her arms around the girl, holding her tight to protect her from the past. "Shh, it's over, Peyton. It's a memory. You're safe now."

"Kate." Peyton gasped for air. "I was drugged and raped. I knew it the minute I woke up. It was all my fault; I should have left with Don. What was I thinking?"

"It wasn't. You didn't deserve for it to happen."

She pulled away and wiped her tear-stained face with the back of her hand. "It wasn't just that I was raped—don't you see? The animal, the one who raped me, is the father of my precious little boy. His father is a rapist! I can't ever let that become public knowledge. When Owen is older, I'd rather he thinks I made a mistake with birth control instead of thinking he was a product of violence."

"You have carried this burden alone, for all these years. I can't begin to imagine how you felt when you learned you were going to have a baby. But I don't understand… Why didn't you tell your mother? She would have offered you a shoulder to lean on."

With a heavy heart, Peyton walked over mounds of soft earth. "How do you tell your mom you are pregnant and that you were raped? At first, I believed it really was my fault." Peyton held up her hand to silence Kate. "Then after deciding to have the baby and give it the best life possible, I didn't want my mom to be reminded every time she looked at her grandchild that my innocence and future had been stolen from me. I wanted her to love the baby as much as I did." She turned to look at Kate. "I'm sure it sounds crazy that I could love the baby, but the best parts of it would come from me. Can you understand? I couldn't take the chance that she wouldn't love my baby, totally and completely."

Kate struggled to find her words. "Peyton, I don't think you gave your mom a chance to love *you*. These last few years, you've punished yourself for something you had no control over. You're a great mother, which confirms you have a great mom, too. You owe it to yourself to tell her the truth. It's time for you to heal and truly move forward with life. You deserve to be happy."

"I'm damaged goods," Peyton cried.

Gently, Kate laid her hand on Peyton's arm. "If you want, I will go home with you. Maybe you should consider seeing a counselor who specializes in this type of trauma." With a comforting smile, she continued. "I've promised I will never tell another living soul, and now that you've shared this with me, I'm here for you, anytime."

"You'd go with me? Why?" Peyton was shocked. First, she had allowed herself to tell a virtual stranger what she had never spoken of and now this same person seemed to be offering unconditional support. "Before today, I wasn't ready to tell anyone. I figured if I told you, then any lingering doubts about Don would be gone and this would just go away."

"Peyton, I have a sister and friends. If one of them were standing in front of me right now, I would be offering the same support. I know you have good friends, but maybe you need a friend who isn't a part of your past. Someone to help you move forward."

The girls trudged along the path, one trying to figure out what to do next, and the other trying to rein in her anger toward a scumbag who belonged in jail, which at this moment wouldn't be productive. The winery came into view and Peyton stopped in the shade of an ancient maple tree.

. . .

"*K*ate, if you are serious and have the time, will you come to my parents' house? Now, before I lose my nerve?"

"Give me a minute to tell Don we need to run an errand. I'll meet you at the car."

Peyton nodded.

Kate's long legs dashed across the deep grass. As she entered the semi-darkened room, she stopped and steadied herself. She made a promise to Peyton and she would keep it. Don wouldn't push for answers, for now anyway.

"Don?"

He came to the office door. "Kate, is everything alright? I saw you and Peyton leave. You've been gone a long time."

"Everything's fine, but she needs my help."

"Did she tell you something about Owen's father?"

"You have to trust me. I made a promise what we talked about won't go any further than me. If she wants to confide in you, she will, but she's waiting and I need to go. I'll be back when I can. Okay?"

"Go. I'll be here when you get back." He kissed her hard.

She pulled him close. Her voice thick with tears, she murmured, "I love you very much." She gave him one more kiss and without a backward glance was gone.

The drive to Peyton's childhood home was brief. Quietly sitting in the passenger seat and fidgeting with a paper clip, she said, "Kate, I'm scared. I'm not sure I should do this. What if Mom hates Owen and me? Me for not telling her, and Owen, well, I'm not sure why I brought Owen up; he's innocent in all of this."

"One thing my parents taught me; love transcends everything—distance, time, even death." Kate thought of her father, certain it was love that kept him tied to their family. "It's time for the truth."

Peyton wore a small sad smile. "I'm not sure what happened between us, but if nothing else positive comes out of today, at least I discovered a nice person can quickly become a treasured friend."

Kate grasped her hand. "And we are friends. Ready?"

Peyton looked toward the house. "I'm petrified by what the next few minutes will bring. Yes." She pushed open the door and stepped out.

Peyton's mother was sitting on the porch swing and greeted them with a smile. "Hi, Peyton. This is a surprise. You're home early." Mary Brien stood on the steps with a paperback book in one hand and her reading glasses perched in her curly dark-brown hair. A smile lit up her warm hazel eyes. She waited for the girls to come up the porch steps.

"Mom, this is Kate Price, Don's wife."

Kate stretched out her hand. "A pleasure to meet you, Mrs. Brien."

Mary laughed. "Please call me Mary. Come, let's sit down inside. Can I get some iced tea for you girls?"

"No, thanks, Mom." Peyton's voice was laced with sadness.

Mary's head snapped in her daughter's direction. "Peyton? What's wrong?" She dropped to an overstuffed chair next to her daughter, who sat on the matching ottoman. Forgotten, Kate slipped into a side chair, letting mother and daughter focus on each other.

"Mom, I have something bad to tell you."

"It's Owen, what's happened to him?"

Kate could hear the panic in Mary's voice. "No, Mom, Owen is fine. He's at daycare. But it does concern Owen." Peyton took a deep ragged breath. "You must promise to love Owen forever, no matter what."

"You're scaring me, honey. Tell me what's wrong. Please." Mary glanced at Kate. "Do you know what this is all about?"

Solemnly, Kate nodded. "I do."

"Mom! Promise me." Anguish filled Peyton's voice.

Mary took her daughter's hands. "I promise, honey, I will love Owen for eternity. Now, please tell me what's wrong."

"I never told you who Owen's father is because… I don't know." Tears coursed over Peyton's cheeks. "I was raped."

Mary pulled Peyton into her arms and the two women cried. Discreetly, Kate left the room.

Mary rubbed warmth back into Peyton's ice-cold hands while the details of that night so long ago came out bit by bit. She listened, heartbroken that her baby had endured a woman's worst fear. When she finally spoke, it was in a firm but gentle voice. "We have to tell your dad. He deserves to know, so he can understand and help."

Horrified, Peyton cried, "No! Daddy will hate me forever."

"Don't underestimate your dad. Your father loves you and he's a good man. I don't keep secrets from him, especially of this magnitude."

Peyton studied the floral pattern on the chair, avoiding her mother's eyes. In a hoarse whisper, she said, "I know." Resigned to the fact that the circle of secret keepers was growing, she looked to Kate for support. It was the first time Mary noticed the chair was empty. "I'll be right back."

Mary leaned back in the chair, her eyes closed, fighting back the tears for her daughter and grandson.

*P*eyton found Kate on the porch swing. Sitting down next to her, she said, "Mom says I have to tell my dad."

"It's understandable. She wants you to have their love and support. How are you feeling now?"

"Actually, relieved, but all I've done is burden my mother and soon my father."

"This is why we have family, to share heavy

burdens that are too much for us to bear alone. Go back inside, and when you're ready, I'll take you back to the winery. I'm not in a rush."

"I don't want to hold you up. I'm sure you and Don have plans. I'll be right out. Besides, I think Mom might need some time to process the bomb I just dropped."

*K*ate wondered how many other girls had been drugged and assaulted, positive that most of those crimes went unpunished. It was hard to comprehend that someone Peyton knew and considered a friend had committed the ultimate act of betrayal. Kate decided to talk to Ellie and said a silent prayer her baby sister would never experience anything like what was done to Peyton.

"I'm ready." Peyton had red-rimmed eyes, her face devoid of makeup.

Kate hugged the young mother. "I'm sorry I pushed you. I got that stupid idea in my head and wouldn't let it go. I know it's a lot to ask, but can you forgive me?"

Fresh tears sprang to Peyton's eyes. "Kate, you helped me face the memory of the worst morning of my life and find the courage to tell my mother. There is nothing to forgive."

"That is really nice of you to say. But I was a jerk. Maybe we can chalk it up to raging hormones or something."

For the first time all afternoon, Peyton laughed. "Sounds good. If all else fails, blame our hormones. I'm sure Don is wondering what is keeping us."

The two girls crossed the lawn for the short drive back to the winery, each lost in her own thoughts. Once there, Peyton stopped Kate from getting out of the car.

"Tell Don about today, but ask him to not say anything to his family, not yet. I'm not ready for it to be common knowledge, but I won't ask you to keep a secret from your husband."

"Are you sure you're ready for him to know the truth?"

"I'm not prepared for what he will think of me, but yes."

"He won't think any differently of you, but he will blame himself for leaving you vulnerable."

"Shoot, I didn't think of that." Peyton released a deep sigh. "I guess once others find out, everyone will have their own ideas. For so long I thought this was just about me, but it isn't, not entirely."

"Don will want to talk to you, but I'll make sure he waits until you're ready. You don't have to worry. He is a very patient man."

With a catch in her voice, Peyton said, "I understand. Pick the right time and tell him. Please?" She gave Kate a quick hug. "Before we go inside, I want you to know I feel freer than I have in a long time. The horror I've felt about someone finding out is behind me. For the first time in years, maybe I can have some peace."

Don met them at the door. "Ladies?" Don looked from Kate to Peyton. Kate noted with the exception of red eyes, they didn't look worse for wear.

"We're fine," Kate reassured him. "We should take off and let Peyton close up for the day. We can see her tomorrow."

The couple took separate cars for the drive to their cottage. Once inside, Kate got a bottle of water and Don grabbed a beer. "I have a feeling I might need this." He followed Kate into the living room and sank into the over-stuffed sofa.

She swallowed hard. "There is no easy way to say this, Don. Peyton was date-raped the night of the bonfire."

"What do you mean, 'date-raped'? She wasn't on a date!"

"After you left, someone passed shots around in small cups and that is the last clear memory she has. A few weeks later, she learned she was pregnant, and given that she hadn't been with anyone, she put two and two together. She was devastated and ashamed and decided not to tell anyone, including her mother, until today. I don't know why she confided in me. Maybe the timing was right, but after we talked, I encouraged her to tell her mom. I know my mom would want to know. That's where we went, to see her mother."

Don was stunned. "Let me get this straight. I left her at the bonfire and some jerk slipped her a drug, just to take advantage of her, and she has no idea who?" He rubbed a shaking hand over his chin, his eyes narrowed.

"No, she doesn't know who did this to her and I don't think that is something she wants to dwell on. She has focused on her blessing from that night—Owen. But this makes it hard for her to trust any guy, which is why she doesn't date." Kate could see Don's temper flare again.

"Oh my God, this is my fault. I should have insisted she leave with me." He leaped to his feet and began to pace.

"Don, you had no reason to think anything

would happen any more than Peyton had reason to be afraid for her safety. She was among friends."

Don went pale. "My sisters are friends with those same guys. They have to be told."

"Sweetheart." The warning tone in Kate's voice stopped him in his tracks. "This is not information for you to share. Peyton didn't want me to keep a secret from you. She will tell Tessa and Anna when she's ready. Until then, you must respect her privacy." She put extra emphasis on the word *must*.

"If something happens to either of them, I won't forgive myself," he growled.

"Your sisters are far too busy to be going to parties, and hopefully people have grown up by now to stop doing that kind of stuff."

"I hope you're right." He stared out the back door.

She understood his concern. "Peyton is telling her father tonight."

"I'm glad. Her parents should know." He grew quiet.

"Give her some time. When she's ready, I'm sure she'll find a way to put the girls on alert without opening the floodgate of questions."

"I have questions and I intend to ask them."

"Let her come to you. I'm not going to remind you again; this isn't about you. It's about Peyton and her alone. She needs your understanding and compassion, not your anger."

"I'm trying to understand, but it's hard. I don't know how a guy could do that to any girl."

"I don't either. But we need to be patient. Peyton took a huge step today. I gave her my number and told her to call anytime."

"She's lucky to have you in her corner." He wrapped his arms around her and held her tight against his chest.

"Actually, I think we're both lucky. I have a new friend, and hopefully she'll find peace."

22

Don walked into the kitchen as Kate was hanging up the phone. He leaned in to kiss his wife. "Who called?"

"I was talking to Mom. I wanted to check on things and let her know we were coming home tomorrow. She informed me there is no need to rush back. Dani handles the kitchen like a pro and has developed a good working relationship with Luke. Mom doesn't think we need to keep looking for a cook either, so basically I'm not needed."

Don gathered her in his arms and nuzzled her neck. "I need you," he murmured.

Kate laughed. "We need breakfast. I still want to go home tomorrow to check for myself. Is that alright with you? Maybe we could have the family for dinner, and if things are really as good as it sounds, pack up some more stuff, and then the next trip here we'll stay longer."

"Sure, that sounds great. Do you want to give Cari a heads-up we're coming or have it be a surprise?"

"Let's not say anything for now. I might change my mind and listen to her to stay right here." Kate smirked and pulled a box of cereal from the cabinet. She placed mugs and bowls and added a couple of bananas to the table. "I'm going to meet the architect again today. There are a couple of things that have been bothering me about the traffic flow in the kitchen."

"Do you need me to swing by and put in

my two cents?" He poured a healthy serving of cereal and added milk.

She frowned as she watched the generous amount of sugar he sprinkled on top. "We're meeting at the winery, so I'll track you down."

He nodded and inhaled his cereal. "I hate to eat and run, but if we're going to Loudon, there are a few things I have to get done." He dropped a kiss on her head and hastened to the door. "See you later, honey. Have a fun day."

Silence settled over the house. "Well, he certainly was in a hurry," she mused. Kate enjoyed a quiet breakfast, jotting notes on her ever-present pad. She tapped her pen and then put it aside. She picked up the phone and hit a speed dial button.

"Ellie? Hi, sissy." She smiled into the phone. "Did I wake you?"

Ellie answered with a yawn, "Oh no, you know I'm always up this early. How's everything in wine country?"

"The house is starting to feel like home,

and we break ground in a week or two at the winery. I just wanted to call and check in. Have you talked to Mom lately?"

"I had dinner with her and Ray a couple of nights ago. You know Mom; she likes it when she's feeding us."

"Was everything okay with her? We talked this morning and she said the shop was running fine. I thought I'd get your input. How is Dani doing?" She doodled on the pad absent-mindedly.

"Ah, so that's the reason for your call. Mom told you everything was running smoothly and your nose is a little bent?" Ellie teased.

"No, that's not what I meant. Sis, you know family loyalty is everything."

"Katie, if things weren't running smoothly, I'm sure she would tell you. She won't let What's Perkin' suffer. Trust her." Ellie yawned again. "It's time for you to have new and exciting adventures. Mom raised each of us to stand on our own two feet. You've worked for Mom since graduation so it's overdue. Now that I've reassured you, tell me, is Don happy in his new job?"

Kate smiled into the phone. "He's thriving. It seems running a major company really is in his wheelhouse. I hate to admit this, but I was selfish, wanting him to work for Shane and live in Loudon." Kate sighed. "I hope he doesn't resent me for dragging my feet. Marriage is a joint venture and I wasn't doing my part."

"He moved to Loudon because he loved you and he wanted you more than a career." Ellie sighed deeply. "I happen to think what he did was the *ultimate* romantic gesture."

"You might be right. If the roles were reversed, I might not have done the same thing. Heck, that's right, I almost didn't." Kate didn't let herself get bogged down in the past. "Oh, I forgot to tell you about Peyton. I bumped into her last week at the market, and she was really cold and rushed off. Then she showed up at our house later in the evening and apologized. So, you know me, I decided to talk to her."

"And… you didn't get pushy, did you?"

"No. I gave her some space. I can't tell you everything, but she told me what happened and asked me to go with her to talk to her mom."

"Did you?"

Kate stared out the window and remembered the way Peyton looked when she shared her secret. It brought tears to Kate's eyes. "Bottom line, she has told her parents about Owen's father and has their love and support."

"That is unreal. Why did she talk to you and not a friend?"

"I think it was easier for her to talk to someone who didn't share history with her. I felt bad accusing her of lying to everyone. And now I can totally understand why she kept things a secret."

"Well, I'm glad it has all worked out. Changing the subject, when are you guys coming home?"

Kate smiled at the word "home." Finding her way to Crescent Lake was the journey home. "I'm not sure. We have to move a few more things here."

"Well, let me know and I'll take some time off to help you pack."

"Thanks, Ellie. I know time is precious with your schedule. Before you hang up, how is your shop coming along?"

"Amazing! The Looking Glass will open next year. I hate to cut this short, but I need to go for a run. I'm up to four miles a day and I'm feeling really good. Maybe one of these days I'll actually like it."

Kate laughed. "Sounds good, kiddo. Regarding running, you already like it or you wouldn't do it. Remember, I know you, little sister, sometimes better than you know yourself."

Ellie chuckled. "Talk to you later, sis, and see ya soon."

Kate and Ellie sat miles apart, smiling, knowing no matter the distance that separated them, the sisters would always be close.

Kate was anxious to talk to Don. She was ready to make the move final. Everyone was going to be fine. Strolling into the winery, she saw Peyton across the room and waved.

"You look pretty today," Kate said.

"I can't tell you how much brighter my world looks now. I don't have secrets from my parents and they have promised to go to counseling with me, however long it takes. I have you to thank for it all. If you hadn't given me a push, well, really a shove—" Peyton shrugged. "Bottom line, if you hadn't shown up, I would still be blaming myself." She reached out and gave Kate a fierce hug. "I can never thank you enough for all that you've done, including going with me to see my mom. Just knowing you were there gave me courage."

"You're giving me far too much credit. You had it in you all the time."

Peyton's head bobbed. "I'm glad we're friends."

"Me too because you're the only friend I have in Crescent Lake that isn't related to me," Kate joked.

"Yeah, you're walking into quite a group." Peyton visibly relaxed.

"Do you know if Don's upstairs? I need to talk to him."

"I think so. At least I haven't seen him go out."

"I'll see you before I leave."

"Alright, and Kate…" Peyton's gaze dropped to the floor. "If my story will help other girls, you can, I mean, if you want to, tell your sister. It's okay."

"Oh, Peyton, I do want to tell her just because I want her to be safe. Are you sure?"

"I'm sure."

"Thank you," Kate said quietly.

Don was sitting at the conference table, studying information projected on the wall screen. He looked up when she walked in.

"Hello, beautiful. I didn't expect you to stop in this morning."

Kate dropped a kiss on his mouth and plopped in Don's lap. "I talked with Ellie this morning and she said Mom is doing great at the shop. So…" She paused. "I'm ready to make the move permanent and we can put the house in Loudon up for sale."

"Well, I must say I'm happy you're ready and feeling comfortable, but I don't think we're going to sell our house. We'll need a place to stay when we go back, and I like the idea that when we have a family, we have a home in Loudon too."

Surprised, she said, "Are you sure, Don? That's a lot of money to have tied up in two houses."

He pulled her into his lap. "We can afford both. And I think it's the right thing to do, at least until we both decide it's time." He gave her a tender kiss. "Are we leaving for Loudon tomorrow?"

"You know me so well. If you can get away, I'm ready."

"Then tomorrow it is."

"By the way, what are you working on?" Kate gestured toward the screen.

"I got tired of looking at numbers on a tiny computer screen, and it's easier to see trends when the numbers are large. So, hence the projector."

Kate laughed. "If you say so, but from what I see, business has been good and you're trying to figure out a way to make those bars grow much taller, maybe hit the ceiling. I'm going to let you get back to conquering the world of wine and I'll take care of spending some money on our new business venture." She gave him a quick kiss goodbye. "See you tonight," she called over her shoulder. Don's laughter followed her out the door.

EPILOGUE

It had been an eventful trip to Loudon. Don and Kate hosted a family barbeque, and in true McKenna fashion, everyone came bearing platters, casserole dishes, and desserts galore. Cari and Ray set up large tables and chairs under a rented tent. With the adoption final, Devin was officially a McKenna. Jake and Sara chased the triplets, who skipped the walking phase and went straight to running. Grace and Charlie were happy to help wrangle the little ones. Luke and Dani came too, as the newest honorary members of the clan. Kate informed the family she and Don were moving to Crescent Lake and that their door was always open to all, at any time. It was a mixture of tears and smiles as the family said goodbye at the end of the evening. After cleaning up and making everything tidy, Kate was exhausted and desperately wanted to put her feet up and take five minutes to relax. Don went to take out the garbage when Kate found herself alone, but not.

"Hi, Daddy." Kate spoke in a tired voice.

"Hi, Katie-bell. It seemed like everyone had a wonderful time tonight. I couldn't help myself. I had to check it out."

"It's going to be different, not seeing them every day. But I'm ready now and I'm pretty lucky Don was patient. I could have lost him with my foolishness."

"But you didn't, Kate. He's just out the back door."

"I have a surprise for him tonight."

"He doesn't know yet?" Her dad smiled at

his oldest daughter. "I have to go, Katie. Remember, I'm always with you. Take care of our family." He faded away.

She wiped the tears from her cheeks and went to retrieve two glasses and a special bottle chilling in the back of the refrigerator.

She carried the tray into the backyard, where her husband was sitting with his feet propped up in front of the fire pit. "Sweetheart, let's enjoy our last night as full-time residents of Loudon."

He took the tray from her and popped the cork. It was only then that he noticed the label. Puzzled, he said, "Sparkling grape juice?"

Kate grinned.

Don passed a glass to her. He bent over to kiss Kate's upturned lips. Clinking glasses, he said, "Here's to our new home, a new life, and our family."

With eyes shining, Kate whispered, "To us."

If you loved Ready to Soar help other readers find this book: **Please leave a review now!**

Are you ready to read more in the McKenna Family Romance Series?

Are you ready to read more about the McKenna Family? Order Love in the Looking Glass. Also don't forget to sign up for my newsletter for a free download at www. lucindarace.com/newletter

LUCINDA RACE

Love in the Looking Glass

SNEAK PEEK - LOVE IN THE LOOKING GLASS

Ellie looked at the clock for the third time in ten minutes. She was banging on the computer keys when the small bell on the door chimed. Ellie froze, unable to breathe. The man who walked in couldn't possibly be a photographer. He looked like he belonged in front of a camera lens.

The man was tall and his biceps strained the fabric of his black short-sleeve button-down shirt. He wore formfitting black jeans and well-worn black cowboy boots. Amber eyes were framed by chestnut-brown hair, which curled at the collar. Deep dimples appeared as he smiled.

Grasping Ellie's hand with a firm, cool grip, he said, "Hello, I'm Padraic Stone."

His deep baritone voice caused her insides to quake.

"You must be Eleanor McKenna?"

Stunned by the pure physical reaction to this man, Ellie nodded mutely. Taking his outstretched hand, she was taken aback by the electricity that surged through her as their skin touched. She looked down. Turning her hand over, she expected to see it red, evidence of the burning sensation.

"Yes, I'm Eleanor McKenna," she said. "But everyone calls me Ellie."

"Since our relationship has become instantly casual, please, call me Pad." He cocked his head. "Did I come at a bad time? You seem to be preoccupied."

"Oh no, not at all. I was just"—she pointed to the screen—"you know, working. Always paperwork to do in business and this one is no exception. You're probably not aware, but my grand opening was last night, and I was checking the sales. Surprisingly, we did a brisk business. My stepdad was in charge of the cash register so I had no idea…" Ellie stopped mid-sentence, realizing she was babbling. "Enough about all of that. Let's talk about your work and if we're a good fit for each other." Ellie blushed crimson, wishing she could retract that last statement. "I mean if my gallery would be suitable for your photos."

Ellie felt Pad's eyes study her as she rambled on. Her hand touched the back of her hair, secured in a chignon. A few tendrils had escaped, curling around her face.

Pad said, "Did you have an opportunity to check my website? I left several prints in the car. If you'd like, I'll go get them. You can choose what you'd like to display, if any."

Ellie stepped from behind the counter. She was used to men giving their eyes free rein at her expense. She stood tall, straightened her shoulders, and said, "I would like to see your photos. Shall I come with you?"

"No, I'll bring them in."

"Then let's go into the kitchen. You can lay the prints on the table. It will be easier to get the full effect without all the distractions in the main room." When Pad returned with the prints, Ellie led the way and gestured to the carafe. "Coffee?"

Padraic poured himself a cup while Ellie studied each photo. She could hear his fingers tapping on the edge of the cup. She tried to ignore him as she immersed herself in each image before moving to the next.

"These are incredible. The way you've captured shadows and light is unique. Where were they taken?"

"The White Mountains in New Hampshire. I like to wander and stop whenever the mood strikes. Typically, I don't have a destination in mind when I pack up and hit the road, just a vague direction—north, south, east, or west."

"What did you do before photography?"

Ellie placed the last framed photo on the table and picked up her cup. "Did you go to art school?"

"I don't have formal training. I was in public service. After a few tough years of seeing too many unspeakable things, I packed it in and picked up a camera."

Ellie sensed he didn't want to talk about his past and respected his privacy. "I must admit I can't wait to get these hung and make the announcement that Padraic Stone originals are available. That is, if you would like me to take your work on consignment?"

"I would. Your place has a good feel, and I think we will work well together." Padraic gathered up the prints. "I'll hang them for you."

"You'll need to sign some paperwork before you leave."

Padraic glanced at his phone. "I have another appointment in the area. Can I swing back either later today or first thing tomorrow?"

"That works too." Ellie walked past Winnie's paintings and noticed Pad smile. "Do you know Mrs. Simpson's work?"

"I've been a fan for a long time." Without elaborating, Padraic set about hanging the photos while Ellie directed how she thought they should be arranged.

Stepping back, Pad slipped his hands in his pockets.

"Perfect." She smiled at Padraic

"I'm assuming you're talking about my work," he teased.

Flustered, she smoothed the front of her blouse and crossed the room to take refuge behind the counter. "The photos are breathtaking." Ellie hit a couple of keys in an attempt to steady her hammering heart. "Stop back at your convenience. I'm open today until four and tomorrow ten till four as well."

Padraic gave a mock salute. "I'll be seeing you."

A FREE STORY FOR YOU

Have you enjoyed Ready to Soar? Not ready to stop reading yet? If you sign up for my newsletter at www.lucindarace.com/newsletter you will received Blends, the love story of Sam and Sherry, right away as my thank-you gift for choosing to get my newsletter.

Can two hearts blend together for a life long love..

His mother's final illness waylaid Sam Price's college dreams, but he's content working in his family's vineyard in a small town in upstate New York. When he finds a woman with a flat tire on a vineyard road, he's stunned to discover it's the girl he'd had a crush on in high school. He'd never been confident enough to ask her out back then. He'd been a farm kid. Her daddy was the bank president. Way out of his league.

Sherry Jones is tired of her parents' ambitious plans for her life. She'll finish her college accounting degree like they want, but how can she tell them about her real love: working with growing things? Then a flat tire and a neglected garden offer her an unexpected opportunity, with the added bonus of a tall, gorgeous guy with eyes that set her senses tingling.

What does a guy with dirt under his nails and calluses on his hands have to offer a woman like Sherry? It will take courage for her to defy her parents and claim her own dreams. Sam and Sherry's lives took different paths, but a winding vineyard road has brought them back together. Are they willing to take a chance to create the perfect blend for a lifelong love?

Blends is only available by signing up for my newsletter – sign up for it here at www.lucin darace.com/newsletter

SOCIAL MEDIA

Follow Me on Social Media

Like my Facebook page
Join Lucinda's Heart Racer's Reader Group on
Facebook
Twitter @lucindarace
Instagram @lucindraceauthor
BookBub
Goodreads
Pinterest

LOVE TO READ?

Cowboys of River Junction

<u>Stars Over Montana</u>
The cowboy broke her heart but he never stopped loving her. Now she's back ready to run her grandfather's ranch…

Hiding in Montana

Orchard Brides Series
<u>Apple Blossoms in Montana</u>
Twenty years later Renee and Hank are back where

they fell in love but reality is like a spring frost and is a long-distance relationship their only option for their second chance?

The Sandy Bay Series
<u>Sundaes on Sunday</u>

A widowed school teacher and the airline pilot whose little girl is determined to bring her daddy and the lady from the ice cream shop together for a second chance at love.

Last Man Standing/Always a Bridesmaid
<u>Barrett</u>

Has the last man standing finally met his match?

<u>Marie</u> *May 2023*

Career focused city girl discovers small town charm can lead to love.

The Crescent Lake Winery Series
<u>Breathe</u>

Her dream come true may be the end of his...
Crush

The first time they met was fleeting, the second time restarted her heart.

<u>Blush</u>

He's always loved her but he left and now he's back…the question, does she still love him?

<u>Vintage</u>

He's an unexpected distraction, she gets his engine running…

<u>Bouquet</u>

Sweet second chances for a widow and the handsome billionaire...

Holiday Romance

<u>The Sugar Plum Inn</u>

The chef and the restaurant critic are about to come face to face.

Last Chance Beach

<u>Shamrocks are a Girl's Best Friend</u>

Will a bit of Irish luck and a matchmaking uncle give Kelly and Tric a chance to find love?

A Dickens Holiday Romance

<u>Holiday Heart Wishes</u>

Heartfelt wishes and holiday kisses…

Holly Berries and Hockey Pucks
Hockey, holidays, and a slap shot to the heart.

Christmas in July
She's the hometown girl with the hometown advantage. Right?

A Secret Santa Christmas
Christmas just isn't Holly's thing, but will a family secret help her find the true meaning of Christmas?

It's Just Coffee Series 2020
The Matchmaker and The Marine
She vowed never to love again. His career in the Marines crushed his ability to love. Can undeniable chemistry and a leap of faith overcome their past?

The MacLellan Sisters Trilogy
Old and New
An enchanted heirloom wedding dress and a letter

change three sisters lives forever as they fulfill their grandmothers last request try on the dress.

<u>Borrowed</u>

He's just a borrowed boyfriend. He might also be her true love.

<u>Blue</u>

Will an enchanted wedding dress work its magic one more time?

The Loudon Series

<u>Between Here and Heaven</u>

Ten years of heaven on earth dissolved in an instant for Cari McKenna when her husband Ben died.

<u>Lost and Found</u>

Love never ends... A widow who talks to her late husband and her handsome single neighbor who has secretly loved her for years.

<u>The Journey Home</u>

Where do you go to heal your heart? You make the journey home...

<u>The Last First Kiss</u>

When life handed Kate lemons, she baked.

<u>Ready to Soar</u>

Kate will fight for love, won't she?
<u>Love in the Looking Glass</u>
Will Ellie's first love be her last or will she become a ghost like her father?
<u>Magic in the Rain</u>
Dani's plan of hiding in plain sight may not have been the best idea.

Cozy Mystery Books
A Bookstore Cozy Mystery Series
<u>Books & Bribes</u>
It was an ordinary day until the book of Practical Magic conked Lily on the head causing her to see stars. And then she discovered her cat, Milo, could talk.

Catnip & Crimes May 2023
The fun continues as Lily practices her magic and needs to investigate another murder.

Tea & Trouble August 2023
A fall festival and reading tea leaves and just

enough to propel Lily into a new murder investigation.

Scares & Dares October 2023
A haunted house and Halloween, what could go wrong in the small town of Pembroke Cove?

ABOUT THE AUTHOR

Award-winning and best-selling author Lucinda Race is a lifelong fan of reading. As a young girl, she spent hours reading novels and getting lost in the fun and hope they represent. While her friends dreamed of becoming doctors and engineers, her dreams were to become a writer—a novelist.

As life twisted and turned, she found herself writing nonfiction but longed to turn to her true passion. After developing the storyline for A McKenna Family Romance, it was time to start living her dream. Her fingers practically fly over computer keys as she weaves stories of mystery and romance.

Lucinda lives with her two little dogs, a miniature long hair dachshund and a shih tzu mix rescue, in the rolling hills of western Massachusetts. When she's not at her day job, she's immersed in her fictional worlds. And if she's not writing romance or cozy mystery novels, she's reading everything she can get her hands on.

www.ingramcontent.com/pod-product-compliance
Lightning Source LLC
Chambersburg PA
CBHW071957190726
48293CB00001B/66